Fool's Gold
The Dream Traveler
Book Four

Ernesto H Lee

Dedication

My writing always starts with my initial ideas for the beginning, middle and end of each of my stories, but these ideas inevitably evolve and change course as I place myself in the minds of my characters.

Within the genre of Time and Dream Travel, this creates a constant challenge in not letting myself get to carried away with my scenarios, and my editor is constantly at pains to remind me, that the notion of *'Suspension of Disbelief'* can only be taken so far.

She is right about this of course, but she is also wrong. The very fact that I am writing about a subject that pushes *'Suspension of Disbelief'* to the max, means to me that this notion has no limits, other than those set by the mind of the writer or the reader themselves.

That is certainly my own preferred take on the subject and, is due in no small part to the fact that it applies as much in my personal life as it does with my writing.

After more than one thousand days of crazy, I still have to pinch myself to believe you are real, Maria. You are my inspiration, my friend, my lover, and most importantly......my utterly amazing, but very slightly bonkers, *'Suspension of Disbelief'*. x

Ernesto H Lee
31ˢᵗ January 2020

*Suspension of Disbelief - The temporary acceptance as believable of events or characters that would ordinarily be seen as incredible. This is usually to allow an audience to appreciate works of literature or drama that are exploring unusual ideas.

Preface

After solving the mystery of Lucy Partington-Brown's disappearance and handing over the ongoing case to DI Miller and Lincolnshire Constabulary, I had been hoping that we could take it easy for a few days before diving into another case. With that in mind, I had set up a meeting for tomorrow to brief Detective Chief Inspector Kevin Morgan on our conclusions and formally request closure of the cold case file. Once that was done, I would have requested that Catherine and I be allowed to take the rest of the week off.

Bloody fat chance of that now. Despite our best efforts in putting Clive Douglas behind bars and cutting off his network of support, he has once again demonstrated that he is far from powerless. Worse still, he has succeeded in getting under my skin by making a threat against the people that I care about most in the world.

He thinks I'll be rattled. And he's 100 percent right. But I'm not just rattled. I'm angry and pissed off at the audacity of the man. I promise myself that, one way or another, I will make sure that Clive Douglas never takes a breath as a free man again.

For now, though, and as much as I would like to ignore him, I need to assume that he is prepared to carry out his threat if I don't at least appear to be trying to help him. Whilst it's unlikely that he will act on his threat so soon after speaking to me, he is a desperate man in a desperate position, which makes him both dangerous and unpredictable. Waiting until tomorrow to speak to Cath and Morgan is not an option.

More importantly, I could never forgive myself if anything were to happen to Cath, Ben, or Maria tonight for a lack of action on my part. I know what I need to do, and I need to do it now.

Sean McMillan
April 25th, 2018

Present Day – Wednesday, April 25th, 2018

I check my watch. It's just past 9:45 in the evening. The lights are still on in the upper-floor rooms of the house and after watching for a couple of minutes, I'm relieved to see the unmistakable silhouette of Maria in her bedroom window. I imagine her sitting at her dressing table brushing her hair and removing her makeup in readiness for bed. I watch a few more minutes. Then, satisfied that she is alone in the house and not in any immediate danger, I get into my car and call Catherine. She answers after three rings and sounds sleepy.

"Hey, boss, sorry, I dozed off on the sofa. I wasn't expecting you to call tonight. Is anything wrong?"

"I hope not, Cath. Sorry to wake you up over what might be nothing, but I need your help. I need you to arrange for a squad car to sit outside Maria Pinto's house tonight and for a uniformed presence outside Benjamin Pinto's ward at Hounslow General hospital. I need you to do that right away please. You understand?"

"Yes, of course," Catherine replies, sounding both confused and concerned. "What's happened though? Are they both okay?"

"They are both fine, Cath. It's just a precaution for now. I had another run-in with my biker friends, and I spoke to Clive Douglas in—"

"What? You spoke with Douglas?" Catherine interrupts. "How? I mean, what did he want?"

"Cath, I don't have time to explain fully, but a threat was made against Maria and Ben. When you have made your calls, get yourself over to the hospital to check on Ben. I'm already here outside Maria's home. I'm going to wait for the squad car to arrive and I'll call DCI Morgan to let him know what's going on. Once we are sure that Ben and Maria are safe, let's meet at my place so that I can bring you up to speed. Call me when you get to the hospital."

"Understood, Sean. I should be there in ten minutes. I'll arrange the uniform cover on the way there."

"Thanks, Cath. Oh, and just one other thing — Douglas threatened you as well, so be careful please, DC Swain. I need you."

There is a short pause and then I hear Catherine take a deep breath.

"Good, if you speak to Clive Douglas again, tell that bastard to bring it on. I'll be waiting for him."

If I've learned nothing else about Catherine Swain in the time we have been together as partners, it is that she is not a woman that is easily intimidated. Neither is she afraid to get stuck in when the need dictates. There are two crooked sergeants that could testify to this fact. If, of course, they were still alive to do so. Catherine Swain does not make idle threats and Clive Douglas would be wise not to underestimate her. I laugh at her comment before telling her to be careful again and ending the call.

Next, I call DCI Morgan to tell him about my conversation with Douglas. As always, Kevin Morgan listens without interrupting. When I finish speaking, he assures me that Ben and Maria are both perfectly safe for now.

"It's a sensible precaution putting uniform on both locations, but you're right, Sean, Clive Douglas is just clutching at straws in the hope of reducing his sentence. If he is going to make a move, it's not going to happen until after you've spoken to him again. I wouldn't worry too much about it tonight. Let's meet after tomorrow's briefing as planned to agree on how to approach this."

Fool's Gold

"Thank you, sir. But just one question, if I may. You said until after I had spoken to him again. So, you think that I should speak with him again?"

"Yes, why not?" Morgan replies. "I don't see any harm in hearing what he has to say for himself. If by some chance he does have something useful for us, we can throw him a few bones to keep him onside until we're satisfied that he has nothing else to offer."

"And if he is just chancing his arm?"

"Well, if that's the case we'll throw him back to the wolves. Either way, the worst that can happen is that you will have wasted a few hours of your time. Let's talk in the morning. Goodnight, Sean."

A few seconds after the call ends, the squad car arrives. Before I can react, it passes me and takes a position on Maria's driveway. With its strobe lights still flashing, there is absolutely no chance that Maria will have missed its arrival. I look up to the bedroom window and, sure enough, Maria is pulling back the curtains to look outside. Thirty seconds later she appears at the front door in her dressing gown. I speak briefly to the two uniformed officers in the squad car to apprise them of the situation and then I try to reassure Maria, who quite justifiably looks worried.

"What's going on, Sean? Why is there a police car here?"

"It's just a precaution, Maria. I can't say too much, but the former Detective Superintendent connected to the death of Paul Donovan contacted me earlier."

"Is that Clive Douglas?" Maria asks. "I remember his name from the newspapers. He was part of the Network that you took down and he came to my house that time, didn't he?"

"Yes, that's him. DS Douglas was the one that showed up here the morning after that thug broke in and attacked me."

7

"But I thought all of that was over, Sean. I don't understand."

"Honestly, it's nothing, Maria. He wants me to speak to him and is using you and Ben as leverage. He's not going to be stupid enough to try anything. I can assure you of that."

At the mention of Ben, Maria starts to panic.

"Did he threaten to hurt us? Oh God, what about Ben? Why are you still here? Please, Sean, we have to get to the hospital."

She is already halfway out the door and I gently pull her back. "Maria, please. Catherine is already on her way there. By now, there should also be two police officers outside the ward. Nothing is going to happen to Ben."

Right on cue, my phone rings and I speak to Catherine. After telling her to come to my apartment, I hand the phone to Maria.

"Here, speak to Catherine. She is at the hospital now and Ben is fine."

Maria takes the phone and while she speaks to Catherine, I move away to give her some space. A few minutes later, she ends the call and I rejoin her.

"Are you okay, Maria? Did she manage to reassure you?"

"Yes, thank you, Sean. I'm sorry for panicking. It's just …"

"Honestly, it's fine and there is no need to apologize. Like I said, Clive Douglas is just using you both to get to me. There really is nothing to worry about. Now go back inside and try to relax. The car will be outside all night as a precaution only. Tomorrow we can decide how to take things forward. Is that okay?"

"Yes, thank you, Sean. Will you call me tomorrow?"

"I will, I promise. Goodnight, Maria."

I wait for the front door to close and then, before leaving, I hand one of the uniformed officers one of my business cards.

"You don't leave until you are relieved in the morning," I instruct him, "and you call me if anything happens here. Understood?"

Both officers confirm their understanding and, content that everything possible has been done tonight, I drive home to wait for Catherine.

■ ■ ■ ■ ■ ■ ■

At just after 10:30, Catherine arrives at my apartment and I buzz her in. I pour myself a Jameson whiskey, but Cath declines and joins me in the kitchen where I make her a coffee.

"All quiet at the hospital, Cath?"

"All good, boss. Ben was sleeping and I didn't see the need to disturb him. The boys in blue will let us know if anything happens. It sounds unlikely though. So, go on, what happened?"

"Like I said on the phone, my biker friends made another appearance."

"You're okay though?"

"I'm fine, Cath. The passenger told me to call Clive Douglas. I guess that means he must have been the guy that made the same comment when I was pushing through the press pack at Meadow Farm. When I told him I wasn't interested, he threw me a cellphone with a number pre-programmed to Clive's prison hotline."

"What else?"

"Nothing, Cath. He threw the phone to me and they left. End of story."

"Arrogant bastard!" Cath exclaims. "Just by having that phone he is looking at another three to five years added to his final sentence."

I reply with a shrug, "Yep, I told him pretty much the same thing. He doesn't give a shit though, and I can see his point. He is already looking at a whole life sentence. Getting a few more years makes no difference to him in the wider scheme of things."

"Even so, boss. Let me call the prison. I can get his cell turned over. At the very least they can take the phone away and cut off his ability to be heard."

"No, not yet, Cath. I was thinking about that on the drive over here and for now it suits me to be able to speak directly to him."

"So, the slippery bastard is offering something?"

"Yeh, something like that. He told me that he has information relating to another major cold case and—"

"And if we help him reduce his sentence, he will share that information," Cath interrupts me. "That is bollocks, Sean! Please tell me that you are not considering this."

"Morgan seems to think it could be worth a visit just to see what he has to say."

"And you agreed?" Cath asks, incredulous.

"It can't hurt. Clive Douglas is more likely than anyone to have information on unsolved cases."

"Sean, Clive Douglas tried to kill you. It was because of him that we both ended up in hospital. For God's sake, you nearly died because of him. Information or not, that bastard deserves to spend the rest of his life rotting in the deepest, darkest hole in England. I refuse to bloody help him."

"Believe me, Catherine. I feel the same. But personal feelings aside, if he does genuinely have information relating to another case, then we have an obligation as police officers to hear him out. If nothing comes from it, we will at least have had the opportunity to see Frank Butler's handiwork close-up. Neither of us have seen him since he was moved from Meerholt Prison. From what I understand, Butler did a real job on his face and that alone must be worth a trip to see him. I for one am looking forward to laughing in that bastard's face, and so should you. He might be locked up, but he is as arrogant as ever. What do you say, Cath? Worth a trip so that we can stare him down together to let him know who is in charge?"

Catherine thinks about it for a second and then slowly nods. "That would be nice, I suppose. But even the thought that we might be helping him reduce his sentence sticks in my throat."

"I promise you, Cath, unless he has something earth-shattering, we will walk away and leave him to rot. Even if he does have something good to trade, it doesn't necessarily mean that we need to help him. Anyway, let's see what Morgan has to say in the morning and take it from there."

"I guess so, Sean. I was hoping to never see that man again, but you're right. No harm in hearing him out, I suppose."

"Good, now finish your coffee," I tell her. "It's getting late and I have a feeling that tomorrow is going to be a long day."

Catherine rinses her coffee cup in the sink, and I walk her to the door. We hug, and I wish her a good night. I'm about to close the door when she turns back around to face me.

"Sean, what time did you speak to Clive Douglas?"

"Sorry, what was that?"

"The time you spoke to him. You called me at 9.48 p.m. What time did you speak to Clive Douglas?"

"I'm not sure exactly. I guess maybe five or ten minutes before I spoke to you. What's your point, Cath?"

"When you called me, you said you were already outside Maria Pinto's house. How did you get there so quickly?"

"Oh yes. Sorry, I should have said. I wasn't in my apartment when he called. I'd paid a visit to Ben in Hounslow General. Maria was also there. I offered her a lift home at the end of visiting hours. He called me just after I'd dropped her off."

Catherine doesn't look convinced, but she nods and then asks about Ben.

"How is he doing?"

"He's doing well, Cath. They think that he may be able to go home tomorrow."

"That's good. And I don't just mean for him, boss."

"Meaning?"

"Meaning that Morgan will be looking for an explanation as to how Ben was able to track you to Tyevale and how he came to be injured."

"I've already explained that, Cath. He called my mother to find out where we were. Ben himself told his mum that it was entirely his idea to try to get involved in the case. I had noth—"

"Yes, you've said that already. I think Kevin Morgan might need a little more convincing though."

"And you, Cath?"

"I'm your partner, Sean. Despite my better judgment at times, I will always have your back. As your friend, though, you need to take my advice and back off a bit from whatever relationship you have with Ben and Maria Pinto. That whole thing with Paul Donovan and Clive Douglas was tough on all of us. But we are cops and tough assignments are part of the job description. It's hard not to get personally involved, but we need to—"

I cut her off mid-sentence. Catherine has me on the back foot and knowing that she is right has me annoyed. "I'm not getting your point, Cath. If you have something to say, you need to spit it out."

"I'm saying that Ben and Maria Pinto were part of a case for us and nothing more. Ben showing up in Tyevale and getting hurt is a complication, but it does not change the need to maintain a professional distance. If there is something else going on that would give Clive Douglas reason to target Maria and Ben to get to you, then I need and deserve to know what it is."

"There is nothing else, Catherine. I went to visit the boy and I offered Maria a lift home. That is as far as it goes."

Catherine stares at me for a few seconds without speaking and then nods.

"Okay, just be careful, Sean. Our job is tough enough already without the added burden of personal complications. I'll see you in the morning for Morgan's morning briefing. Sleep well."

Catherine leaves and once again I am left feeling like a complete shit for lying to her.

Tomorrow is going to be an interesting day.

■ ■ ■ ■ ■ ■ ■

As always, the morning briefing starts promptly at 9 a.m. We have been out of the office for over a week, so I should be paying attention to the case updates from Morgan and the other case officers, but my mind is distracted by the call to Clive Douglas and Cath's reminder that Morgan will want a full explanation on Ben Pinto's involvement in our last case.

Towards the end of his briefing Morgan congratulates us for our work on the Partington-Brown case and invites me to give a short case summary to the assembled audience. I defer to Catherine who gladly takes the opportunity to share the case details with our colleagues.

At the end of her presentation, Morgan ends his briefing by announcing that the Promotions Selection Board has promoted Detective Sergeant Sarah Gray to the rank of inspector with immediate effect and she will be assuming the lead coordination role for all departmental cases as team detective inspector. It's a well-deserved and long overdue promotion and the news is met with congratulations from the whole team.

As the applause dies down, Morgan stands up and beckons for us to follow him.

"DS McMillan, DC Swain, my office please. You too, please, DI Gray."

■ ■ ■ ■ ■ ■ ■ ■

We take our seats in Morgan's office and after checking a few emails, he turns his chair around to face us.

"Well you two, that was quite the can of worms you opened up in Tyevale. Impressive work, though, in getting a grip on the case so soon. You will be pleased to know that the Home Secretary has already given the go-ahead to close the case from our end. You will no doubt, however, be called in due course to give evidence against Lucy Partington-Brown and Edward Wells for the litany of offences that your investigations turned up. I should imagine that it's going to take the boys and girls in Lincolnshire Constabulary quite some time to pull everything together on that little lot. That's quite a workload they have there. They can thank you pair for that."

The intonation of the last statement makes me feel uneasy, so I stay quiet and let Morgan carry on.

"In fact, you two are getting quite the reputation. Isn't that right, Sarah?"

"Yes, sir. Quite the pair of superstar detectives we have here. Two major cases solved in extremely quick succession. That's very impressive."

"It is impressive, Sarah. But solving cases doesn't give any of my officers carte blanche to tear up the rule book or to go rogue on me, does it?"

"No, sir, it doesn't," Sarah replies.

Morgan is staring at both of us, but I know that his comment is aimed at me.

"Before we discuss how to handle Clive Douglas, why don't you start by telling me how the hell Ben Pinto ended up seriously injured in hospital, Sergeant McMillan? What in God's name was he doing in Tyevale at the scene of your investigation? And don't even think about giving me any kind of cock and bull story, son."

His direct way of asking has me slightly flustered and for a second, I am lost for words. Sarah Gray breaks the silence.

"Anytime soon would be great, DS McMillan. DCI Morgan asked you a question."

"Uhm, yes, ma'am," I stammer, before gathering my thoughts and turning back to face Morgan.

"As I told you previously, sir, Ben Pinto had been considering dropping out of university to join the police service. His mother was concerned and asked me to speak to him. She asked me to convince him to stay in university to finish his journalism course."

Morgan frowns. "It would appear that your advice fell on deaf ears, DS McMillan."

"Sir?"

"He ignored your advice and followed you to Tyevale," Sarah Gray interjects.

"Did you tell him where you were going?" Morgan asks me.

"No, sir. Of course not. Maria and Ben Pinto were introduced to my mother at our commendation ceremony. They exchanged numbers and Ben got our location from her. I swear, sir, I had no idea of Ben Pinto's intention to follow us to Tyevale. Please call Maria Pinto. She can corroborate what I am telling you."

Morgan raises his eyebrows. "Thank you for the advice, sergeant. I have in fact already spoken with Ms. Pinto and luckily for you she has indeed corroborated your story. No doubt if I speak to the boy, he will say the same?"

"Yes, sir. I believe he will. He is extremely sorry and has assured me that this won't happen again."

"I hope not, for your sake, DS McMillan. You can count yourself lucky that the boy is on the mend and heading home today."

I'm shocked that he knows that Ben is being released today and my face shows it.

DI Gray smiles and says, "Don't look so shocked. You're not the only one around here who is on top of things, DS McMillan. We didn't get where we are today by not being in the know."

Morgan nods his agreement and then turns to Catherine. "Anything you would like to add on this subject, DC Swain?"

"No, sir. I think everything has been covered," Catherine replies.

Morgan shakes his head at Catherine's reply, but he is looking directly at me again when he speaks.

"Well, that remains to be seen, DC Swain, but let's leave it for now, shall we?"

It's a rhetorical question so neither of us answer and after a few seconds to make the point, DCI Morgan gets down to business.

"Okay, let's talk about our old friend, Clive Douglas."

"Yes, sir. I was thinking that—"

Before I can continue, Morgan holds a hand up to stop me and it is clear that the decision has already been made.

"I was discussing this with DI Gray this morning. We both agree that it is worth a trip up to Leeds to speak with Douglas. Who knows what secrets he still has locked up in that head of his?"

I nod my agreement. "Yes, sir. It's definitely worth a shot. If we get going now, we can be there and back by the end of the day."

"Good, don't let me keep you," Morgan says.

"Sir?"

"I mean, get on your way, son. Call DI Gray on the way back here and don't make Douglas any promises. Understood?"

"Understood fully. Thank you, sir."

Without another word, Morgan turns back towards his computer screen and DI Gray escorts us out. Before we leave, she offers some advice.

"I don't need to remind you both just how cunning Clive Douglas is. He clearly still has connections and just because he is locked up don't make the mistake of thinking that he is any less dangerous than he was on the outside. Be careful with him. Whatever he tells you, it will be purely for his own advantage. Keep that in mind and you will be fine."

We thank DI Gray for the advice and then head to the underground garage to get my car. Without waiting for an invitation, Cath opens the passenger side door and climbs in.

"Oh, right, I'm driving then, am I?" I ask her sarcastically.

Catherine smirks and fastens her seat-belt. "Fair's fair, Sean. I did pretty much all the driving on the last case. I'm sure you can handle a trip to Leeds and back. Be a good boy and I might buy you a late lunch on the way back. Come on, if you put your foot down, we can be there by two."

■ ■ ■ ■ ■ ■ ■ ■

Despite our expectation of a short drive after passing Leeds, Her Majesty's Prison Yarwood is actually located a further fifty miles north-west of Leeds's city center. What isn't a surprise, though, and given its Category A high-risk prisoner status, is its actual location well away from civilization on the edge of the North Yorkshire moors. The prisoners incarcerated here are the worst of the worst and include those classed as highly dangerous to the public or national security in the event of an escape. This categorization could almost have been made for Clive Douglas.

Despite the prison's ominous-sounding status, in the middle of spring the drive in to HMP Yarwood is both picturesque and charming. However, I suspect it would be far less appealing during the winter. Imagine, if you can, the scene from An American Werewolf in London where two young American tourists are wandering in the fog and rainswept desolate moors after dark. I can easily imagine this place would be pretty much the same as that in the winter.

■ ■ ■ ■ ■ ■ ■ ■

At just after two in the afternoon, we arrive at a barrier positioned around one hundred yards from the entrance to the prison. From outside, the prison reminds me very much of the old black and white pictures of Colditz Castle during the Second World War. After a close check of our identification by the prison officer on duty, the barrier is raised and ahead of us a huge pair of steel gates barring the main entrance to the prison swing open. I park the car inside a grim-looking central courtyard, which is surrounded on all four sides by high granite-walled cell blocks and offices. We get out of the car and Cath wastes no time in saying exactly what I am thinking.

"Bloody hell, Sean! This place makes Meerholt nick look like a holiday camp. Christ, I bet even the cockroaches try to break out or top themselves!"

Cath sniggers at her own joke and I nod my agreement.

"Yep, if he wasn't such a target at Meerholt, I'm sure Clive Douglas would be quite happy to go back there. Come on, let's go and see what he has to say for himself."

We are led into the reception area and the officer manning the desk stands up to meet us.

"Detective Sergeant McMillan, Detective Constable Swain, it's good to meet you both. My name is Senior Officer Wilkinson. Welcome to HMP Yarwood."

I shake his hand.

"Great, nice to meet you also. I take it that you were expecting us, and you know why we are here?"

Wilkinson nods and smiles. "Yes, of course. I also recognize you both from the newspapers. That was a great piece of work you did. Particularly with the two bent screws from Meerholt. Really, a great piece of work!"

I feel embarrassed at his obvious admiration and hope he will stop there. He doesn't.

"You put away the two screws that were on the take, Senior Officer Phillip Cartwright and Officer Brendan Taylor. By fingering that pair, you prompted a big shake up within the prison service, which was long overdue in my opinion. There are too many like that pair abusing their positions of responsibility and damaging the reputation of the honest hardworking officers — who, I must add, are very much in the majority. There is still a long way to go but putting those two away has opened a lot of eyes and at least got the ball rolling in the right direction."

Pleased his speech is finally over, I thank Officer Wilkinson for his kind words and ask him to arrange for us to meet privately with Clive Douglas.

"Yes, of course," Wilkinson replies. "Let me show you through to one of our interview rooms."

He comes out from behind the reception desk and escorts us through a series of security doors before showing us into a small windowless room. Inside, there is a small table and four chairs bolted securely to the bare concrete floor, but otherwise the room is empty.

"Make yourself comfortable. Prisoner Douglas should be here in a few minutes. Two of my officers will wait outside during your meeting. Knock when you are ready to come out."

Wilkinson leaves us to get Douglas and I roll my eyes at Catherine.

"I'm not sure about getting comfortable, Cath, and I don't suppose we will be getting offered a tea or coffee anytime soon. My God, this place is bloody grim."

Catherine nods and shrugs her shoulders. "That's probably a good thing, boss. If what we have seen so far is anything to go by, I'm pretty sure the refreshments wouldn't be up to much anyway."

We take a seat on the side of the table facing the door and a few minutes later Clive Douglas is brought in by two hard-looking prison officers. He looks much smaller than I remember. If not shorter, he has definitely lost weight and his face is completely devoid of emotion. A couple of seconds pass as I size him up and then I gesture for him to take a seat. The escorting officers take up their positions outside.

My first impression is of a man who is desperate and broken. My second impression instantly proves how wrong a first impression can be. As soon as the door is closed, Douglas sits upright in his chair and smiles. .

"Sean, my boy, so good to see you. And you, Catherine, I can honestly say that I have never seen you looking quite so lovely. This is such a lovely surprise seeing you both. What brings you up to this neck of the woods?"

The old Clive Douglas's sarcasm and arrogance are well and truly back, if indeed they ever left in the first place. I am about to say something in reply, but Cath beats me to it.

"Looking good yourself, Clive. That new scar really suits you. And that whole half an ear thing — well, that is just so you.

20

Keep up the sarcasm, and I will be happy to arrange for someone to take the other half."

At the mention of the injuries inflicted on him by Frank Butler, the smile quickly leaves Douglas's face and he instinctively lifts a hand to his mutilated left ear. Just as quickly he recovers his composure and drops his hand back to his lap. He looks at me and smirks knowingly before turning back to face Catherine and chuckling to himself.

"Just having a bit of fun with you, DC Swain. No need for threats. We are all friends here."

Before Catherine can say anything else, I kick her foot under the table, and I tap the top of the table to turn Clive's attention back towards me.

"Enough of the screwing around, Douglas. If you have nothing to say worth hearing, then we can end this meeting right now. Let's not forget, though, who asked for this meeting. You said that you had information about another major cold case. What is it?"

A look of seriousness passes across his face, but, with nowhere else to go, Clive Douglas is in no particular hurry and he won't be rushed. For a few seconds he makes a show of stretching his neck and shoulders and trying to get comfortable in his seat, finishing this time-wasting routine by loudly cracking his knuckles. I lose my patience.

"You have five seconds before we leave and have your cell tipped to find your phone, Douglas. Do you bloody well have any information or not?"

He nods his head and then leans across the table. "I have information, Sean. I have lots of very good information and not just about one unsolved case. It's not for free, though. You scratch my back and I scratch yours."

"You want our help in reducing your sentence?"

"No, I want your help in getting me full immunity from prosecution and assisted resettlement for me and my wife."

Cath leans forward and laughs in his face. "Keep bloody dreaming, Clive. There is no immunity for a murderer. The best you can hope for is a free Zimmer frame and a place in a retirement home when they let you out in thirty or forty years."

Unfazed by Cath's comment, Douglas leans back in his chair and smirks at me again. "You really need to keep her under control, Sean. I have something worthwhile to offer. But fair is fair and, like I said, it's not for free."

I nod in agreement. "Maybe so, but like DC Swain just said, you are being held, amongst many other things, for the premeditated murder of Paul Donovan. That single charge alone automatically excludes you from immunity to prosecution. Surely you already know that, Clive."

Now he looks flustered and he hesitates before replying, "But ... but what I have is literally pure gold, and this is just the first of—"

I hold up my hand. "Clive, stop there. Quite frankly if you were to sit here now and tell me that you had conclusive evidence to finger the real Jack the Ripper, or evidence proving who was really behind the assassination of JFK, there would still be zero chance of full immunity for you. You're a murderer, Clive. Do you really think they are going to change the law for a crooked murdering piece of shit like you?"

I'm slightly disappointed with myself for losing my cool so quickly, but any feeling of disappointment soon disappears when Douglas sits back and makes light of it with a small laugh.

"Oh well, you can't blame a fella for trying, can you, Sean? I knew full well that immunity was off the table. I do want a reduction in my sentence, though, and a move to a Category C prison. What I want first, though, is an immediate transfer to a London prison while you make the other arrangements. That's not for me you understand; it's for my wife. She doesn't drive and traveling by train is hard for her. Agree to that and we can do business. What do you say?"

"What I say is that you are living in cloud cuckoo land, Clive. Before we can even begin discussing the possibility of a move or a reduction in sentence, you need to give us something that we can work with. You know the rules as well as I do. You give and we give back, not the other way around. Tell me about this pure gold. If it checks out, then we can see about getting you a move back to the London area as a first step."

"You can guarantee that?"

I shrug my shoulders and let out a small laugh. "No, no I can't. But I can guarantee that you will stay rotting in this shithole forever if you don't give us anything or even think about trying to fuck us around. It's your choice, Clive. Give us something to work with or stay here. It's all the same to me."

He makes a pretense of thinking it over, but we all know that he doesn't have any real choice if he wants to get out of Yarwood. He clears his throat and leans forward across the table again.

"I'm sure that you both know about the 1983 Brinks Mat robbery from the Heathrow Trading Estate. Six robbers got away with twenty-six million pounds in gold bullion, diamonds, and cash. Only two of the six suspects were ever caught and convicted and only a small amount of the gold bullion was ever recovered. The remaining amount would be worth in excess of seventy million quid today."

"And I suppose you know where it is, or where it might be?" I ask sarcastically.

Douglas bursts out laughing. "No bloody idea, Sean. I was still a snot-nosed Detective Constable in 1983. I haven't got a clue about the Brinks Mat case. I was never directly involved in it."

Catherine is already on her feet and touches my shoulder.

"Come on, boss. This asshole has brought us here on a wild goose chase. Let's go."

I'm inclined to agree with her, but before I can stand up, Douglas tells Catherine to wait.

"Hold your horses, princess. I was just setting the scene. Sit down. I promise you, you will want to hear this."

I nod to Catherine who reluctantly sits back down, and I tell Clive to get to the point. He takes another deep breath before continuing.

"Well, as you can imagine, the Brinks Mat robbery was a huge embarrassment to the police, but more importantly it eventually resulted in the collapse of Johnson Matthey Bankers and a huge insurance payout from Lloyds of London."

"And why exactly would that interest us?" Catherine asks.

"Because, DC Swain, some of the board members of Johnson Matthey were senior politicians. Some of those same politicians were also Lloyds of London names. As I'm sure you can understand, these people don't like their names being attached to bad news and they certainly don't like losing their money."

I stop him to ask a question.

"Just to be clear, when you say Lloyds of London names, you mean the private individuals who underwrite and spread the insurance risks?"

"Correct, Sean. They know the risks, but it doesn't make it any easier to accept when the odds go against them."

"Okay," I reply. "But I still have no idea where you are going with this. I suggest that you move on and make your point soon, or we will be leaving."

"The point I am making, Sean, is that the Brinks Mat robbery was so embarrassing for certain senior members of the government that the then Home Secretary ordered a complete press blackout on a second major heist at Heathrow just less than a month later. As far as Joe Public was concerned it never happened."

We remain quiet and Clive continues.

"But it did happen and whilst it wasn't on the same scale as Brinks Mat, this one was still significant and was carried out when the police were still trying to get to grips with the first robbery. You can understand then why the Home Secretary was so keen to make sure it was kept under wraps."

"Really?" I ask. "Do you seriously expect us to believe that after one of the most audacious robberies in UK history, there was a second robbery in the same location less than a month later and it's been kept secret from the public all this time?"

"And with the Heathrow Trading Estate crawling with coppers?" Catherine adds. "Not possible. Heathrow would have been an active crime scene for months after a heist of that magnitude. No criminal in their right mind would have come within ten miles."

Douglas nods. "Yeh, you would think so, wouldn't you? You're right, DC Swain. After Brinks Mat, there was a heavy police presence around that trading estate for months. But it was also a time when the police were up to their eyes in one of the most complex investigations of modern times and, like you, they weren't expecting anyone to have the nerve to try and rob the place again. How wrong they were."

"So, go on then. Give us some details," I prompt him. "If this really did happen, then we need something firm that we can look into. We need dates, names, what was taken etcetera. You do have that information, yes?"

"I get my move back to London?" Douglas counters.

I don't have the authority to agree to anything yet, but I don't want him to clam up on us, so I tell him what he wants to hear.

"If what you have checks out, then yes. Until then you stay here. What have you got?"

Douglas leans back in his chair and then with a smug look on his face he tells Catherine to take out her pocketbook.

"I'm not going to give you too much at this stage, but it will be enough to get you started. The Brinks Mat heist was on November 26th, 1983. The second robbery was on December 24th, 1983."

"Christmas Eve?" Catherine exclaims. "Seriously?"

"Yep, not a very merry Christmas for the boys in blue that year, though," Douglas replies with a grin.

"The same crew that hit Brinks Mat?" I ask him.

"No, they were long gone. It would have been crazy for them to hang around. No, this was a couple of small-time blaggers who were put onto it by someone in the know."

Catherine looks up and asks, "Just three suspects?"

"Yep, just three of them involved. The first was—"

"Hang on," I interrupt. "You said that this was another major robbery, but you're telling us that only three people were involved?"

"That's right, Sean. The whole thing was beautiful in its simplicity. You know yourself that the more people are involved in these things, the greater the risk of someone talking. This was just two fellas, in and out before the security or police even knew what hit them."

"You just said three were involved," Cath says.

"Correct, but only two carried out the actual blag. The third just put them onto it and supplied the intel."

"Okay, so start there, who was the brains of the operation?" I ask.

"No, you get that after my move to London. For now, you can have the names of the blaggers and what they got away with."

It's more of a question than a statement and for a few seconds I say nothing. Douglas knows, though, that he already has us both hooked. I look to Cath and she nods her agreement.

"Fine, give me the names and the haul. If that checks out, then you will get your move to London. After that I want the third name and any other information you have. Clear?"

"Crystal clear, Sean."

"Okay, start with the names."

Douglas straightens up and loudly clears his throat again.

"Okay, the first guy was Patrick 'Paddy' Newman. He would have been around thirty-five at the time. Usual kind of record, starting with shoplifting, vandalism, and burglary in his teens and progressing to armed robbery by his late twenties. Not the sharpest tool in the box apparently, but a bit handy if you know what I mean."

"A thug," Catherine says.

Douglas smiles at her. "I prefer the phrase, not afraid to get stuck in. A shoot first, ask questions later kind of guy, if you know what I mean."

"And where would we find him now?" I ask.

"No idea, that's your job. Ask around, it shouldn't be too hard to track him down."

I ignore the attitude and continue, "Okay, and blagger number two?"

"Michael Davies," Douglas replies. "A couple of years younger than Patrick, but old school friends and long-time partners in crime. Michael was the calmer of the pair. The voice of reason, if you like."

"And his whereabouts now? I suppose you don't know that either," says Catherine.

Douglas sits fully upright and leans towards Catherine.

"Wrong, DC Swain! I know exactly where Michael Davies is. Would you like me to tell you?"

I answer on Catherine's behalf and don't spare the sarcasm. "Yes, please. That would be ever so kind of you, Clive."

In response Douglas laughs and says, "You will find Michael Davies in the same place he has been since February 1984 ... Highgate Cemetery."

He waits for a couple of seconds in expectation of a reaction to this news, but when there is none, he continues speaking.

"Okay, so just over a month after the heist, and for no apparent reason, Paddy Newman walked into a pub in broad daylight and put a bullet in Michael's face. There was obviously some kind of falling out. Presumably it was over the proceeds of the robbery."

"You say presumably. You don't know for sure?"

Douglas shakes his head. "No. There were plenty of witnesses to the shooting, so Paddy Newman was pulled soon after for the murder and in connection to the robbery, but he kept his mouth firmly shut about both. He served twenty-two years of a life sentence. He would have been released sometime around 2007."

"And you don't know where he is now?" Catherine asks.

Douglas looks at Catherine and smirks. "You need to pay attention, DC Swain. I told you two minutes ago that I don't know where he is. Why don't you refer to your notes?"

Douglas is deliberately trying to wind Cath up, but she keeps her cool and says nothing. I ask again about the third suspect.

"If you want to move back to the London area, then I need that name."

"Not going to happen, Sean. I've told you enough already to be going on with. You get the third name when I get my move."

I nod and carry on. "Fine, tell us about the haul. What did they get away with?"

28

"Around two million in cash, five million in gold bullion, and another three million in precious gems. The cash and gems were found under the floorboards at Newman's mother's house, but the gold bullion has never been found."

Douglas leans over to leer at Cath's legs before sitting back with a smirk. "I'm no expert, DC Swain, but I reckon that bullion would be worth at least twenty million in today's money. That would buy a lot of pairs of Jimmy Choo's, princess."

I'm about to say something, but Catherine holds up her hand to stop me. "It's okay, boss. Let him get his kicks while he can. It must be hard knowing that by the time he next gets to touch a woman he will be well past getting it up. Isn't that right, Clive? By the time you get out, it will have shriveled up and fallen off."

Catherine laughs and Douglas looks to me in expectation that I will intervene.

"What? You don't think you deserved that?" I ask him.

Clearly offended and without waiting for permission, Douglas stands up.

"We are done here, McMillan. That's good information I have just given you. But that's it for now. Until you get me back to London, you get nothing else. You know how to get hold of me."

I stand up to block him. "We're done for now on this case, but there is one other thing. You need to stand down on Maria and Ben Pinto. If anything happens to them, I promise that you will stay in this shithole and never see the light of day again. Do we understand each other?"

He agrees and then without another word he knocks on the cell door and calls to be let out. The door opens and I nod to the two prison officers, who lead Douglas away.

We wait for the door to close and then Catherine says, "So, do you think he is full of shit, boss?"

29

I laugh at her comment. "I think that's a given, Cath. But in his situation, why would he bring us all the way here just to feed us a line of bullshit? He knows with just a couple of calls and a search of the crime database that we can easily find out if he is telling the truth about this blag. No, I think, for once, Clive Douglas might actually be telling the truth. Come on, let's get out of here. I'm bloody starving."

■ ■ ■ ■ ■ ■ ■

On the way back to London, Catherine calls DI Sarah Gray to tell her about our meeting with Douglas. I call Maria to let her know that she is in no danger and that the police officers watching over her and Ben will be leaving. Understandably, she is not completely reassured, but she trusts that I would never leave either of them exposed.

When we finally arrive back at Blackwell Station it is already getting late, but DI Gray is waiting for us and invites us into her office. As we take a seat, she places a thin Manilla case file onto the desk.

"It's not much, Sean. But it does look like Douglas was telling the truth. This is Operation Hush."

"Operation Hush?" I ask quizzically.

"I think somebody's idea of a joke," DI Gray responds. "If what Clive Douglas says is true about the Home Secretary wanting this one kept quiet, then perhaps Hush Hush would have been more appropriate. Whatever the reason, the robbery was real enough and the rest of the information he gave you also seems to check out. The two named suspects were Patrick Newman aged thirty-six and Michael Davies aged thirty-four. They went to the same school together in Fulham and were known partners in crime. The file confirms a third, as yet un-named, suspect, who is still officially classified as at large."

"Anything about the robbery proceeds, ma'am?" Catherine asks.

"Yes, pretty much what you were told by Douglas. A large amount of cash, gold, and precious gems. The gold has never been recovered."

I point to the file. "I don't suppose there is a current address in there for Patrick Newman?"

"Unfortunately, no. Just the address of the bail hostel he was sent to after his release from prison. I did a bit of digging though. I don't have an address, but he collects his pension every Tuesday from the main post office on Fulham High Street. If I were a betting woman, I would say that from there he probably heads straight to the nearest pub. Here, take the file home tonight and see what you make of it. Let's regroup in the morning to see if this case merits looking into further."

I take the file and stand up to leave. Catherine asks me to wait. She turns to DI Gray.

"About Clive Douglas's request for a transfer back to the London area, now that we know the case is real, it may be to our advantage to have him somewhere close by, ma'am."

Sarah nods her head. "Yes, perhaps you are right, Catherine. Leave it with me. I will speak to the boss to get his opinion. I will let you both know the decision in the morning."

We leave DI Gray working on her computer and, after making a copy of the file for Catherine, we separate. I drive home to review the file contents for something that might give me a reason to travel tonight.

■ ■ ■ ■ ■ ■ ■

After a quick shower and a change of clothes, I call to order Chinese food and then I pour myself a large whisky and spread out the file contents on my coffee table. Everything is as expected and more or less corroborates what Clive Douglas told us earlier today. After the robbery, there was a full investigation that drew a complete blank until the untimely death of Michael Davies.

With multiple witnesses to the shooting, in a pub called the Bluebell, Paddy Newman was quickly identified. Within hours he was picked up drinking in another pub nearby, the Fox and Hounds, and after the discovery of the cash and jewels at his mother's house, he was interrogated non-stop by the Serious Crimes Squad for almost two weeks about both the robbery and the murder.

Throughout the questioning he confirmed the existence of a third offender, who seemed to be the ringleader, but insisted that he had never met him and did not know his identity. He also maintained throughout that he did not know the whereabouts of the missing bullion. With no further leads to go on, he was formally charged with the premeditated murder of Michael Davies and the heist at Heathrow.

After his conviction, the investigation continued intermittently for another two years before it was finally relegated to the ranks of the many other unsolved cases in the Metropolitan Police archives.

■ ■ ■ ■ ■ ■ ■ ■

My takeaway arrives and without finding anything useful yet, I push the file to one side and switch on the television to watch the ten o'clock news. The big stories are of Kim Jong-Un crossing into South Korea for an historic summit, a hit-and-run driver ploughing his car into a group of pedestrians outside a Birmingham mosque, and William and Kate revealing the name of their third child to the world's press.

Unbeknownst to him, young Prince Louis Arthur Charles Windsor was fifth in the line of succession to the British throne. Through a mouthful of soy-soaked noodles, I wonder to myself if the monarchy will still be around when Prince Louis is grown up.

I finish my dinner and then reopen the file. I take out the notes relating to the murder of Michael Davies. He was shot dead by Newman at 7:47 p.m. on the evening of Saturday February 4th, 1984 in the Bluebell Pub. I have no idea if the Bluebell Pub is still standing, but the address is also in Fulham and not too far from where Paddy Newman now collects his pension. It's likely then that this was one of the favorite watering holes of Newman and Davies. It's the only lead so far to tracking them down in 1984, and definitely worth a visit, but I need something more to give me a better idea of what date to aim for.

I skim through the file contents for another ten minutes before I find what I am looking for. Both suspects have rap sheets as long as my arm, but it is the entries from December 1983 that interest me the most. I slowly run my finger down the page from Michael's file and when I reach the entry for Friday December 9th, I stop and congratulate myself.

"Fucking bingo, Sean! I bet they went straight to the pub after this. I'll bet my life on it."

I read the entry again and then I cross reference the same entry in Newman's file. Both entries match exactly. Newman's car was pulled over at just after 5 p.m. for a routine traffic stop. After running their details, it was discovered that Newman was driving without insurance or tax and Davies had numerous warrants out on him for unpaid traffic violations. Nothing particularly serious in the scheme of things, but enough to haul them both off to jail for a couple of hours. The entry notes that they were both bailed and released at just after 7:30, with a court date set for March of the following year. Subsequent events would obviously dictate that neither of them would ever make that court appearance for traffic offences. I, however, now have a solid date to aim for tonight.

I close the file and say to myself again, "Yep, they would have headed straight to the pub after they made bail, I'm sure of it."

I pour myself another drink and then I take a long hard look at the mugshots of Paddy Newman and Michael Davies in readiness for my trip back to Fulham circa December 1983.

I'm not particularly tired and have only had two glasses of whiskey, but with each subsequent experience of dream travel, these factors are seeming to become less and less of a necessity. With the faces of my two suspects clear in my mind, I lie down on my sofa, close my eyes and begin my chant.

"December ninth, 1983, December ninth, 1983, Dec—"

Barely a few seconds have passed before a blinding light engulfs me and I am there.

The Past – Friday, December 9th, 1983

Since the mid-sixties, the London borough of Hammersmith and Fulham has been a stronghold for successive Labour-party-dominated councils, with the exception of an eight-year period under Conservative control between 2006 and 2014.

Like many London boroughs, the ethnic mix in Fulham has seen a significant shift from predominantly white British in the seventies and eighties to an eclectic melting pot of white British, white non-British, Caribbean, African, and Asian in 2018.

Standing here now, though, on the edge of a bustling street market, just off Fulham High Street in 1983, the majority ethnic group is still very much white British.

I watch for a few minutes and notice that — whilst there are also a good few Asian, African, and Caribbean faces amongst the passersby and stall holders — the eastern Europeans who came to London in their droves from 2007 following the expansion of the European Union are now very much conspicuous in their absence.

I pick up a newspaper from a newsstand and, after checking the date, put it down and check the time on my watch.

"Just after 6 p.m. They were arrested at 5 p.m. and released a couple of hours later. I'd better get going," I mumble to myself.

The newspaper vendor hands some change back to one of his customers and then turns towards me.

"Sorry, pal. What was that you said?"

As he speaks, he looks me over, but there is nothing much to see and he doesn't make any comment about how I look. Without time to plan, I have deliberately dressed down in a pair of plain gray-flannel jogging bottoms with a matching gray hoodie. My running shoes are also my least flashy pair and unlikely to attract any interest or attention.

I smile and shake my head. "Sorry, just talking to myself. Ignore me, mate."

The vendor looks unimpressed as he reaches forward to straighten up the newspaper I had been looking at.

"You don't want this then?"

"Um, sorry, no," I reply. "Could you point me in the direction of Fulham police station though?"

"What am I, a bleedin' information desk?" he responds, screwing up his face.

Begrudgingly, he points away to the right and says, "It's that way. Down through the market. Turn right at the end and onto the high street. Keep walking and it's on the left."

I try to thank him, but he turns to serve his next customer and waves me away with the back of his hand.

"Yeh, yeh, whatever. Next time you just want directions, go and bother some other mug." Then to the woman he's serving, he laughs and says, "Cheeky bastard! Do I look like bloody Citizens Advice to you, love?"

■ ■ ■ ■ ■ ■ ■

I leave the newspaper vendor to his grumbling and head off in search of the police station. It is already getting dark, but the market is busy with pre-Christmas shoppers, party-goers and people making their way home from work. Although it is cold, the addition of piped Christmas music and gaudy red and green decorations throughout the market contributes to an overall happy and festive mood.

Even the buskers scattered along the length of the market don't seem to mind that they are competing with the Flying Pickets' surprise hit, 'Only You', which seems to be blasting out from every café and pub. It was the Christmas number-one song in 1983 and, depending on your point of view, it has either been entertaining or driving people nuts at Christmas ever since.

Although I have a job to do, I still take time to marvel at the eighties fashions as I wander through the market. Much of what is on display is a glaring reminder of some of my own recent travels. In 1983, the Skinheads, Punks, and the Soccer Casuals were very much in their glory days and all are present in and around the market in large numbers.

Today, though, there is no hint of menace. For all these groups, a big part of who and what they are is looking good and being seen. Hanging about in a public place is, I guess, an essential element of being seen. No point after all in looking good if there isn't an audience around to appreciate it.

I find the punks particularly fascinating with their bondage trousers, oversized multi-colored mohawk hairstyles, chains, piercings, and crazy makeup. I couldn't pull the look off myself, but I do admire them for having the guts to dress so outrageously outside of Halloween.

I keep walking until I reach the end of the market and am just about to turn right onto the high street, when I am stopped in my tracks. I look back towards a group of five young men who have just passed me heading into the market. Without thinking I turn and loudly blurt out a name, "Darren?"

A sharply dressed young casual spins around on his heels and says, "What was that, pal? How the fuck do you know my name and who the fuck are you?"

If I was slightly unsure before, now I know for certain. He can't be more than fourteen or fifteen years old, but the Tottenham shirt poking out from under his jacket confirms beyond doubt that I am now looking at Darren 'Daz' Phillips five or six years before I first meet him in 1989.

I'm not sure who is more taken aback at this chance meeting, but I am sure that it is more than just coincidence. In any case, meeting him has given me an idea. While he is still trying to work out who I am, his mates gather round and a stocky young man asks him, "What's going on, Daz? Who is this old prick?"

In answer to the question, I take out my warrant card and quickly flash it under their noses. I don't allow them to get a good look, but it is enough to make them hesitate and back away. Darren, though, stands his ground and I take a step forward.

"It's Darren Phillips, isn't it? What are you doing in Fulham? This is the stomping ground for the Chelsea, Fulham, and QPR crews. You're taking a bit of a risk coming here wearing Spurs colors, aren't you?"

Still unsure of who I am and what I want, he at first hesitates to answer. When he does answer, he is playing up to his audience and is the Darren that I know and love.

"I don't know who the fuck you are, copper, but I haven't done anything wrong and where I choose to go is my bloody business. So, fuck you and fuck any other crew that wants to have a pop. I fucking shit Chelsea, Fulham, and Queer PR."

Then, with a wink to his mates, he adds, "Are we done here, pal? Because it's Friday night and the birds aren't gonna shag themselves."

His colorful blending of the English language and youthful bravado has me struggling to stifle a grin, but I hold it back and, after staring him down for a few seconds, I ask, "How would you and your mates like to earn twenty quid each for ten minutes' work?"

Darren screws up his face. "What? What the fuck are you on about, pal?"

"I think he wants a gang-bang," one of Darren's mates chips in with a laugh.

"Yeh, he looks like a right fucking nonce," another of them adds.

They all join in the laughter and Darren nods and grins. "Is that it, pal? You want us all to nosh you off?"

I shake my head and Darren turns towards his gang. "My mistake, lads. He wants to nosh us off."

They all piss themselves laughing and as Darren turns back to face me, I step forward and slap him hard across the face with the back of my hand.

The laughing stops instantly. Darren and his mates are frozen to the spot with the shock of the assault, but Darren quickly composes himself. His initial look of shock turns to a look of defiance. I know that I only have a few more seconds to press my advantage before the rest of them have time to gather their wits.

"Okay, Darren, now that I have your attention, let's talk business. Do you and your girlfriends want to earn twenty quid each for doing what you do best, or do I call my mates to haul you all down to the station? It's your choice. Easy beer money, or Friday night in the nick getting fucked around?"

"But we've done fuck all wrong," one of Darren's mate's protests.

"Yeh, and we could have you done for assault," another of them adds. "You're not a bloody copper. Let's see that badge again."

I point at each one and snap at them to button it. "You lot, shut your bloody pie holes. I was talking to the organ grinder, not his monkeys." Then to Darren, "You lot like a good scrap, right?"

While he is still thinking it over, I take five twenty-pound notes from my wallet and hold them out in front of me. Darren looks me up and down and then cautiously takes the money, "So, what is it you want us to do?"

I smile and nod. "Good, do you know where the Bluebell Pub is?

■ ■ ■ ■ ■ ■ ■

After going over the plan once more with Darren and his boys, I leave them and continue on to Fulham Police Station.

I arrive at just after 7 p.m. and take a seat in a bus shelter on the opposite side of the street from the station entrance.

For thirty minutes, I watch as a steady stream of squad cars and meat wagons arrive to offload or pick up the flotsam and wastrels of London. Most I imagine are the inevitable Christmas party drunks that the festive season brings out year after year.

Unused to smashing back so much booze in such a short space of time, the usually quiet and reserved office workers, secretaries, bankers, and lawyers miraculously transform into the brawlers and gropers that fill the cells across the country during every public holiday or special occasion in the UK.

The only difference between 1983 and 2018 is the ratio of men to women in the cells. In 2018 the women are just as likely as the men to be involved in a scrap and even to start one. God only knows what it will be like in another thirty years.

At 7.35 p.m., a bus passes, momentarily blocking my view of the station entrance. As it moves away, two men appear on the station steps and I stand up to get a better look.

Both men are unmistakable. Even from this distance, I can see that Paddy Newman is a big lad. He is at least six inches taller than Michael and twice as broad. Both are wearing black woolen caps and are similarly dressed in dirty jeans, donkey jackets, and scruffy steel-capped boots. I remember from their files that neither of them was in permanent employment, but both were known for taking casual laboring work on construction sites.

Michael turns up his collar to keep out the early evening chill and then they turn left and walk in the direction of the market. I lift my hood over my head before I cross the street to follow behind from a discreet distance.

I'm gambling on them going to the Bluebell Pub. If I'm wrong and they go somewhere else, I will have just pissed away my money and Darren and his mates will have a good laugh and a few pints at my expense. I have a good feeling, though, and after walking for ten minutes, I smile when I see the signboard for the Bluebell up ahead.

They go inside, and I hold back for a few minutes to give them time to get a drink and relax. Happy that enough time has passed, I take a deep breath to steady my nerves and enter the pub.

■ ■ ■ ■ ■ ■ ■ ■

While the elderly barman pulls me a pint, I turn and casually scan the bar area.

For a Friday evening close to Christmas, the Bluebell is quieter than I would have expected it to be. After taking a quick look around, though, it's not really that surprising.

If I were to call this place a shithole, I would be doing an injustice to shitholes. With its tired and filthy décor and its equally tired and filthy clientele, cesspit would be a more fitting description for the Bluebell Pub.

Being quiet, however, may work in my favor tonight. With what I have planned, I don't need any have-a-go heroes or bystanders getting involved or getting hurt.

I need to get a move on, though. Darren and his mates wouldn't normally be seen dead in a place like this, and I don't want them to attract any attention until I am ready. Unfortunately, their current behavior is making it highly likely that they will attract attention.

Darren and his mates are gathered around a video game playing Space Invaders. Disappointingly, and despite my earlier instruction to keep a low profile, they are knocking back the pints and loudly egging each other on. To make things worse, Darren turns towards me and nods to where Paddy and Michael are sitting.

Thankfully, the two men are deep in conversation and don't look up from their drinks. I turn back to face Darren, drawing my hand across my throat to indicate that they should shut the fuck up. Then I walk towards the bathroom, indicating for him to follow.

After checking that we are alone, I ask what the hell they are playing at.

"What part of 'keep a low profile' did you bunch of numb-nuts not understand? It's bad enough that you're all drinking under-age without you also feeling the need to make enough bloody racket to wake the dead. If you screw this up, you and your mates are going to be spending Christmas in the cells. Do you understand me, Darren?"

Darren still has his drink in his hand and instead of answering immediately, he chugs the rest of his pint and then carefully places the glass down on the edge of one of the sinks.

"It seems to me that this is screwed up already, pal."

"What do you mean?"

"What I mean is, have you seen the size of one of those fellas? He's got hands like bloody shovels. You said it was easy money. Give them a few slaps, you said. You didn't say anything about spending Christmas in bloody Accident and Emergency. You said—"

"Whoa, stop right there, Darren. There are five of you boys and only two of them. Don't tell me you're scared of—"

"You said that you were going to step in on their side, so that's three of you," Darren interrupts me.

I laugh and shake my head.

"Okay, so it's five against three. Don't tell me that you don't fancy your chances against three old codgers? Anyway, I told you already, as soon as I step in you can all make yourself scarce. I'll make sure that none of you get seriously hurt. Any more questions or concerns or can we get on with it?"

"Just one question," Darren says. "What's this all about? Why don't you just arrest them if you need something from them?"

"None of your bloody business," I reply.

"Okay, so how about you at least tell me who you are?"

"Also none of your bloody business, Darren. Now get out there and earn your twenty quid. I'll be watching from the bar. So make sure it looks good."

Another twenty minutes pass before the right moment presents itself. Thankfully for all concerned, it is Michael that gets up to go to the bar for fresh drinks and not Paddy. I nod to Darren who places himself directly behind Michael. As he turns to go back to his table, Darren accidentally on purpose shoulder barges him and sends the drinks flying.

Only a small amount of the beer ends up on Darren, but the wheels of this act are now well and truly in motion and nothing and no-one is going to stop them moving forward. As the drinks fall to the floor, Darren theatrically lurches backwards and looks down with disgust at his very lightly soaked Fila tracksuit bottoms. He then looks back up at Michael who is wiping himself down with a beer towel.

"You stupid old dickhead. Look what you've bloody done! These cost me a bloody fortune, mate. You need to watch where you're bloody going, grandad."

Michael puts down the beer towel and calmly straightens himself up.

"And you need to mind your bloody manners, son."

"Or what?" Darren taunts.

The reply comes from behind him and is far more menacing.

"Or you are going to find yourself on the end of my fist, boy. I saw what happened and I think you're the one that needs to look where he is going."

Then Paddy adds, "Now, be a good boy and apologize to my friend and offer to buy us two fresh drinks before I lose my patience."

The atmosphere in the pub is now electric and for a moment I think that my plan may have gone to shit. Despite having his mates nearby, Darren looks unsure of himself and I'm worried that he may be about to apologize.

I needn't have worried though. After a few seconds of uncomfortable silence, he looks first to Michael and then to Paddy before he turns to pick up a freshly poured pint of lager, which he offers to Michael.

"There you go. No hard feelings, mate."

Michael looks at the drink and shakes his head.

"You're going to have to do better than that, son. I'm a bitter drinker, and that's lager."

With a fake look of confusion, Darren lifts the glass to his face and makes a show of carefully inspecting the drink. Then he nods and smiles, before hurling the contents of the glass in Michael's face. At the same time, he skillfully sidesteps to avoid Paddy's giant fist crashing into the back of his head.

Darren's boys waste no time piling in and as the brawl erupts in earnest, I pick up my glass and move further down the bar to wait for the right moment to get involved. For a minute or so, Michael and Paddy hold their own, but even at such a young age, Darren and his boys are tough little bastards and competent scrappers. With the tide turning against my targets and no-one else stepping into help, I take a swig from my glass and nod to the barman who is about to call the police.

"No need for that. The cavalry is already here."

Unsure of who I am, he hesitates, and I tell him again. This time there is no misunderstanding the insistence in my words. "I said, put the phone down, old man. Nobody needs the coppers getting involved, do they?"

The barman drops the handset onto its cradle, and I smile and push my empty glass across the bar.

"Good, now fill that up. I'm going to be thirsty when I'm done."

Two of the boys have a firm grip on Michael's arms, whilst a third is jabbing body shots into his ribs. I start on this lad first. I kick downwards into the back of his knees and as he falls, I slam my fist into the back of his head. At the same time, Michael gets one arm free and manages to land a belter of a punch in the face of the lad still holding him. The punch sends the boy careering backwards and with his second arm released, Michael falls to the floor with the wind knocked out of him.

Unsure of whether he is supposed to hit me or not, the third guy hesitates just a moment too long. In the interest of keeping it real, I slam my knee upwards into his bollocks and follow it up with an elbow to the back of his head. The three of them don't wait to find out what happens next. They leg it out of the door and I help Michael back to his feet.

On the other side of the bar, Darren and the fifth boy are going at Paddy with a pair of pool cues. Although he doesn't appear to be badly hurt, Paddy is doubled over with his arms over his head to protect himself. I know, though, that if he manages to get back to his feet fully, he could quite easily do some serious damage to his assailants.

I leave Michael to regain his senses and rejoin the fight by landing a half-hearted punch on Darren's shoulder. He turns to confront me, and I pull him forward into a bear hug. The last guy is already running and before Paddy can get to him I push Darren away towards the door.

"Go on, ya little bastard. Get the fuck out of here before I rip your bloody head off."

In no mood to let him off so easily, Paddy gives chase, but I have seen Darren run before and I'm quietly confident that he won't be caught.

Sure enough, a few seconds later, Paddy storms back into the bar with a face like thunder.

"Those little bastards. If I see them around here again, I'll bloody tear their heads off and shit down their necks. What the fuck was that all about, Mike?"

Michael is at the bar holding a handful of ice over a small swelling above his right eye. Unlike Paddy, he doesn't seem to be concerned about what has just happened. Quite the opposite in fact. In answer to Paddy's question he puts down the ice and has a small laugh to himself.

"Ah forget it, Paddy. Just a bunch of kids that have had their first sniff of the barmaid's apron. No different from us when we were that age. Fuck em, let's get another drink."

Paddy is still raging and considers for a moment going back outside, but then he thinks better of it and reluctantly says, "Ah sod it," under his breath before joining Michael at the bar.

Spotting two freshly poured pints of bitter settling on the drip tray, Michael reaches into his wallet to pay, but the barman shakes his head and nods in my direction.

"With the compliments of the fella at the end of the bar, gents."

Despite coming to their rescue, Paddy eyes me with suspicion. Michael, however, raises his glass and invites me over. I offer my hand and Michael introduces himself. Paddy ignores my invitation to shake hands, but I do get a begrudging nod of acknowledgment.

Picking up on this, Michael laughs and slaps me on the back.

"Aww, pay no mind to the big fella. That's his way of saying he likes you. He's really quite friendly when you get to know him. Isn't that right, Paddy? Go on, shake hands with the man. That's the least you can do after he got stuck in like that to help us."

Paddy is clearly still angry about the fight, but, not wishing to argue with Mike, he nods and holds out one of his huge hands.

"The name's Paddy, Paddy Newman. Thanks for your help. Although we could have taken those little bastards on our own, you know. But thanks anyway. What did you say your name was?"

"It's Sean. Sean Smith," I reply. "And it was no problem. I've never been one to stand around when it's an unfair fight. Besides, it's been a while since I had a good scrap. It's good to know that I've still got it."

Paddy still looks unconvinced, but Michael is already sold on my story and slaps me on the back again.

"Fucking too right, pal. We showed those little bastards, didn't we? Come on, come and sit with us. We owe you a couple of jars."

He points me towards his table and then turns back to the barman and calls out, "Barkeep, more beers and a round of whisky chasers, my good man."

■ ■ ■ ■ ■ ■ ■

While Michael pays for the drinks, Paddy takes the seat opposite and thanks me again for stepping in to help.

"I'm serious about what I said at the bar, Sean, we could have taken those little fuckers. I was just getting warmed up. But I do appreciate your getting stuck in. Most fellas would have just let them get on with it. So, what's your story, Sean? I don't recall seeing you around here before."

There is more than a hint of suspicion in the question, but I am saved from answering for now by the arrival of Michael carrying a tray laden with three fresh pints and three whisky chasers.

"Enough of the chit chat, ladies, give me a hand with these."

A pint and a chaser are placed down in front of me and Michael proposes a toast, "This is to ... sorry, what did you say your name was again?"

Paddy is looking directly at me when he answers for me, "It's Sean, Sean Smith apparently."

"Oh yeh, that's right," Michael says. "Right, this is to our new mate Sean and to kicking the shit out of those little assholes."

We smash back the whisky chasers and then Michael asks what we were talking about.

"I was asking Sean what his story was," Paddy says.

Although this time it's not a direct question, they both look at me in the expectation that I am about to tell them my whole life story.

I briefly feign innocence and then I ask them what they would like to know.

"Well, we know that you're a bit handy with your fists, but that's all we know," Michael says. "So how about you tell us where you are from and what you do. You're a London boy, but you're not from Fulham, are you?"

"No, you're right about that, Mike. I'm originally from Feltham, but I'm living in Hounslow now."

"So, what are you doing around here then?" Paddy asks.

I shrug my shoulders. "Ah, you know how it is. There's not much work around anywhere just now, so I thought I'd cast the net a bit wider."

Michael nods. "Yeh, I hear you, Sean. So, what is it you do?"

"This and that," I reply.

"How about being a bit more specific?" Paddy grunts.

Michael tuts and says, "Ah, for fuck's sake, calm yourself down, Paddy. Sean is okay. Isn't that right, Sean?"

"No, it's okay," I say "It's a fair enough question. I don't really have a trade to speak of. I mostly do casual work. A bit of kitchen work, a bit of laboring. Anything I can get, really."

"Fair enough," Michael says. "Any luck today?"

"No, not a thing. I've been banging on doors since eight this morning and all I've got to show for it is sore feet."

Michael is about to speak when I add, "With my record, I'm used to it, though." Then for extra effect I laugh and say, "Fuck, with my record, I wouldn't even give myself a job."

This extra comment seems to lighten the mood with Paddy, and he sits up straight in his chair.

"So, you've done time then?"

Both lean forward in anticipation of my answer. I deliberately hesitate, and Michael gives me a knowing look.

It's okay, Sean. You're amongst friends here. What were you in for? Nothing minor, I hope?"

They both chuckle at Michael's joke and then Paddy asks again, "Go on then. What was it, Sean?"

"Nothing very serious," I reply. "A couple of stretches in a Borstal for theft and vandalism. Then two stretches up north for burglary, assault, and car theft."

Paddy sits back in his chair and laughs. "You're right, it wasn't very serious, was it, Sean? What do you think, Mickey? Is he a regular Al Capone or a regular—?"

Before he can finish the quip, he is interrupted by a shout from the bar. The barman is holding up the phone and when he doesn't get a response, he repeats what he has just said, "Michael, it's a call for you. They didn't give a name but said that it's important."

Neither of my companions seem to be surprised by the call and this is confirmed when Michael says to Paddy, "That must be 'T'. You stay here with Sean. I shouldn't be long."

No sooner has Michael left the table when Paddy also stands up. "No offence, Sean, but I need a piss. I'm sure you can amuse yourself for a few minutes, but if you do get bored, I recommend reading the back of the beer mats. There are some interesting facts on them about the flora and fauna of Africa."

As he walks away to the bathroom, I raise my eyebrows and sarcastically thank him for the advice.

With Paddy out of the way, I turn my attention towards the end of the bar where Michael is on the phone. Unfortunately, he has his back turned to me, so there's no chance of picking anything useful up without taking the risk of moving closer. I rule this out as too risky, and instead pick up one of the beer mats and turn it over.

A few minutes later, Paddy plonks himself back down in his seat and I tell him that he was right.

"Right about what?" he asks.

"The flora and fauna of Africa. It's very interesting. Did you know that in Madagascar there is a man-eating tree called the Yateveo?"

My apparent naivety seems to work in my favor and, in a sign that Paddy is warming to me, he laughs and says, "Jesus, Sean, how bloody long was I gone? Bloody man-eating trees, for fuck's sake."

Concentrating fully on Paddy, I don't notice that Michael's call has ended until he retakes his seat next to me.

"What are you two dickheads rabbiting on about?"

"Sean was just telling me about some tree in Africa that eats fellas alive. I was just about to tell him about a couple of birds I know who do much the same thing."

50

Paddy laughs at his own joke, but sensing that Michael has something to say, he stops and asks if everything is okay.

"Yep, all good," Michael replies. Then turning to me, "In fact, that was an old friend on the phone, Sean. If you meet us back here tomorrow morning, we might be able to put a bit of work your way. That's if you are interested, of course?"

This first trip couldn't have gone any better, but not wishing to sound overeager, I deliberately sound hesitant in accepting the offer to meet again.

"What kind of work? It's nothing dodgy, is it? I don't want to get mixed up in anything heavy, Mike."

Michael looks to Paddy, who gives him a nod.

"Nothing dodgy and nothing heavy," Michael reassures me. "Maybe just a bit of driving and a bit of moving some stuff around. An honest day's work for a decent wedge of cash in your hand. What do you say?"

I nod and smile. "Okay. Yeh, that sounds good. So, I come back here, yes?"

"Yep, come in tomorrow morning around eleven. We can give you the details over a fry-up and a cup of tea."

No sooner have I said that it sounds perfect when Michael stands up and tells Paddy that they need to get going.

"Sorry, Sean, I would love to stay and finish my drink, but we have business to attend to. Eleven o'clock tomorrow morning, okay? And don't be late."

Without another word they leave, and I am left alone at the table. To be sure that they are not still hanging around outside, I take another five minutes to finish my pint before I also leave.

I set off to find Darren.

■ ■ ■ ■ ■ ■ ■ ■

The time is just after 9:20, but it's already bitterly cold and I shiver as I step out onto the street. With tonight's plan already complete, I should now be finding my way home. But before I do, there is still one loose end that needs to be tied up. I retrace my steps to where I first bumped into Darren and his crew at the entrance to the market.

When I get there, I'm pleasantly surprised to find all five of them waiting for me, exactly as I had instructed.

Darren is sporting a cocky smirk as he steps forward to meet me.

"You look surprised to see us," he observes.

"I am. And for the second time tonight," I reply. "I was surprised that you turned up in the Bluebell at all, and I'm even more surprised that you're here now."

Darren raises his hands in mock indignation. "What are you talking about, mate? We made a deal and took your money. That's a matter of honor where we come from."

Before I can respond to this obvious line of bullshit, Darren laughs and says, "Nah, but seriously. We're here because you seem to know all about me. And you said that there might be a bit more work for us if we did okay. Is that right?"

I look beyond him to where his boys are leaning against a graffiti-covered wall.

"You did okay, I guess. What do you say, lads? Would you be up for a bit more cash, if it were on offer?"

They all nod, and I point to the young guy who was on the receiving end of my knee to his bollocks. "What about you, numb-nuts? If I give you some more work, are you going to get stuck in, or are you just going to stand there again like a spare prick at a wedding?"

Clearly embarrassed in front of his mates, his face flushes red and he blurts out a feeble apology. In fairness to him, though, it was just the luck of the draw. It's highly likely that the other lads, including Darren, would have also hesitated to hit me.

Whether they would or wouldn't have hit me is irrelevant, though, at this point. I have a part to play and no time for sympathy. I laugh at his discomfort and call him a dickhead before turning back to Darren.

"Okay, Phillips, give me a telephone number where I can get hold of you."

I scribble the number down in my pocketbook, and then I read it back to him to confirm.

"Yeh, that's it. But for fuck's sake, be discreet, will ya? That's my mum's number. She will go apeshit if she thinks I'm in trouble with the old bill."

I give Darren a look to tell him I don't really care, and then I say, "Yeh, whatever. Go on then, piss off. I'll be in touch if I need you."

Without needing to be told twice, my new recruits disappear into the market and are soon out of sight.

■ ■ ■ ■ ■ ■ ■

I continue walking until I come across a pair of dossers who have bedded down for the night in a shop doorway. Both look me up and down with suspicion and one of them loudly objects when I push him over to make room for myself.

"What the fucking shit! This is our place. Piss off and find—"

The sight of my last twenty-pound note waving in his face instantly silences the grumbling. He greedily reaches forward to snatch the note from my hand, but I quickly pull it away and point to the cheap bottle of Vodka poking out from under his filthy and torn puffer jacket.

"Give me a big swig of that and a place to sleep and the money is yours."

Twenty quid for a swig from a five-pound bottle of Vodka is a great deal under any circumstances. I know it and they know it. Seduced by the lure of easy money, the second dosser straightens up and snatches the bottle from his friend. He hands it over and they both watch with fascination as I chug a quarter of the contents before I hand it back.

As promised, I hand over the money and with the Vodka already having the required effect to dull my senses, I slump backwards onto the pavement next to the dossers who are already burrowing back down into their sleeping bags to keep out the winter cold. It's not yet 10 p.m., but the temperature is already close to freezing. Within another few hours it will be well below that. Under any other circumstances, only a madman would be out on such a night without adequate clothing or protection.

For my purposes, though, it suits just fine. The cheap Vodka has helped make me drowsy and with any luck I will soon be oblivious to the cold. I take a final look up to the stars before pulling my hood down across my face and sarcastically thanking my friends for their hospitality.

"Truly, gentlemen, it has been an honor to meet you and to stay at such a fine establishment. If the breakfast is as good as the hospitality, I shall be leaving you a glowing review on Trip Advisor."

My words are met with a chuckle and one of my hosts leaves me with his own final comment before he rolls over to face the wall. "You're off your bloody rocker, mate. You'll bloody freeze to death if you stay like that tonight."

"Thanks, buddy. I certainly hope so. Sleep tight, don't let the bed bugs bite."

I close my eyes to begin my journey home.

Present Day – Friday, April 27th, 2018

I'm surprised to find that DCI Morgan is absent from the morning briefing. Instead, it is led by DI Sarah Gray. She keeps the briefing to exactly one hour, but there is no mention of the information received from Clive Douglas, or the fact that we are looking into it.

With the briefing over, DI Gray asks us to join her in her new office and she wastes no time in getting down to business.

"I spoke to the boss last night about your trip up north to see Clive Douglas. We both agree that the information he has provided so far is worth looking into further."

"So, the case is officially reopened?" I ask.

"Not quite, Sean. We need to get approval from the Crown Prosecution Service and the Home Secretary to make it official, but there is nothing to stop us from having a bit of a discreet dig around for now. Obviously, if you do turn up anything concrete it would be a big help in pushing along an official sanction to investigate."

"And Clive Douglas, ma'am?" Catherine asks. "Can we get him back to London?"

Sarah smiles and hands Catherine the copy of Clive's transfer order. "Already done, DC Swain. The boss briefed the Chief Superintendent and he spoke to the Home Office last night. By now, our friend Clive should already be settling in to his new accommodation."

Given that the Home Office is not generally known for its efficiency, the speed of this transfer gives me confidence that we are onto something big. For approval to be given overnight, it can only mean that someone high up the ladder has taken an interest in the case. I can't help but wonder, though, if that interest is in solving the case or making sure that it is quickly and quietly closed back down again.

I quickly dismiss the thought and put my skepticism down to my own recent experiences with the Network and those in power. I check the transfer order and then turn to DI Gray.

"That's great news, ma'am. If it's okay with you, we'll head straight over to speak to him. We need to get that third name and anything else he might know that could help us."

She nods her agreement. "Yes of course. Go easy though, Sean. This is still not an official investigation. If you make any slip-ups, Clive Douglas will have his legal counsel all over us. That's not a position that any of us want to be in and not a position that the boss will be able to defend easily."

I'm not quite following her point, so I ask her to explain, and I instantly wish that I hadn't.

"DS McMillan, the original investigation was called Operation Hush and, as you know, it was deliberately kept under wraps to prevent any embarrassment to Margaret Thatcher's Conservative Government in 83/84. If you go digging into this and it goes belly up for any reason, Jeremy Corbyn and his Labour cronies will be all over it. If that does happen, you can be sure that they will leave no stone unturned if it means there is even the slightest chance to embarrass the current Conservative Government. Are we following each other, sergeant?"

Feeling very much like a chastised schoolboy, I blush slightly. Behind me, I swear I can hear Catherine giggling slightly at my discomfort. With her point made, Sarah asks me to keep her updated and then she excuses herself to go to another meeting.

I turn to face Catherine, who I know is itching to say something sarcastic. Before she gets the chance I hold up my hand to cut her off.

"Don't, Cath! Not unless you want me to arrange an immediate transfer for you to traffic duties on some godforsaken Scottish island for the rest of your career."

Wisely she stays quiet for a few seconds. Then, with a smirk, she says, "I guess this means I'm driving, boss?"

■ ■ ■ . ■ ■ ■ ■

Just over two hours later we take our seats in one of the interview rooms to wait for Clive Douglas to arrive. Sensing something might be wrong, Catherine touches my hand and asks me if I am okay. "You look like you've seen a ghost, mate. I guess it must be tough coming back here."

"It is," I reply. "I'm fine, though. It just seems a bit surreal. The last time I was in this room was when you came to see me with DCI Morgan and Jean Monroe after the discovery of the Network ledgers and the mobile phone footage of ACC Butterfield shooting Darren Phillips."

"But that turned out to be a good thing," Catherine points out.

"If you call us both ending up in hospital a good thing, then yes, I guess it was a good thing," I say with a small laugh.

My laugh is enough to break the tension.

Hearing the sound of footsteps approaching, I straighten up and tell Catherine to put her game face on. "Here we go. I think our boy is here. Let me lead and you chip in when you feel it's appropriate. And Cath, don't let the bastard wind you up ... okay?"

In response, she playfully sticks her tongue out and then quickly straightens her face as Douglas is escorted into the room by two prison officers. One of the escorting officers is Patrick Bayliss. When he sees me, he smiles and remarks that I am looking well.

I stand up and shake his hand. "Thank you, PO Bayliss. I have you to thank for that. After all, it was your call to DC Swain that helped save my life."

Slightly embarrassed, he shakes his head and says, "It was nothing, DS McMillan. I'm just glad to see that you've made a good recovery." Then with a smile he adds, "Oh, and it's Senior Officer Bayliss now."

I reach out my hand again to congratulate him on his promotion, but we are interrupted by an impatient cough and the usual sarcasm from Clive Douglas.

"This reunion is all very touching, but do you think we can move this on, ladies? I have a reservation for lunch today and I would hate to keep my guests waiting."

Not rising to the bait, Officer Bayliss tells him to sit down and be quiet. "And don't you worry about lunch, Douglas. Keep on with the attitude and I will arrange for a private reservation in solitary for you."

The second remark is enough to wipe the smirk off Clive's face and he sits down without another word. I thank Bayliss again and ask him to wait outside until we are finished.

■ ■ ■ ■ ■ ■ ■ ■

Clive is looking a lot less cheery than at our last meeting.

"You're looking tired, Clive. I'm sorry about the overnight move, but you did say that you were in a hurry to get back. How's the new accommodation? Meeting your expectations, I trust?"

My sarcastic question is ignored and, staring directly at me, Douglas asks his own, "Was it your idea, Sean? Or was it hers? He looks at Catherine and nods to himself. "Yes, I think it was DC Swain's idea. She always did have more imagination than you, McMillan."

"What are you talking about?" I ask him.

"I think he means bringing him back to Meerholt," Catherine supplies with a shuffle of her eyebrows.

"Oh, right," I reply. "That was nothing to do with us. Just a happy coincidence I think. Probably down to some do-gooder in the Home Office wanting to return you to the bosom of your loving friends. How are you settling in so far?"

For a few seconds, Douglas just stares at us, then he says, "Fuck you, McMillan. I'm doing just fine and if you want me to help you anymore than I already have, I suggest that you make sure it stays that way."

"Consider it done," I say. "Just say the word and I will get you moved back into solit—"

"No, no bloody solitary. I'm staying out on the wing and you make sure that nobody comes at me. It's that or nothing, McMillan."

I look to Catherine and then back to Douglas. "You know, out on the wing I can't guarantee your safety one hundred percent. You're an ex-copper and a bent one at that. Frank Butler has been moved on, but there are plenty of others here who would love to have a pop at you."

"I know that, McMillan. I'm not bloody stupid. I've already made a few arrangements for myself, but it wouldn't hurt to have a word with the screws to keep an eye out for me."

Catherine leans towards me. "We can do that, can't we, boss?"

I nod my agreement. "Yes. I'll speak to SO Bayliss on the way out. Now, if there is nothing else, you promised to tell us about the third suspect."

"Not so fast, there is one other thing first."

This asshole is pissing me off already, but I need him to remain cooperative. I keep my composure and ask him what it is. When he smiles, I know already that he is just trying to remind us who currently has the upper hand. His response confirms it.

"Nothing too difficult, sergeant. Just a nice cup of tea and half a dozen digestive biscuits — chocolate ones, please."

Without my needing to ask, Cath gets to her feet to speak to Officer Bayliss. As she passes Douglas, he tells her that he takes two sugars and a splash of milk. For good measure he calls her "princess" and deliberately focuses his eyes for too long on her legs. Thankfully, she doesn't rise to it or say anything to wind him up.

There then follows five minutes of uncomfortable silence before Bayliss finally returns with the tea and a small plate of biscuits.

After confirming that there is nothing else we need, Bayliss excuses himself and locks the door behind him as he leaves. Douglas looks dismissively at the plate of biscuits and comments to us that they are not what he asked for.

"Next time you come here, make sure that you bring chocolate digestives. I'm not a big fan of custard creams."

I reach forward to pick up the plate. "You don't want these then. Will I take them away?"

His hand quickly covers the plate. "No, no, in the interests of our new-found partnership, I'm prepared to overlook it this one time. Just get it right next time please."

"Fine, can we carry on now?" I snap.

Douglas nods and picks up a custard cream to dunk in his tea. Then he smiles and says, "Ready when you are, Sean."

■ ■ ■ ■ ■ ■ ■ ■

With Catherine poised to take notes, I briefly refer to my own pocketbook. I then pick up from where we finished during our last meeting.

"Okay, so what you told us checks out so far, but if—"

"Of course, it checks out," Douglas interrupts me. "If it didn't, I would still be in Yarwood nick, wouldn't I?"

Then he points to Catherine's right hand and adds, "You might want to get that checked out. I think you might have chipped your nail polish, darling."

Despite the continued provocation, Catherine remains calm and doesn't take the bait. Knowing we won't get anything more out of him, I call for Bayliss to take Douglas away.

As soon as he is gone, we both sit back down, and I tell Cath that it went as well as we could have possibly hoped for.

"Really? You think that went well, Sean? The bastard was taunting us again."

"Yep, he was, Cath. Did you really expect anything different?

"Well, no … but … Christ, Sean, that man makes my blood boil."

"Mine too, Cath. But he is right, we need him. So, for now, let's keep him on side and thinking he's important. At least until we have what we need."

"What about the transfer request to Cat C?" Cath asks me.

"No harm in starting the paperwork. He did give us the name, after all."

"No, he gave us a name," Cath corrects me. "For all we know he could have pulled that name out of his backside."

"I don't think so, Cath. He badly wants that transfer."

My confidence that Douglas is telling the truth is further bolstered by the reference made by Michael Davies last night in the Bluebell Pub. Before he stood up to take the call at the bar, he had clearly said to Paddy that it must be "T". This is too much of a coincidence, even in my twisted world.

"You may be right," Catherine says. "I still don't bloody trust him though. That bastard would say anything to make his life easier."

"I know. I don't trust him either. Come on, let's get back to the station and see what we can dig up on this Pinois guy."

I hand Catherine the car keys and playfully suggest that we stop at a supermarket on the way back to the station.

Looking confused at my suggestion, she asks why we need to go shopping.

When I answer, I can barely control my laughter.

"For the chocolate digestives of course …, Miss Fuzzy Knickers."

Completely unfazed, Catherine waits patiently for me to finish giggling and then with a perfectly straight face she asks if I am quite finished.

Trying to stop myself from grinning, I reply, "Yep, I'm done."

"That's good, Sean. Because it's a close-run thing, you know."

Now it's my turn to look confused.

"Close run thing? I don't get you."

My confusion is soon cleared up as Cath puts me firmly in my place in the way that only she can.

"It's a close-run thing between you and Douglas to decide who is the bigger asshole!"

She then hands back my car keys.

"It looks like you're driving, mate. I don't think I could concentrate in these fuzzy knickers."

■ ■ ■ ■ ■ ■ ■

After more than three frustrating hours of trawling through every possible database and resource with no success, I push my pocketbook to one side and drop my pen.

"This is not right, Cath. It's one thing having a clean record, but to have no record at all is fishy beyond belief. We've checked every information resource known to man, including the electoral roll and tax records and nothing even comes close.

"It's not like there are even that many variations on the name Terry. We've already searched Terry, Terence, Teddy, and Theodore at least half a dozen times. There are plenty of hits alright, but none with Pinois as a surname."

Catherine doesn't say anything. Instead she flicks through her notes from the earlier meeting with Douglas until she reaches the part where Clive had referred to Terry's parentage.

For a couple of seconds, she taps her index finger over the entry and then her face lights up.

"What's up, Cath? Are you having one of your lightbulb moments or something?"

"Well, just a thought actually. Our suspect is mixed English and French. What if we are looking at this in the wrong way?"

"Go on."

"Well, for the last three hours, we have been working on the assumption that Terry might be short for something else. That could of course still be the case, but what if it is short for a French name and not an English one?"

Without explaining herself further, Catherine turns and types the name Thierry Pinois into the Police National Computer database.

Almost instantly a link appears on the screen. Cath clicks on the link and the mugshot of a thick-set, balding, white guy in his mid to late thirties opens. Despite Clive Douglas saying that the third suspect had a clean record, this guy has a criminal record as long as my arm. It includes everything from shoplifting to armed robbery, but interestingly the last recorded entry is for common assault in 1978, which makes me wonder for a moment whether we are barking up the wrong tree entirely. Of course, the lack of later entries could indicate that either he kept his nose clean after 1978, or he just didn't get caught for later offences.

On balance and given his record, I think that the second scenario is the more likely of the two. Reasonably confident that we are onto something, I tell Cath that she is a genius.

"This has to be our suspect, mate. How on earth did you think of the French connection? That was a lightbulb moment and a half."

Ever modest, Cath brushes off my compliment. "It was nothing. I'm sure it would have come to you soon enough. So, what now, boss? Can we pay him a visit?"

"Damn right we will, but not today. It's getting late, and I don't know about you, but I could do with the weekend off."

"Are you sure, boss? I don't mind putting in a few hours over the weekend."

"No, honestly, Cath. We could both do with the break. It's been an intense couple of weeks, and I don't think we need to worry too much about Mr. Thierry Pinois running away. It's been nearly forty years since the robbery, so he must be nearly eighty by now. If he does run, it won't be very fast. Let's regroup with clear heads on Monday. We can pay him a visit after the morning briefing."

Cath is already on her feet and picks up her handbag, "Great, I was actually hoping you were going to say that. I'm meeting up with the girls tonight to hit the town and we're planning on hitting it hard. I would invite you, but you know how it is, boss."

"Too much testosterone for you all to handle?" I ask smugly.

She rolls her eyes. "Yeh, that's it. The girls are a delicate bunch. Enjoy your weekend, mate, and give my regards to Maria."

Too easily caught in the trap set for me, I stupidly try to protest my innocence.

"What? No, I'm not—"

Realizing too late that Cath is just baiting me, I cut myself off mid-sentence and shake my head.

"Yeh good one, Cath. For your information, I'm actually going to have a quiet weekend in."

"Yeh, of course you are, mate," Cath says with a knowing look. "Anyway, I would love to stay and chat, but I have a date with my hair stylist. Have a good weekend, Sean."

As she turns to leave, I shake my head at being caught out so easily.

"You too, Cath. Try not to fall down the stairs on your way out."

■ ■ ■ ■ ■ ■ ■

All in all, it's been a productive couple of days. This case hasn't yet been officially classified as reopened, but I'm feeling confident that we already have the names of all three original suspects. More importantly, I have made what I hope will be a fruitful contact with Michael Davies and Patrick "Paddy" Newman in 1983. The potential offer of work after the mysterious call from "T" is just too coincidental for it not to be linked in some way to the robbery. There is of course only one way to find out for certain. So, tonight, I plan to travel back to 1983 again to take Michael up on his offer of breakfast and to find out more about "T" and what kind of work is on offer.

I also have some other unfinished business that I want to take care of this weekend. When I said to Cath that we could both do with a break, it wasn't just to keep her out of the way. I am genuinely in need of some rest and recuperation and as the saying goes, all work and no play makes Jack a dull boy. Coincidentally, it also makes Sean a dull boy and with this in mind, I pour myself a drink and settle down on my sofa to make a call.

■ ■ ■ ■ ■ ■ ■

Feeling as nervous as a schoolboy on a first date, I take a sip of my drink to steady my nerves. I scroll through my contacts and place the call. By the time she answers, my heart is banging like a drum and there is a bead of sweat on my forehead.

When Maria says hello, I hesitate for a moment too long and she starts to worry.

"Sean, is that you? Is everything okay? I just got home a couple of hours ago with Ben."

"No, no. Everything is fine," I reassure her. "I was just checking in on you both. How is Ben? I thought he was meant to be getting out yesterday."

"Yes, he was. He had a slight infection, though, so they kept him in for another day to be safe."

"But he's okay now?"

"Yes, he's fine, Sean. He's up in his room now fiddling around with his laptop. I think he is keen to get back to his studies."

Hearing this is great news. The more Ben concentrates on his studies, the less time he will have to focus on getting into my business. I'm under no illusions, though, that I am off the hook as far as dream travel and working together is concerned. The sooner I find a solution to this problem, the better it will be for all of us.

"Good. That's really good to hear … and uhm … uh … I mean, you're also okay, Maria?"

"Thanks. I'm doing okay and I'm much happier now that Ben is home."

Failing to find the right words or the nerve to come straight to the point, I awkwardly repeat myself, "Good. That's really good to hear. I … I mean …"

In a repeat of Wednesday evening, Maria tells me to calm down and to take a deep breath.

"Sean, I told you already. I'm really not that scary, I promise. If you want to ask me out to dinner, then go ahead and ask. The worst that could happen is that I say no."

"And would you?" I ask her.

"Would I what?" she says with a laugh.

"Would you say no if I asked you to come to dinner with me?"

For what seems like an eternity there is complete silence and I swear I can hear my heart pounding in my chest. In reality, it is no more than a split second before she answers the question.

"No, I wouldn't say no," she says slowly.

I nervously ask, "So, is that a yes then?"

Maria laughs again and calls me an idiot. "Yes, Sean. I think in a completely awkward and roundabout way, it's a yes. What night are you thinking of?"

"How about tomorrow around eight?"

"That would be lovely. Should I meet you somewhere?"

"No, that's okay. I'll pick you up at eight and whisk you off to somewhere nice, if that's okay with you?"

"That's perfect, Sean. I'm looking forward to it now. So, I'll see you tomorrow at eight, yes?"

"Absolutely," I reply. And then after a few seconds of awkward silence. "Okay, so I'll see you tomorrow at eight then."

"Yes, you just said that." Maria laughs again. "Goodnight, Sean."

"Goodnight, Maria. Pass on my regards to Ben."

"I will. Take care, Sean."

■ ■ ■ ■ ■ ■ ■ ■

The call ends, and with my plan for the weekend now set, I am confident that I have more than enough time to accomplish everything I need to before Monday morning. I pour myself another drink and after an hour of channel surfing, I take a shower and change back into my hoodie and jogging bottoms.

My wallet and warrant card are next to my Taser on the side table by the bed. I pick up all three, but then decide against taking the card. It's unlikely to happen, but If I am searched and the card is discovered, it would be game over immediately. It's a risk not worth taking and I'm not expecting to need my warrant card tonight anyway. I put it away in the bedside table drawer and put my wallet in my back pocket. Lastly, I stuff the Taser into the top of one of my socks.

Ready to go, I turn off the lights and lie down on my bed. The images of Michael and Paddy are crystal clear in my head. Tonight, no chanting is necessary.

The Past – Saturday, December 10th, 1983

The question comes from behind and it is a couple of seconds before I get my bearings.

"Are you lost, pal? This is a private area."

In front of me there is a neat stack of empty beer kegs and I realize that I am standing in the storage yard to the rear of the Bluebell Pub.

I turn to face my questioner who immediately recognizes me and mumbles an apology.

"Oh, sorry, I didn't realize it was you."

The pajamas, dressing gown, and slippers make the barman from last night look slightly comical and the heavy steel crowbar looks awkward and unwieldy in his frail old hands.

I look down at it and raise my eyebrows. "Really?"

Embarrassed, he slowly lowers it to his side and apologizes again.

"Sorry, I thought you were a burglar or a pikey. Those fuckers are always on the hunt for kegs to sell for scrap. Two times already this mon—"

I hold up my hand to stop him.

"Is this your place then?"

'Yes, it's my pub. I'm the landlord."

"What's your name?" I ask him.

He replies, but is obviously hesitant and is shaking slightly, "It's … um, Maurice."

"Um Maurice, that's a strange name," I say with a grin. "And why are you shaking, Um Maurice?"

"No, it's just Maurice. Maurice Stevens. I'm the landlord."

"Yeh, you said that already. So, why are you shaking, Maurice Stevens?"

"Because it's bloody cold out here." The answer is accompanied with a look to suggest to me that he is stating the obvious.

Now that he mentions it, I'm actually feeling quite cold myself. To his great relief, I tell him that we should go inside. "I was looking for Michael and Paddy. I was drinking with them last night. Are they here?"

"Yes, they're both here. They said you might be coming."

He leads me down a short corridor and into the bar area. A table is already set with five place settings. In the center of the table, there are two serving plates piled high with sausages, bacon, grilled tomatoes, eggs, toast, and fried bread. Paddy is the first to see me and is not shy in expressing his annoyance.

"You're bloody late, Smith. You were told to be here for eleven."

Sitting opposite Michael and Paddy is an elderly woman whom I assume is Maurice's wife. Whoever she is, it is clear from their plates that they have started breakfast without me and the clock on the wall behind the bar shows that it is 11:45. I apologize and make up a feeble excuse about my bus being late. Looking irritated at my tardiness, both men say nothing for a few seconds, and it is the woman who finally breaks the silence.

"Well, you're here now. Sit yourself down and help yourself, love. There is plenty to go around."

I sit down and Maurice also takes his seat and introduces me to his wife. "This is my missus, Annie. Annie, this is Sean. This is the fella that got stuck in to help Mick and Paddy last night."

Unimpressed by my heroics, Annie just smiles and says, "That's nice, dear. Can I get you a cup of tea, Sean?"

Paddy answers on my behalf, "Actually we have a bit of business to do, Annie. Why don't you both get dressed and go out for a little walk? I'll get Sean his tea."

Not needing to be asked twice, Maurice and Annie get up and leave us alone.

As soon as the door to the bar area is closed, Michael retrieves a package from under the table and places it down in front of me.

I reach over to take the package and ask what it is. Paddy, though, places his shovel of a right hand on top of it before I can pick it up.

"Not so fast. I want to know that we can rely on you for this job."

"What do you mean?" I ask.

Michael points to the clock. "We need to know that if we bring you in on this job that you're not going to let us down, Sean. If we say be somewhere or do something at a specific time, then that's exactly what we mean. Do you understand?"

I nod my head. "Of course. I promise, I won't let you down. It was the bloody buses this morning."

"Fuck the buses," Paddy growls. He tosses me a set of car keys. "You can use my car until after the job is done. It's the red Cortina parked outside. Don't get pulled in it, and do not fucking damage the paintwork. Do I make myself clear?"

I nod again and Michael asks me again if they can trust me. "This is important, and I want you to be very clear about what is going to happen to you if you let us down or screw up."

I return the question with a blank stare and Michael gestures towards Paddy. "Well, let me put it this way, Sean. If you screw up and put us at risk, Paddy here is going to rip off your arms and legs and beat you to death with the bloody stumps. And don't for a second think I'm joking. I've seen him do it."

Looking at the size of his hands, I have absolutely no doubt that Paddy could tear a man apart. I nod my understanding and Michael says, "Okay, let's get on with it then."

He reaches for the package, but Paddy stops him.

"Wait. Can we have a quick word outside, Mike?"

Michael looks unsure and Paddy gestures to the door.

"It won't take a second, Mick."

Both men get up to leave while I make a show of helping myself to bacon and a slice of toast. The door to the corridor closes behind them and I immediately jump to my feet and rush to the door. With my ear pressed against one of the flimsy wooden panels, I can easily hear what is being said on the other side.

"What's on your mind, Paddy?"

"I'm not sure about this fella. He's a bloody halfwit."

Michael laughs. "I know that. That's what makes him perfect."

"No, it makes him a bloody liability," Paddy says. "We don't need him. It's a simple enough job. Why risk having someone else involved? It means another cut of the take as well."

"I agree. But he's our insurance," Michael replies. "If anything does go wrong, he's handy with his fists. If it goes really wrong, we offer him up as the sacrificial lamb while we make ourselves scarce."

"And if it goes to plan? How do we guarantee he doesn't open his mouth or go flashing the cash around? We hardly know him and he's not the sharpest tool in the box."

"Don't worry about that, mate. He won't be getting any cash to flash. He's expendable."

There is a short silence and then Paddy laughs and says, "Fuck me, Michael, you're a cold bastard."

"Yeh, I am, and that's not the only thing. Come on, let's get back inside, my tea will be getting cold."

I make it back to my seat a split second before the door opens. Through a mouthful of bacon and toast I ask if everything is okay.

"All good," Paddy says. Then he gestures to the package on the table. "Go on. Open it."

I pull away the sellotape and tear open the brown paper. The package contains black trousers, a black tie, a white shirt, and a black pullover embroidered with the familiar logo of Securicor Security Services.

Masquerading as security officers to get into the depot at Heathrow is no surprise to me. This was detailed fully in the case file, but for the benefit of the act, I hold up the pullover and feign innocence. Michael smiles and says, "Nothing to worry about, just a bit of driving work, like we said."

"Driving work?"

"Yeh, trust me. It's nothing heavy. I think you're bright enough to figure out from that uniform what we're planning, but you're just going to be doing the driving. Me and Paddy will be handling everything else. It's an easy payday, Sean. You up for it?"

Of course I'm one hundred percent up for it. But I can't appear too keen. "Yeh, that sounds okay," I say slowly, "but what's my cut?"

"How does fifty grand sound?" Paddy asks.

They have no intention of ever paying me a penny or letting me walk away after the heist, but they don't know that I know this, so I smile and nod enthusiastically. "That sounds bloody brilliant. Thanks, lads."

"Good, try the kit on for size," Paddy says and points to the bathroom. "You can get changed in there, if you're shy."

I'm not shy, but I do have a Taser stuffed in my sock and I can't risk them seeing it. I carry my kit to the bathroom and strip off. The jacket is a little tight but everything else fits well. There is also a long black wooden baton in the package. I straighten my tie and then I slip the baton into its holder on my belt. I go back to the bar and both men look at me clearly pleased with themselves.

"Bloody hell! You look like a completely different bloke in that get up. Very bloody convincing."

Paddy nods his agreement. "T was right, Mike. These uniforms will open the door for us, no problem."

I seize the opportunity to ask who "T" is, but I am immediately cut off by Paddy.

"You don't need to know that."

"Sorry, I just ..."

Michael laughs "That's okay, Sean. We don't actually know who T is either. All you need to know is that it's T that is giving the orders on this job. We only communicate by phone. It's all very mysterious and it's best that you don't ask questions. Okay?"

"Sure thing, Mike. That's fine by me."

I sit down at the table and ask what exactly it is they want me to do.

Paddy says, "One step at a time, Sean. Better you don't know just yet. Here, take this."

He hands me a clear plastic wallet that has a clip on it to attach to a shirt or pullover. Inside the wallet there is an ID card belonging to a Stuart Mark Goldsmith. His date of birth is April 12th, 1953, making him thirty years old. This is close enough to my own age, but apart from having short dark hair, his picture looks nothing like me. More worryingly, he is only 5'2" tall.

"I don't think this will work," I say. "I'm much taller than that."

"Don't worry," Paddy replies. "You'll be driving when this gets checked and we all look the same height sitting down."

"But I don't look anything like this fella," I protest.

"This should help." Michael retrieves a green canvas bag from under the table and passes me a black helmet with a clear full-face visor. "We will all be wearing these on the day. Just keep your head down and you will be fine."

I take the helmet and put it down in front of me. "Okay, so what now?"

Michael chucks me the bag. "Nothing. Put your kit in there. Then go home and lie low for a couple of weeks. Give him some spending money, Paddy."

"What?" Paddy protests, none too pleased.

"Come on, give him a few hundred quid to tide him over until the job."

Begrudgingly, Paddy takes a bundle of cash from his jacket pocket and peels off three hundred pounds in ten-pound notes. I take the cash and Michael tells me that I need to meet them back here at 9 a.m. on December 24th.

"That's Christmas Eve," I say.

"It is," Michael replies. "So, if you were planning to go carol singing, cancel it. Make sure you are here bang on nine, Sean. Don't fucking let us down."

"Of course. I mean, no. I won't let you down, Mike."

Mike nods. "I know you won't. Go on then, off you fuck."

I'm almost at the door, when Paddy tells me to wait. I turn around and he points at my uniform. "Take that off and put your own clothes back on, ya bloody muppet."

Playing the fool has served me well up to now but trying to leave in the uniform was unintended. I blush and go back to the bathroom to change. When I get back to the bar, Paddy is alone at the table. I say goodbye, but he barely acknowledges me. I do, though, hear him call me a fucking idiot under his breath as I step through the door and out onto the street.

∎ ∎ ∎ ∎ ∎ ∎ ∎

His red Cortina is parked around fifty feet from the entrance on the opposite side of the street. I stash the bag containing my kit behind the front passenger seat and after a quick check in the mirror to make sure I am not being followed, I pull out onto the high street to find somewhere reasonably close to park the car out of sight until I need it again.

I already have a destination in mind and ten minutes later I pass the sign that signals my arrival into the Clem Attlee council estate. It's a concrete jungle of 1960s high- and low-rise tower blocks and for my purposes it is a perfect hiding place.

Each tower has its own block of garages and I quickly find one that is both open and seemingly abandoned. Confident that I am not being watched, I drive in and park. As expected, the light is not working, but in the corner of the garage I can make out a pile of rusting paint cans and a mildew-covered drop sheet, which I use to cover the car.

After checking that the drop sheet is completely covering the exhaust, I pull down the garage door and make my way carefully through the gloom back towards the car. With my hands held out in front of me, I lift up one side of the cover, then I get back in and start the engine.

With nowhere else to go, the fumes from the exhaust soon fill the canvas and permeate through the chassis and into the car. The toxic mix of carbon monoxide, sulfur dioxide, nitrogen oxides, formaldehyde, benzene, and soot quickly has me gasping for breath and my head feels like it is ready to explode.

Satisfied, that there is enough petrol in the engine to finish the job of sending me home, I retrieve my Taser from my sock and jab the prongs into the side of my neck. I pull the trigger and the result is near instantaneous. I barely even have time to register the pain before I am gone.

Present Day – Saturday, April 28th, 2018

The sunlight cutting through the gap in my bedroom curtains causes me to squint and I fumble blindly for my cellphone on the bedside table. It has already stopped ringing but, still half-asleep, I lift it to my ear and mumble hello. There is no answer, so I drop the phone and close my eyes.

A few seconds later it rings again, but it only rings once and I don't recognize the ring tone. Confused and disoriented, I screw my eyes tightly shut and roll over to try to get back to sleep. When it rings again it is accompanied by loud banging and a muffled voice.

It finally dawns on me that someone is ringing my doorbell. I jump up with a start and rub the sleep out of my eyes. The banging on the door is now constant and I can clearly make out my name.

"Okay, okay, hold your bloody horses," I call, irritated. "I'm coming, for fuck's sake."

I make my way to the door and pull across the security chain, whilst muttering, "If that's you, Cath. This had better be bloody good. I told you to take the weekend off."

The door is barely half-open before Ben pushes his way inside.

"Sorry to disappoint you, Dad. It's only me."

My outstretched hand stops him from going any further.

"Whoa, just hang on there. What are you doing here?"

"Do I need a reason to visit my old man?" Ben replies sarcastically.

"Actually, yes you do," I reply. "And cut the dad shit. I'm not in the mood."

Ben looks me over before saying, "Yeh, I can see that. What the hell are you wearing? You look like a poor man's Chav.

Where were you last night? Or should I say, when were you last night?"

I'm about to tell him to mind his own business, but he has already turned and gone inside. I close the door and find him in the kitchen rifling through my cupboards. Before I say anything, I watch with mild fascination as he switches on the kettle and drops two slices of bread into the toaster.

"Don't mind me, Ben. You just help yourself."

He takes the milk from the fridge and smiles.

"Thanks, Dad. I will."

I shake my head. "Okay, I'm confused, did you actually want something, or did you just come here to ransack my cupboards for food?"

"Sean, don't be so cynical. Can't a son come and see his dad without there needing to be a reason?"

"Not when it comes to me and you," I reply. "What do you wa—"

The toast pops up and Ben holds up a hand to stop me.

"One second please."

I watch patiently as Ben slathers each slice of toast with a liberal coating of butter. He then takes a large bite before turning back to face me.

"What was that you were saying, Pops?"

Ignoring his obvious attempt to wind me up, I ask again, "What do you want?"

Unhurried, he takes a sip from his tea and then places the mug down on the counter. "That's an interesting question, and the answer comes in two parts."

"Okay, well you have my attention," I say. "What's the first part?"

He stares at me for a second and then says, "What are you playing at, Sean? And don't give me that look of innocence. Mum told me that you are taking her out tonight. I'm not happy about this. In fact, I'm—"

With the shoe firmly on the other foot, I smile and sarcastically reply, "What? I thought you would be happy that your mum and dad were going out for the night. I thought—"

Ben takes me by surprise when he snaps, "No, Sean! You can't mess around with people's lives like that. It's not right. This is my mum and I won't let you mess her around and break her heart. God only knows why, but she really likes you."

His next words are full of emotion and heartfelt.

"Please, Sean. Please don't hurt her. You hurt her once before. Please don't do it again. She doesn't deserve it."

This outburst is completely unexpected, and I now feel like a complete shit for trying to mock him. I feel particularly bad given his honesty in revealing that Maria really likes me. I allow him to compose himself before I speak again.

"Listen, Ben. I do really like your mum and I'm patently aware of the situation I left her in. That was never intentional, but despite everything, it's a situation that I would never consider putting right."

Ben is looking confused, so I continue. "Putting right that wrong would mean taking you away from her. You were what kept your mum going all those years. You were her reason for getting up every day. You are the best part of her life and I can't be sorry for that."

He still looks skeptical. "We're not talking about me, though, are we? We're talking about my mum. Why should I trust you, Sean? You ran out on her once before. What's to stop you from getting your end away and then ditching her again?"

"Ben, I can't answer that. But I promise you this. Getting your mum into bed and running away afterwards is not my intention. Your mum is an amazing woman. I knew that the very first time I met her. I know only too well that I badly messed things up. Now, I just want to get to know her. If you give me a chance, you have my word that I will take it slowly."

He thinks it over for a few seconds and then says, "You'd better, Sean, because I'll be watching you. I swear to God, if you hurt her, I will ruin you."

As he speaks, he absentmindedly rubs his shoulder. I assure him again of my intentions and then I take the opportunity to deflect the conversation in a different direction. "Maria said that you had a mild infection. Is it still causing you some pain?"

He shakes his head. "It's nothing. Just a bit sore every now and then. Particularly when it gets cold."

Obviously keen to change the subject himself, Ben points to my jogging bottoms. "I take it you travelled last night?"

I'm about to lie when he holds up his hand. "Don't, Sean. For a copper, you're a shitty liar. You didn't go clubbing dressed like that and you stink of exhaust fumes. What was it, the old carbon monoxide poisoning trick?"

My face gives me away and Ben smirks, "I'm right, aren't I? You gassed yourself to death. Go on then, what are you working on?"

"That's none of your business," I tell him. "You said you were here for two things. What's the second thing?"

He takes a bite from his toast and then smirks. "I'm here about your business."

"What? Haven't you had enough? Ben, you nearly died. You've only just been released fro—"

"You're right, Sean. I did nearly die. I nearly died saving you from that nutter with the shotgun. You owe me."

"For fuck's sake, Ben. How many times do we need to go through this? It's too bloody dangerous and you're not ready."

"So, get me ready."

"What? No. It's not happening. Christ, what is it that you don't understand about you nearly died? Maria would never forgive me, and I could never forgive myself if something else were to happen to you. You're my ..."

I hesitate mid-sentence and Ben tells me to finish what I was going to say. "That almost sounded for a second like you were going to call me your son, Dad."

"Of course, you're my son and I care about you. Despite you also being an annoying, know-it-all little shit, you're growing on me. Good enough?"

Ben smiles. "Good enough for now. You can finish whatever you are currently working on, and I promise not to get involved, but I want in on the next one. Is that fair?"

I really don't have a choice in the matter, so I reluctantly agree. "Fine, but only when you are fully fit, and this time you do exactly as you are told. Understand?"

Happy to have the upper hand, Ben smiles and puts two more slices of bread into the toaster. "Sorry, I'm bloody famished. I was planning to get a Maccers breakfast, but I overslept."

Until now, I hadn't even considered the time. If McDonalds have finished serving breakfast it must already be past eleven. If it is, then this is the latest I have slept in a long time. I ask the time and Ben checks his watch.

"It's just after one. Is this you just getting up?"

I think to myself, Christ, I must have really needed the sleep to have slept for so long. I don't answer his question, but I do point to the toaster. "Hurry up and get that down your neck, greedy boy. I've got things to do."

"Sure, give me ten minutes," Ben replies.

At the same time, he pours himself another cup of tea and switches on the television. Realizing that there is no point trying to push it, I tell him that I am going to jump in the shower.

"Just let yourself out when you're done, mate."

I don't get any response, but from inside my bathroom, I can hear MTV playing at almost full volume. Ten minutes after getting into the shower, the music stops, and I hear the door to my apartment close.

■ ■ ■ ■ ■ ■ ■ ■

It's been over a month since my last haircut and I want to look my best when I pick Maria up this evening. Italian Tony has been my regular barber for the last five years and is well used to the fact that I am not one for small talk about the weather or the state of the economy.

Also, and in my humble opinion, getting a haircut is one of the rare occasions when it is socially acceptable for a guy to sit in silence. So, when my phone vibrates in my pocket five minutes into my haircut, I ignore it and let it ring off.

After the third bout of vibration, Tony stops cutting my hair and tactfully asks if I want to take the call. "It could be important, Sean."

I retrieve the phone from my pocket, but it's not a number that I recognize. "It's okay, Tony. They'll send a message if it's important."

I put the phone away and Tony picks up his scissors to continue. Less than five seconds later it vibrates again, and I hear the tone that signals the arrival of a message. I tell Tony to carry on, but I take out the phone to read the message.

Sean, my boy. I hope my information was of some use to you. Call me back please. Clive D.

"You need me to stop again?" Tony asks.

"No, it's nothing important," I reply. "You crack on. He can wait."

■ ■ ■ ■ ■ ■ ■ ■

Thirty minutes later and sporting my fresh new haircut, I get into my car and start the engine to keep warm while I make my call. The first time my call goes unanswered. The second time it is picked up immediately, and Clive Douglas is in top form.

"Hello, Douglas residence. May I ask who is calling?"

"You're very chirpy for a man facing the rest of his life in prison," I reply. "Or am I missing something?"

"Well, there's no point being a miserable bastard, is there, Sean? And besides, now that we are working together, I have a feeling that good things are on the horizon for me."

"Let me just stop you there, Douglas. We are not working together. You are providing information in return for a few perks. Nothing more, nothing less. Once this case is done, our business is done. Understood?"

There is a short pause before he says, "Sure, understood."

"Okay," I say. "This is not the number you had before. You got yourself another phone?"

"Of course,," he replies. "I could hardly bring the other one from Yarwood, could I?"

"Of course not. I'm impressed how quickly you got your hands on another one though. You really are a resourceful man, Clive."

"Thanks, Sean. Although I've told you that many times before."

"That wasn't a compliment," I say.

Clive laughs. "Well, if it's all the same with you, I'll take it anyway."

"What is it you want, Douglas? You have some new information?"

Again, there is a short but noticeable pause before he replies, "Nothing that I am prepared to share right now. I was just wondering if you'd had any luck tracking down Terry Pinois, and if you had started the application for my transfer yet."

I reply with a question of my own, "I'm confused, Clive. Terry Pinois or Thierry Pinois?"

"Ah! So, you have had some luck," Clive exclaims. "Was that you or was it the fragrant Ms. Swain?"

Not in the mood for banter, I ask him if he knew it was Thierry and not Terry.

"No, I didn't," he replies. "Now that you say it, though, it makes sense with the French connection."

"So, you didn't know Thierry?"

"Like I said, all of this was well before my time. I've told you what I know."

"Somehow, I doubt that. I think you know a lot more than you have told us so far. I think you knew perfectly well that it was Thierry and not Terry. I think—"

"You think what you want, McMillan. You know how this works. Once I stop being useful, you drop me like a stone and leave me to rot. Get moving on that application and we can talk again."

"So, you do know—"

Before I can finish speaking, Douglas cuts off the call.

"Fucking asshole," I curse under my breath.

■ ■ ■ ■ ■ ■ ■ ■

After getting home, I spend a couple of hours in the afternoon reading through the case file and my notes. So far, we appear to have made good progress, but we are a long way from cracking the case and there are some major pieces of the puzzle still missing or unclear. To help my focus, I take out my pocketbook and make a list of the knowns and the unknowns.

1. Suspects – Michael Davies, Patrick "Paddy" Newman – Confirmed. Plus Thierry "Terry" Pinois – most likely the third member of the gang, but not confirmed.

2. Is Thierry Pinois the brains of the operation? Is he "T"? – Most likely, but not confirmed.

3. The suspects carried out the robbery disguised as Securicor Guards. They took the place of two genuine guards, then drove a real Securicor vehicle into the depot and picked up a planned shipment of cash, jewels, and gold without the need for threats and violence – this is fact and clearly detailed in the case file.

4. So, what happened to the real guards? Were they involved? Was anyone else involved? Why weren't Mick and Paddy challenged by the police or security guards at the depot? Why weren't they questioned after the robbery? There is no mention of any of this in the case files.

5. What happened to the gold? Why has none of it ever been recovered? If Thierry took the gold as his share, why has none of it ever appeared on the open market? It is a huge amount of gold to not raise suspicion, even when melted down.

6. Why did Paddy kill Michael after the robbery? Did he think that Michael had double crossed him over the gold?

7. Is it really true or even possible that neither Paddy nor Michael knew the true identity of "T"?

8. Does Clive Douglas know more than he is saying? <u>Almost certainly</u>.

I read through the list twice more. Whilst right now the knowns are thin on the ground compared to the unknowns, I'm pleased at the progress we have made in such a short space of time.

I think to myself, but do not note in my pocketbook, that if they take me along as the driver, the case file will change to four suspects. Three to carry out the raid and the mysterious "T" directing operations.

I'm confident that talking to Thierry and Paddy on Monday and Tuesday will help fill in a few more of the blanks. All in all, it's been a productive couple of days and I'm content.

I tidy away the case file and check the time. I have just over an hour before I need to leave to pick Maria up, so I pour myself a large glass of Jameson. I hold the first sip of whisky in my mouth for a few seconds to savor the flavor. Suddenly feeling romantic, I stand up and lift the lid on my retro turntable.

It's been a long time since I played anything from my record collection, but tonight it seems appropriate to get ready to the sound of something smooth on vinyl. The Rat Pack can always be relied upon to set the mood, so with the volume turned up to maximum, I shave and shower to the dulcet tones of Frank Sinatra, Dean Martin, and Sammy Davis Jr.

■ ■ ■ ■ ■ ■ ■

I'm barely out of the taxi before the front door of her house opens and Maria steps out to meet me. Thankfully, Ben doesn't follow her. He stays just inside the door and I meet Maria halfway down the path. For a woman approaching fifty she is as stunning as the day I first met her in 1994. Her hair is thick and luxurious, and her skin is almost flawless, with only the faintest of laughter lines around the corner of her eyes. She is wearing the lightest of makeup, but it is enough to accentuate her natural beauty. I'm momentarily lost for words and am only snapped out of my trance when Ben loudly wishes his mother a good night. "Have fun, Mum. But not too much fun." And then to me, "Make sure she gets home by midnight, Sean. She doesn't look great as a pumpkin."

Before I can respond, Maria tells Ben not to wait up and to go back inside. Then she takes my hand and leads me towards the cab. "Ignore my son, Sean. Keep me out as long as you want. I'm a beautiful pumpkin."

Under my breath, I say, "Yes, I think you probably are."

Maria asks what I have just said. I squeeze her hand and point to the passenger door, "I said your carriage awaits, Cinderella."

■ ■ ■ ■ ■ ■ ■

Thirty minutes of small talk later, the taxi pulls up outside Gordon Ramsay's discreet flagship Chelsea restaurant on Royal Hospital Road. Before the driver has even had the chance to engage the handbrake, I get out and dart around to Maria's side to open the door. As she steps out, I take her hand and I'm rewarded with a beautiful smile and a compliment.

"Quite the gentleman, aren't you, Sergeant McMillan?"

Then she catches sight of the brass plaque on the wall to the side of the restaurant entrance. "Wow, three Michelin stars! You weren't joking when you said you were going to whisk me off to somewhere special. This place is vegan, is it?"

Catching the look of panic in my eyes, she struggles to hold a straight face and bursts out laughing. "I'm sorry, Sean. I couldn't resist that."

"So, you're not a veg—" I splutter.

She cuts me off by leading me towards the entrance. "Far from it. I'm as carnivorous as they come. Come on, I've been saving myself for this all day and now I'm starving."

■ ■ ■ ■ ■ ■ ■ ■

If I was awestruck by her beauty earlier, I am doubly so now. In the taxi she had kept her coat on, but in the warmth of the restaurant she takes it off and hands it to the cloakroom attendant. As the waiter leads us to our table, I can't help but admire her figure so perfectly wrapped in a delicate ivory lace knee-length dress, and her legs that are accentuated so well by her matching shoes. More than once, I find myself asking If I am good enough for her.

We take our seats and, with me still deep in thought, Maria reaches across the table for my hand.

"Sean, the waiter was asking if we would like to order some wine," she prompts me.

"Oh yes. That would be nice. You like wine, Maria?"

She nods and smiles. "I have been known to partake of a nice glass of red every now and then."

I order the wine and the waiter suggests that we might like to share a half dozen oysters as an appetizer.

I look to Maria for approval and she turns to the waiter and smiles. "Thank you, that would be lovely. Do you have fresh lemon and Tabasco?"

As soon as the waiter leaves us, I tell Maria that she is a woman after my own heart. "Oysters are just not the same without lemon and Tabasco. I'm so glad that you like oysters. It can be a bit embarrassing eating them on your own. What with the slurping and all."

She smiles at my comment but doesn't say anything. Instead she passes me one of the menus and opens the other one for herself. "Let's see what else is good, shall we?"

I look up from the menu twice to find Maria staring at me before she quickly looks away. She doesn't seem to be embarrassed, but I do get the feeling that there is something on her mind. When I catch her for the third time, she holds the stare and takes a deep breath.

"Can I ask you something?"

I nod. "Yes of course you can. You can ask me anything."

There is a short delay and then she asks, "What are we doing here, Sean?"

I know full well what she means, but I try to brush it off. "We're having dinner. Is that oka—?"

"No, I don't mean dinner. I mean, us, Sean. What are we doing here? I'm at least twenty years older than you."

"Does that worry you?" I ask her. "Because it doesn't worry me. We're just two good friends having dinner over a glass of wine." I point to the empty wine glasses. "Or at least we will be when the wine gets here."

She reaches over to touch my hand. "Is that what we are, Sean? Two good friends having dinner. Is that as far as it goes?"

For a moment I'm at a loss for words and then I say, "You're a beautiful woman, Maria, and I'd be a liar if I said I wasn't hoping for more. I promised, though, to … well, what I mean is, I'm happy to take things slowly."

The raised eyebrows give away the fact that I have been caught out and Maria laughs. "Ben said that you were a shitty liar. That was just after he told me that he had paid you a visit to warn you off."

My face starts to flush and just in the nick of time, the waiter arrives with our bottle of wine. He offers the bottle to Maria, who gestures to me. "Please pour for the gentleman first. I think he needs it more than I do."

Feeling decidedly uncomfortable, I wait for him to pour the wine and take our orders for dinner. As soon as he is out of earshot, I try to offer an apology, but Maria stops me and raises her glass.

"It's touching to have my son looking out for me, but I'm my own woman, Sean. You are a good-looking guy and I think it is fair to say that, despite the age gap, I find you more than a little fascinating. So, here's to good friends and to taking things slowly."

Hugely relieved to be off the hook, I join Maria in the toast. As I place my glass back down on the table, I silently mouth the words, thank you to her. She squeezes my hand again and says, "Now, take a breath and relax. I think I see our oysters coming and I'm in the mood for slurping."

■ ■ ■ ■ ■ ■ ■ ■

Two hours later, we finish the last of the wine over an amazing caramelized apple tarte Tatin with a side order of decadently creamy Tahitian vanilla ice cream. The dessert comes with two long spoons and, clearly in a playful mood, Maria points to something behind me. When I look back confused, she uses her spoon to place a small blob of ice cream onto the end of my nose, before she breaks down in a fit of the giggles.

I'm unsure if it is the wine or the effect of my boyish charms that has made her feel so comfortable with me. Whatever it is, it has made an already good night even better. The food and the wine have been amazing, but the company has been perfect. I wait for her to stop laughing and then I raise my eyebrows and say, "Really?"

I then make a comical attempt to lick the ice-cream off the end of my own nose. My attempt, of course, ends in abject failure and, reacting in exactly the way I had hoped for, Maria leans across the table and gently dabs my nose with her napkin. By now her lips are no more than a few inches away from mine and it takes all my willpower not to pull her forward and to kiss her.

Sensing what I am thinking, she smiles and hands me the napkin. "Here, I think you can take it from there. Shall we get a nightcap?"

I nod and tell her it's a great idea. Maria excuses herself to go and freshen up and I find us a place at the bar. Shortly afterwards she rejoins me and that's when, carried away by how well the evening is going, I slip up and say something incredibly stupid.

"I'm getting myself a whisky. Do you still drink Bacardi and Coke?"

The words are barely out of my mouth before I feel myself beginning to blush. Thankfully, Maria is more surprised than suspicious. She thinks about it for a second and then says, "Wow, I haven't had a Bacardi and Coke in years. What on earth made you say that? If I didn't know better, I would say that you had been nosing through my old photo albums, Detective Sergeant McMillan. Is that it? Have you been checking up on me, Sean?"

Hugely relieved that she is making light of it, I laugh and say, "No, nothing like that. I think you must have mentioned before that you used to drink Bacardi."

She looks unsure and shakes her head, "No, I don't think I did." Then she shrugs and says, "Oh, I don't know. Maybe you're right. No Bacardi tonight, though. I'll have a gin and soda please, Sean."

■　■　■　■　■　■　■　■

By the time we get back to Feltham, it is nearly one in the morning. I take Maria's hand and walk her slowly to the door. She turns to face me and, reluctant for the night to end, I keep a firm grip on her hands as she playfully tries to pull away.

"Okay, Casanova. This is as far as you go for tonight."

"Yes, I know that," I reply. "I'm just making the most of the last few minutes. Is that okay?"

Maria turns her head to the side and looks into my eyes. "That's more than okay, Sean. This has been a lovely evening. Thank you."

"It really was my pleasure, Maria. You are an amazing woman. I hope we can do this again sometime soon."

"I'll be disappointed if we don't," Maria replies.

Taking the plunge, I pull her into my arms and our lips meet. Our kiss is deeply intense, and it teases my senses with the promise of something more. I would desperately like to take it further, but my promise to Ben and to my better self takes precedence. Reluctantly, we break our embrace and Maria kisses me on the cheek.

"Go safe, Sean. Give me a call in a few days."

I say goodnight and Maria turns to unlock the door. I'm just about to get back into the taxi when she calls my name and says that she has another question.

I turn around and smile. "I told you earlier, Maria. You can ask me anything."

She looks like she is thinking hard about something and for a moment it seems she may have changed her mind. Then she asks, "Why me, Sean? You could have any girl you wanted. So, why me?"

Her question reaffirms everything I know about this beautiful woman already and it makes me smile before I answer, "I could give you one of a million reasons, Maria, but you would think that I was just laying on the charm."

"And aren't you?" she asks.

I laugh to myself. "Maybe just a little bit. But it comes naturally with you, Maria. And if you want to know why you, just go inside and take a look in the mirror. Your answer will be right there in front of you."

Maria shakes her head and smiles. "I was right, you are a bloody charmer. Goodnight, Sean."

Present Day – Monday, April 30th, 2018

My week starts with an early morning run along the banks of the Thames, followed by a shave and a long hot shower. Feeling confident of a productive day, I gather up the case file and notes and I head into the station. It's barely 8 a.m., but Cath is already in the office hard at work and has clearly been there for some time.

She stands up and hands me a cup of coffee. "Morning, boss. I was in early, so I made a start on getting an address for our target for today."

"And I assume by the big stupid grin on your face that you've found one?"

Cath wiggles her eyebrows. "Does the tin man have a sheet-metal cock?"

"What?"

"It's like, do bears shit in the woods, Sean. Only better."

"Yeh, I get it. Thanks for the explanation, Cath. And thanks for the coffee. So, where are we heading to? Not too far, I hope."

"We're staying north of the river. The last known address is Ponders End in Enfield. I googled it and it's just over an hour's drive at this time of the morning."

I nod and say, "It should be less than that if we make a move after the morning briefing. By then the worst of the morning traffic will hopefully have cleared."

"Actually, I hope you don't mind, Sean, but I bumped into DCI Morgan when I went for the coffee. He was interested to find out how we were getting on and when I told him that we had a name and an address for our third suspect, he told me that we should skip today's briefing. He's keen for us to get something credible as soon as possible that can be sent to the CPS and Home Secretary to get the case reopened officially. Sorry, I was just about to tell you."

"No, that's fine," I reassure her. "It's not like we have anything to share with the rest of the team this morning anyway. Did Morgan say anything else?"

"Just that you should tread carefully, Sean."

I shake my head. "For fuck's sake, does everyone in this office think I'm a bull in a china shop? In fact, Cath, don't answer that. I don't think I could cope with one of your witticisms so early in the morning."

Catherine smirks and says, "Fair enough, shall we get going then?"

"Yep, let's strike while the iron is hot," I tell her. "Did you confirm how old he is now?"

Cath refers to her pocketbook. "Not as old as we first thought, but old enough. Date of birth is February 16th, 1942, so by my reckoning he is seventy-six."

"Yeh, you're right. He is old enough. I think it might be best if you do most of the talking."

■ ■ ■ ■ ■ ■ ■

The Pinois residence is in the more affluent part of town, within spitting distance of the River Lee, the Ponders End Lock, and the King George V reservoir. The house itself is early twentieth century Georgian. Although not as grand in style and size, it reminds me very much of the house once owned by Assistant Chief Constable Maurice Butterfield in Cobham.

We stare at the front of the house for a few seconds and then I ask Cath what she thinks of it.

"There's got to be at least five bedrooms and I bet it's got a sizeable bit of land at the back. A detached house of that size in this area has got to be worth at least a million quid, boss."

"Yep, I was thinking much the same, Cath. Not bad for an old lag that has kept his nose clean since 1978. No cars on the drive, though. You think he might be out?"

In reply, Cath opens her door and starts to get out. "Only one way to find out, Sean. Come on, let's go and wake the old fella up."

■ ■ ■ ■ ■ ■ ■ ■

I try the doorbell twice, but with no response I suggest that we try around the back. The gate to the side of the house is unlocked and we make our way to the back of the house.

At the end of the garden, a woman is tending to a lush patch of red and white rose bushes. As we approach, she appears completely oblivious to the fact that we are there. Being careful not to startle her, we stop around ten feet away before Cath announces our presence.

"Good morning, I'm sorry to creep up on you, but we're police officers and we were hoping to speak to Thierry Pinois. Is he home?"

Far from being startled or alarmed by our sudden arrival in her garden, the woman continues to tend her roses for a few more seconds. She then slowly turns around and carefully sizes us both up.

"I'd like to see some identification, if you don't mind?"

Catherine smiles politely and offers her warrant card for inspection. "Yes, of course. I'm Detective Constable Swain and this is my colleague Detective Sergeant McMillan. And would you mind telling us who you are please?"

The woman is in her mid to late fifties, but she still has the trim figure of a much younger woman. Her luxurious black hair is tied back with a yellow ribbon, but I can see some flecks of gray and white. It would be easy to imagine her as a carefree and beautiful young woman, but the look on her face now hangs heavy with the burden of long and hard years. There is also something else in her look that is hard to miss. As she hands back Catherine's warrant card, she straightens herself up and I can almost smell defiance in the air.

"Am I under arrest, officers?"

I step forward slightly and say, "I can't think of any reason why we would need to arrest you. But then we don't know who you are. Would you mind identifying yourself please?"

She stares at us both for a second and then says, "I'm Rosemary Pinois. This is my house."

"And Thierry Pinois is your ..." Catherine asks.

"Thierry is my father, Detective Constable Swain. He's not home, though, and he hasn't been home for quite some time."

"And do you know when he might be home?" I ask. "Or could we get his contact number? It's important that we speak to him."

Rosemary smiles and then nods her head. "I'm sure that it is. To come looking for him after all this time it must be very important."

Her face then hardens, and we are both taken by surprise at what she says next and the use of profanity. "I know already that you're both a pair of comedians. But tell me, which one of you is the fucking clairvoyant?"

I'm about to ask her to explain herself, when Catherine stops me. "Your father has passed away, Ms. Pinois?"

Rosemary tuts and gives Cath a look of disdain. "Passed away? That's a bloody good one. What kind of second-rate coppers are you? Don't they teach you how to read in Police College anymore? I'm sure it must all be in his file in black and white, or have you whitewashed that in the same way that you did with his murder?"

Cath looks lost for words and I tell Rosemary that we really have no idea what she is talking about. "We came here to speak with your father in good faith. We really had no idea that he was dea ... I mean that he was no longer with us. Please tell us what happened. When was it?"

She clearly thinks that we are lying, but at the same time I can see that she wants to vent at us. She wipes a bead of sweat from her face and takes a deep breath.

"You know full well what bloody happened — or you ought to. Let me refresh your memory. On May 4th, 1979, my dad left home at just after six in the evening for his job driving a cab. I was seventeen years old and, for the first time in my life, Mum and I were happy and secure in the knowledge that he wasn't out getting up to no good. It was the first time in his life that he had an honest job and we didn't need to worry whether he was going to get arrested or get hurt. He was just driving his ca ..."

Her voice falters for a second and then she regains her composure. "Well, you already know what happened next. He was ambushed and murdered in cold blood by one of your licensed killers. The lying bastard said he thought he was reaching for a gun, but Dad wasn't armed. He was trying to find his license in the glove box. I know that for certain. It made no bloody difference though. They still killed him and at the inquest they recorded a verdict of lawful killing."

Catherine starts to offer her condolences, but she is quickly cut off. "Save it. I've absolutely no interest in your phony sympathy. It meant nothing to me and my mother back then and it certainly means nothing to me now. So, if there is nothing else, I'd like you to leave please. There is nothing for you here."

Before we can say anything else, Rosemary walks past us towards the house. We watch as she goes inside and we wait for her to close the back door before I turn to Catherine and say, "Well, don't we look like a right pair of fucking numpties? What the hell just happened there?"

Catherine looks like she is ready to explode. "I'll tell you what just happened, Sean. We have just been played and I've a damn good idea who the player is."

"You think it's Clive Douglas?"

"Damn right I think it's him," Cath snaps. "If he has been playing us, I swear to God, Sean, I will shove his digestives so far up his ass, he will be tasting biscuit crumbs in the back of his throat for a week."

"Jesus, Cath, that's an image that's not easy to forget. I think that you could be right, though. Come on, we have work to do."

■ ■ ■ ■ ■ ■ ■ ■

We are so shell-shocked by the news of Thierry Pinois's death years before the robbery that we barely talk on the way back to Blackwell Station. As soon as we get back, I invite Catherine into my office and close the door.

"Listen, Cath. Not a word of this to Kevin Morgan or Sarah Gray until we have had a chance to find out what the hell is going on."

Cath looks at me with disbelief that I think she would say anything. "This is as much on me as it is on you, Sean. Believe me, I have no intention of speaking to anyone until we have made some sense of what has just happened. If it gets out that we were looking for a suspect who was killed four years before the blag even took place, we will look like a right pair of mugs. This must be down to Douglas. He was the one who put us on to Thierry, or Terry, or whatever his bloody name is."

I tell her that I'm inclined to agree, but, at the same time, Douglas sending us off on a wild goose chase makes no sense.

"It just doesn't add up, Cath. Douglas is not stupid. Why would he risk a cushy move to Cat C by spinning us a line of bullshit?"

"Boss, I have no bloody idea. But I do know that he's playing some kind of twisted game with us."

"To achieve what?"

"I don't know, Sean. Maybe to discredit us, or to make us look stupid. You know him as well as I do. Clive Douglas doesn't do anything without good reason. I'm telling you, though, he is sending us on a bloody wild goose chase."

If I didn't have my link to Michael and Paddy, I would be inclined to agree with her and drop both the case and Clive Douglas like a hot stone. But I do have the link and whatever game Douglas is playing, I am confident that I can find out what it is.

"You could be right, Cath. But let's not pull the plug just yet. If he wants to play games, then let him. We've played his games and beaten him once before and we can beat him again. Let's do some digging ar—"

"Sean, I've got a bad feeling about this. We should cut him loose and send him back to Yarwood to rot."

"And we will, Cath. I promise. Just work with me on this. Let's have a dig around this afternoon to see what we can turn up. Then tomorrow morning, let's see if we can catch up with Paddy Newman when he goes for his pension. If we are still at a dead end by tomorrow afternoon, I promise we will speak to Sarah Gray to reassign us to a new case. Sound fair?"

Catherine shakes her head and is reluctant to continue. "I don't know, Sean. I really have a bad feeling about this, and we know how dangerous he is. I'm really not sure."

"Just one more day, Cath. If we get nothing, I promise, it's over. I need you, buddy. I can't do it without you. Please, Cath. What do you say? One more day, yes?"

She thinks about it for a few more seconds and then reluctantly nods. "Okay, but this is against my better judgment. One more day and then we cut that asshole loose, okay?"

I smile and touch her hand. "I promise. Now, let's get to work. I have a few ideas where we can start."

Cath sits down and I show her the notes I made on Saturday afternoon. She reads through them and then hands back my pocketbook. "Well, I guess question number two has been answered. Thierry Pinois was not the brains of the operation. Why do you refer to him as 'T' though?"

"Sorry, what was that, Cath?"

"In your notes, you have written, 'Is Thierry Pinois the brains of the operation? Is he 'T'? You also mention it again, when you ask if it is really possible that Michael and Patrick didn't known the real identity of 'T'."

Realizing that I have slipped up letting her look at my notes, I shrug and play down the relevance. "Oh, that was me just being lazy, it was easier to put 'T' instead of Terry every time. Remember, after we first spoke to Douglas, we thought we were looking for Terry."

Cath shakes her head and raises her eyebrows. "That's right, but you wrote these notes on Saturday. We already knew on Friday that we were looking for Thierry and not Terry."

I'm trying to think of what to say next when Cath smiles and shakes her head. "It must have been a bit of a boozy night on Friday, was it? You can never think straight when you're hungover, Sean."

I laugh more out of relief than amusement. "Yeh it was a bit of a heavy one actually. Anyway, that question is irrelevant now. Thierry is out of the frame and we have no main suspect. We need to get cracking and come up with something before Morgan or Gray come looking for an update."

Cath opens her own pocketbook. "I'm ready, boss. Tell me what you're thinking."

"I want you to find an address for the Securicor head office here in London. Then get over there and have a dig around in the employee records and time sheets for December 83."

"Am I looking for anything in particular?"

"Yeh, it's bothering me that there are no witness statements or interviews from any of the Securicor staff in the case file, and also how easy it was for the blaggers to get in and out without being challenged. If this was a scheduled collection, then there must be a record somewhere of which guards were assigned on that day. See if you can find out who should have been on the pick-up on the day of the robbery. If any of them are still alive, try and dig up the contact details. I'd be interested to have a little chat to find out where they were on that day."

Cath asks if there is anything else she should be looking for. "Do you think it is worth us trying again to search the files for any other Pinois with a criminal connection?" she suggests. Maybe Douglas was telling the truth about the surname, but was wrong about the Christian name? Let's face it, Pinois is not exactly a common name, is it?"

"Wow, that sounds like you're giving our Clive the benefit of the doubt, Cath. You could be right though. In fairness, it was us that put Thierry in the frame initially and not him. Once you're done at Securicor, have another go at the database to see if there are any other possible suspects. Let's not totally discount Thierry Pinois though."

Catherine is looking confused. "Where are you going with this? Thierry was six feet under pushing up the daisies long before this job was even thought of."

I smile and say, "It's just a thought really. There's probably nothing in it, but what if he had a son? What if there was a Thierry junior keen to follow in Thierry senior's footsteps?"

Cath raises her eyebrows. "Okay, that's a possibility, I guess. Alright, I'll look into that as well. What's your own plan, boss?"

"Me, I'm going to see what I can dig up on the supposedly lawful killing of Thierry Pinois, and then I might give Clive a call. Okay, let's regroup back here later. Message or call me if you turn up anything interesting."

■ ■ ■ ■ ■ ■ ■ ■

Not unexpectedly, it takes most of the afternoon negotiating a series of dead ends and calling in favors before I am finally able to get hold of a copy of the Investigation notes pertaining to the death of Thierry Pinois.

When it does finally arrive, it is delivered personally by a sergeant from the central records department, who asks me to sign for the package.

"This one goes way back, DS McMillan, but then I suppose that goes with the territory for you guys."

I sign the docket and hand back the pen. "Yep, that's why they call it a cold case, sergeant. Is everything in here?"

He nods. "Yep, the file looks complete. Some parts have been redacted though. Good luck finding what you are looking for."

I stop him before he can leave. "Wait a second please. Is it common for this kind of file to be redacted?"

"No, not common at all," he tells me. "And when a file is redacted, there is usually a note in the file to say when it was done and by whom. No note in this file, though."

I thank him for the information and before leaving, he points to the package. "Just one other thing to consider. It's also been redacted by hand, which is very unusual."

■　■　■　■　■　■　■

I rip open the side of the package and place the file on my desk in front of me. Before opening it, I think back to our earlier meeting with Rosemary Pinois. She had made a comment to suggest that the case file had been whitewashed. Earlier that comment had meant nothing to me, but in the current context, I'm now wondering whether she might have had a point.

I open the file and start reading through the documents in order. The first statements are from the officers in the armed response team involved in the incident. All names, ranks, and service numbers have been redacted, but they all describe an operation to intercept Thierry Pinois who was suspected of being on his way to carry out an armed robbery. Given Thierry's history, there is no great surprise at the context of the operation. I do, however, swear under my breath when I read the name of the second occupant of the car.

"Fuck, no wonder she was angry. Not only was her father shot dead by the police, she was actually in the bloody car when it happened. This is significant."

I flip through to find the witness statement from Rosemary Pinois. I quickly check each page for any sign of redaction, but it appears to be clean and I start reading. It reads exactly how she had described things this morning. In her statement she says that her father was on his way to his new job as a taxi driver.

She also says that before going to work, he was taking her to meet friends in the West End. Just before dropping her off, his car had been boxed in on all sides by unmarked vehicles. With armed police on all sides pointing weapons, Thierry had been instructed to lower his window and identify himself. Rosemary then states that he clearly shouted to the police officers that he was going to reach into the glove box for his driving license. The rest I know already.

Thierry was shot dead by a trigger-happy young firearms officer who incorrectly believed that he was reaching for a weapon. I check the inquest notes and they confirm a verdict of lawful killing on the basis that the officer concerned had genuine reason to believe that the victim was armed. Unfortunately, again, the details of the officers involved in the incident are fully redacted in the inquest notes. I put away the contents of the file and I call Cath, who confirms that she is already on her way back to the station.

■ ■ ■ ■ ■ ■ ■ ■

By the time she reaches my office, it is getting late, but neither of us are particularly concerned about knocking off just yet. Cath is looking especially pleased with herself, so I hold onto my own news for now and let her start.

"Go on then, mate," I say. "I can see that you're itching to tell me what you've found out."

She drops her handbag on my desk and sits down. "Well, it was a bitch of a job trawling through the mountain of manual records in the Securicor archive, but I finally managed to unearth a copy of the schedule for the day of the robbery."

Cath takes out some sheets of paper from her bag and passes them across the table. "I wasn't allowed to take the originals, but they made copies for me, plus a copy of each man's Securicor ID badge. Interestingly, there were three guards suspected of involvement in the robbery, so Clive was wrong about that too."

As she speaks, I notice with a sinking feeling the three names highlighted on the time sheet, confirming that my second trip back to 1983 has altered the timeline to involve an additional suspect in the robbery. This is where things start to get tricky and I make a mental note to be careful when discussing the case with Cath or anyone else.

I pick up the identity card copies and although I know it already, I read the first name out loud, "Stuart Mark Goldsmith."

The second and third names are Peter Edwin Lane and George John Benson.

"So, these are the three guys that were scheduled for the Heathrow Depot pick-up on the day of the robbery?"

"Yeh, it seems that way, Sean. I asked around in the head office to see if anybody remembers them, or anything about the robbery, but I drew a complete blank. Anybody working for Securicor in 83 has either long since retired or moved on."

"What about a current address or number for any of them?"

"Nothing. Again, I drew a complete blank. No address, no medical history, no banking records. Nothing. It's almost as if they all dropped off the end of the earth after December 83."

"No, there has to be something, Cath. What about friends or family? There must be someone that knows something. Three young guys don't just disappear without a trace and nobody asks why."

"I know, boss, I looked into the family angle and this is where it all gets a bit funny. I did a full background check on them. All had completely clean records, which is no surprise given the job they were doing. What is a surprise, though, is that they were all unmarried, both parents deceased, and, as a final coincidence, all three were only children."

"And apparently no friends or close associates to give a shit about them if they were to disappear, Cath. Are you thinking what I'm thinking?"

Cath nods. "Yep, I'm thinking that George, Peter, and Stuart were targeted because they were—"

"A bunch of losers?" I cut in.

Cath frowns at my lack of sensitivity. "That's not exactly what I was going to say, but yes, something like that. With no friends or close family pushing for answers, it is far less likely for any investigation into their disappearance to go on for any longer than is necessary. That would have suited our perps just fine, boss."

"So, where do you think they are, Cath?"

"My guess, Sean, either paid off and spirited out of the country or murdered and disposed of."

Given what I know about Michael's intentions for me after the robbery, I'm fairly certain which of those options is the more likely scenario. I shiver slightly at the realization that my interference may have inadvertently caused the death of one of the three missing security guards and Cath asks if I am okay.

"Uhm, yes, I'm fine thanks. If you're right, though, this adds a completely new and worrying dimension to the investigation. Robbery is one thing. Triple murder is something else entirely. From here on, we need to tread extra carefully. What about the robbery itself? Did you come across anything in the archives about that or any indication that any of the Securicor staff were interviewed or gave statements afterwards?"

Cath shakes her head. "Like I said, absolutely bugger all, mate. Possibly a result of Operation Hush, maybe?"

"Yeh, maybe. If the authorities were that keen to keep it under wraps back then, it would make sense that Securicor was ordered to destroy any records or documents relating to the robbery. It still doesn't explain why there was nothing in the case file though. What about my hunch on Thierry junior? Anything on that, Cath?"

She shakes her head again and says, "Sorry boss, no luck with that. It was just mum, dad, and daughter. Unfortunately, no young protégé to carry on the Pinois family business."

"Fair enough, Cath. It was a bit of a long shot anyway. Good work though."

Cath smiles and then asks me how I got on. In response I hand her the Pinois killing investigation file. "The details of the firearms officers have been redacted, but otherwise it seems to be complete. The big surprise is that Rosemary was in the car when Thierry was killed."

Cath looks shocked at this revelation and I point to Rosemary's statement. "It's true, Cath. She was right next to him in the passenger seat."

"My God, Sean. It's no wonder she was hostile to us this morning. In such close confinement, it's likely that she would have been splattered with his blood. Christ, she was just a kid."

I let Cath digest this latest news and then I take back the file. "Okay, so we have the names of the real security guards and we know that Rosemary was present when her father was killed, but other than that we really don't have much else to go on.

"Not a total waste of a day, but not a great one either. I think we should finish up and meet tomorrow with clear heads for our date with Mr. Patrick 'Paddy' Newman."

I'm about to put away the files when Cath suddenly stops me and picks up the investigation file and takes out the inquest notes. She holds one of the sheets of paper up to her nose and inhales.

I'm about to ask what she is doing when she holds up her hand and tells me to wait. She takes another sheet of paper and again lifts it to her nose before handing it to me. "I knew I could smell something, Sean. If this case file is nearly forty years old, then how the hell can I still smell the ink? These notes have been redacted recently."

I take the sheet of paper and hold it to my nose. Although it is faint, the smell of ink is unmistakable. I shake my head in disbelief. "Shit, Cath, were you a bloodhound in a previous life? If you're right about this, then it confirms beyond doubt that we are being played. And if it is Clive Douglas, then he must have somebody on the inside helping him."

"That reminds me, did you speak to him again, boss?"

"No, I didn't get around to it, Cath, and with this latest development, talking to him again can wait. For now, I need you to get these notes over to forensics to see if they can tell us how old the ink is. See if they can also find out the names and badge numbers hiding under the redactions. They've been redacted for a reason and I want to know why. Once you've dropped them off, get yourself home. Call me if you get any updates tonight. Otherwise let's regroup at eight tomorrow."

"What about DI Morgan and DS Gray? We were meant to give them an update, boss."

Given the current lack of progress, I had been hoping to avoid speaking to Morgan and Gray tonight, but Catherine is right. If I don't speak to them, it is almost certain that at least one of them will call. I pick up my cellphone and I tell her that I will call DI Morgan now. She watches as I place the call, and I say, "Go on, Cath, you get yourself over to forensics. I'll call you later if there is anything new."

As soon as she is gone, I cut off the call to Franco's Pizzeria and pick up my car keys. Updates can wait; I have somewhere to be in 1983.

■　■　■　■　■　■　■　■

Unsure of exactly where to go tonight, I use the drive home to replay the previous few days in my head. From the first call to Clive Douglas on Wednesday evening to the discovery of the fresh ink in the case files earlier, I try to picture every small detail to see if we might have missed something important.

When I get to my apartment, I take out my pocketbook and look back through my previous notes. The biggest of the current unknowns is still the question of who is "T"?

Although we know that Clive Douglas is not to be trusted, I can't help but think that there was some semblance of truth in what he told us about Terry Pinois when we met him in Meerholt Prison. In fact, now that I think about it, after asking him about Terry or Thierry, he never specifically said that Thierry was our man. All he said was, So, you have had some luck. Could this mean that we are still on the right track with the Thierry connection? If Douglas is playing us, then it would suit him to drip feed us information until he is ready for his endgame.

The key to this case is still finding out who "T" is. I'm certain of this. Tonight, I need to travel back to my first encounter with Michael and Paddy, but this time I will follow them to see what business they had to attend to after leaving the Bluebell.

I change into my jogging bottoms and hoodie. Then I crack open a new bottle of Jameson and settle down to watch a movie. Two hours and half a bottle later, my eyelids are drooping, and it is time to go. Feeling too lazy to get up and go to the bedroom, I lie back on the sofa and close my eyes. I focus on the image of Darren Phillips entering the market and within seconds my body shivers in reaction to a sudden drop in temperature.

The Past – Friday, December 9th, 1983

A second blast of cold air cuts right through me and forces me to open my eyes. I'm at the edge of the market looking down the high street for Darren but something feels wrong. Although the time feels right, there is no sign of Darren or any of his crew, and I start to wonder whether I may have arrived on the wrong day completely. I'm about to ask someone what day it is when I hear a familiar voice behind me.

"Cor, look at the size of the puppies on that one. I bet she'd give a lovely tit-wank."

To my great relief, I have missed them by literally just a few seconds. I turn to see Darren and his boys less than twenty feet away, heading into the market.

"Oy, Phillips, stop right there, you little prick!"

My shouted insult has the desired effect and stops them dead in their tracks. Their walk back towards me is calm and unhurried, but the body language tells me that they are ready for a fight. They gather around and Darren pokes me in the chest.

"What was that, pal? Who the bloody hell are you? And how the fuck do you know my name?"

Before I can say anything, the stockiest of his mates says, "He looks like a bleedin' nonce to me, Daz. Is that it, mate? Are you a bleedin' nonce?

In answer to the question, I take out my warrant card and quickly flash it under their noses. I don't allow them to get a good look, but it is enough to make them hesitate and back away slightly. As before, Darren stands his ground. So, I look him up and down before saying, "It's Darren Phillips, isn't it? I know all about you and your mates, you little scrote."

Still unsure of who I am and what I want, he at first hesitates to respond. When he does, he is playing up to the audience and is as cocksure as ever.

"Is that right, copper? You think you know all about us, do you? Go on then, tell us. What is it you know?"

I step forward and point to each of them in turn. "I know that you are all light-fingered little fuckers and you like a bit of aggro at the football."

Darren looks to his mates and laughs, then turns back to face me. "Is that it? Is that the best you've got? Do me a bleedin' favor, mate. That's old news. We haven't done anything wrong and this is just harassment now. Come on, lads, we're leaving."

They turn to leave, and I reach for Darren's arm. "Hang on, not so fast, Phillips. How would you and your mates like to earn twenty quid each for ten minutes' work?"

My offer of cash causes Darren to screw up his face. "What? What the fuck are you on about, pal?"

The stocky lad nods his head and laughs. "I knew he was a fucking nonce. I think he wants a gangbang with us."

They all laugh, and Darren says, "Is that it, pal? Are you a bum bandit?"

I shake my head and Darren turns towards his gang.

"I think he might be a bit shy, lads."

They all piss themselves laughing again and I wait for Darren to turn back to face me before I step forward and slap him hard across the face with the back of my hand.

As expected, the laughing stops instantly, and I watch as Darren composes himself after the initial shock of the assault. I let things play out for a few more seconds and then I say, "Okay, Darren, now that I have your attention, let's talk business. Do you want to earn twenty quid each for doing what you do best, or do I call my mates to haul you all down to the station? It's your choice. Easy beer money, or Friday night in the nick getting fucked around?"

"But we've done fuck all wrong," one of Darren's mates protests.

"Yeh, and we could have you done for assault," another of them adds. "You're not a bloody copp—"

I hold up my hand and cut him off. "I suggest you lot shut your bloody pie holes." Then directly to Darren, "If I want to, I could have you all pulled in tonight for sexual harassment and attempted kidnap."

"What? What the fuck are you on about?" Darren exclaims.

His mates join in the chorus and I shout again for them to keep quiet.

"You lot. I've already told you once to button it. Now listen to me, Phillips, I heard what you and your mates said you were going to do to that girl and her puppies."

I'm trying hard not to grin, but Darren looks worried and shakes his head. Then desperately trying to maintain the bravado, he appeals to his mates, "Is this joker for real, lads?" Then to me, "You can't be serious. We were just having a bit of fun. She never even heard what I said."

Pressing my advantage, I move closer so that my face is no more than six inches away from Darren's. "Well, I don't find it particularly funny and I don't think she would either. Threatening to kill her puppies and then to kidnap and jerk off over her tits is serious, Phillips. That's a long stretch in the scrubs for all of you."

They all now look worried and while Darren desperately tries to think of something to say, I take five twenty-pound notes from my wallet and hold them out in front of me.

"Or we could forget all about that little incident and you can earn yourself some easy money. You lot like a good scrap, right?"

Obviously relieved not to be getting arrested for puppycide and sexual assault, Darren looks me up and down and then cautiously takes the money. "So, what is it you want us to do?"

I smile and nod. "Good lad. Do you know where the Bluebell Pub is?"

■ ■ ■ ■ ■ ■ ■ ■

After going over the plan for what needs to happen in the Bluebell, I tell Darren that he also needs to steal a car and to wait for me outside after the fight.

"I take it that you do know how to steal a car, Phillips?"

He grins and says, "Of course, I bloody do. There isn't a car been made yet that I can't get into. Any particular model you would like, sir?"

I shake my head. "No, just make sure that it's not too flashy and it's got a full tank of gas. Now, one last time. Are you all clear about what I need you to do?"

None of them speaks, but they all nod to confirm that they understand. I smile and say, "Good, if you manage to do this without fucking it up, I might be able to throw some more work your way. Just make sure that you all get stuck in, and don't be shy about sticking one on me. It needs to look real."

That last part was aimed particularly at the lad who was unfortunate enough to be on the receiving end of my knee in his nuts on the last trip. They all nod again, and I smile.

"Great, now fuck off and make sure that you are there on time."

■ ■ ■ ■ ■ ■ ■ ■

From here, everything else plays out exactly as it did before, with the exception of one small and painful detail.

After the fight, Michael stays at the bar to pay for the new round of drinks and Paddy joins me at their table. "We could have taken those little fuckers you know," he says, "but thanks anyway. How are your balls doing? That was a hefty kick that little bastard got in on you."

Yep, and don't I know it. My eyes are still watering and I'm now regretting giving the instruction to make it look real. I tell him that I'm fine and Paddy nods. "Yeh, don't worry about it. It was a lucky shot. Anyway, what's your story, Sean? I don't recall seeing you around here before."

■ ■ ■ ■ ■ ■ ■ ■

Fast forward another ten minutes and we agree to meet back in the pub for breakfast the next morning. Michael stands up and tells Paddy that they need to get going.

"Sorry, Sean. I would love to stay and finish my drink, but we have business to attend to. Eleven o'clock tomorrow morning, okay? Don't be late."

As before, they leave without saying another word, but this time I can't afford to hang around. I'm on my feet before the door has had time to close behind them.

■ ■ ■ ■ ■ ■ ■ ■

I hold back in the doorway of the pub and watch as my two suspects climb into Paddy's red Cortina, which is parked on the opposite side of the street. Unbelievably, Darren is parked right behind them and has clearly misunderstood my instruction not to steal anything too flashy. I wait for Paddy to pull away and then I cross the street and climb into the passenger seat.

"Really, Darren, a practically brand new metallic black Ford Escort XR3i with the world's shiniest alloy wheels and the world's biggest rear spoiler. This is not flashy at all, is it?"

He grins and says, "You've got to admit, though, it's a bloody cool motor. Anyway, enough jabber, I take it you want me to follow that pair of pricks?"

I nod my head. "Don't lose them and don't get too bloody close."

■　■　■　■　■　■　■

We follow them through the London traffic for more than thirty minutes and more than once they appear to be doubling back on themselves or deliberately covering the same ground.

The next time they do it, Darren looks at me and says, "Do you think that they know they are being followed?"

I shake my head. "No, they have a job coming up soon. They are just being careful. They don't know we are following them."

For a second Darren takes his eyes off the road. "What job is that then? It must be something big to have an undercover pig tailing them. No offence, of course."

"None taken, Darren, and mind your own bloody business. Just keep your eyes on the road and let me worry about whether they have seen us or not."

He turns back to face the road and shrugs. "Yeh, yeh, okay. I don't suppose I'm allowed to know your name, though, am I?"

"Would it shut you up if I tell you?"

"Yeh, it would," Darren replies. And then adds with a laugh, "Well, for at least sixty seconds anyway."

I turn and call him a dickhead.

"If you must know so badly, it's Sean. Now, slow down, it looks like we might have arrived."

Paddy indicates to turn left, and the Cortina disappears down a narrow alley at the rear of a small shopping parade.

I don't know the area, but thankfully Darren does. He stops suddenly and parks in front of an Indian takeaway restaurant.

"I didn't tell you to stop, Phillips. Come on, we're going to lose them."

"No, you won't, Sean. That alleyway leads to a couple of old lockup garages and a dead end behind these shops. If we follow them in, they will spot us for sure. You're going to have to go on foot from here, mate. I'll keep the engine running."

"And how do I know you won't just piss off as soon as I'm gone?"

"Because I'm having too much fun, Sean. And because you said that you might have some more work for us."

I shake my head and tell him that he is full of shit, but strangely enough, I do actually believe him. I tell him to keep the music down and then I leave him to keep an eye on the car while I go to find Paddy and Michael.

■ ■ ■ ■ ■ ■ ■ ■

For a moment I consider following them directly into the alleyway, but then decide against it and turn back towards the Indian takeaway. Inside the restaurant, I push past the half dozen customers waiting at the counter and flash my badge.

"Police. Do you have a rear exit into the alley behind?"

The young man behind the counter doesn't say anything, but he does lift part of the counter and points towards the kitchen. I thank him and he goes back to serving his customers completely unconcerned at the sudden arrival of a police officer.

In the kitchen it's a different story completely. Four middle-aged Indian guys hard at work preparing the orders in hellishly hot conditions become frozen to the spot the second they see me. One of them has a cigarette hanging from the corner of his mouth. When I show him my badge, his mouth opens, and the cigarette drops into an uncovered pot of something nasty-looking.

They clearly think that I am either an immigration officer or from the council hygiene department. Looking around the filthy kitchen, it's easy to see why they would be worried. I'm almost tempted to give them a bollocking about the state of the place, but I can't afford to hang around.

"Don't panic, I'm not here for you lot. Where is the back door?"

Obviously keen for me to be gone, all four guys raise their hands in unison and point towards the exit. I leave them to it, making my way down a short narrow corridor that is made even narrower by sacks of rice and drums of cooking oil stacked against the walls on either side.

The exit door is unlocked, and I cautiously look out towards the end of the alley. Two hundred yards from where I am standing, Paddy's car is parked in front of one of the garages and I can see a small chink of light escaping from the gap under the door. Next to Paddy's Cortina, there is a white Ford Sierra and I wonder if this could belong to the mysterious "T".

I watch for another five minutes trying to work out how to get to the end of the alley without being seen if they come out of the lockup, but in the end the decision is taken out of my hands when the door suddenly opens. Paddy and Michael are alone, but the light remains on in the lockup, so I assume that whoever owns the Sierra must still be inside. Paddy starts his engine and I duck my head inside the corridor as the alley is suddenly illuminated by the lights from his car. Ten seconds later, the Cortina flashes past the door and I watch as it disappears back out onto the main road.

With Paddy and Michael gone, my focus now is on finding out who and what is in the lockup. A few more minutes pass before the light goes out and I hear the door opening.

Someone leaves the garage, but the lack of light makes it hard to see who it is. I hear the door to the Sierra slam shut, and knowing that I may not get another chance, I take a risk and keep watching as the car moves towards me. It starts to pick up speed and with the headlights blinding me, I know that I will have less than a second to see who is driving as it passes my hiding place. I'm concentrating so hard on the lights that I am taken completely by surprise when a hand touches my shoulder and I spin around ready to defend myself.

Darren is standing behind me with a stupid grin on his face. Too late, I turn back towards the alley, but the Sierra has already gone. To say I am annoyed at missing the opportunity to possibly find out who "T" is would be a huge understatement. I drag Darren out into the alley, and I point towards the main road.

"You absolute fucking dickhead! One of my best leads has just disappeared into the distance thanks to you. I bloody well told you to wait in the car, didn't I? Why are you here?"

"I was worried," Darren replies.

"Worried. Worried about what?"

"About you," Darren says. "When I saw the two old pricks leave and you didn't come back, I thought they might have done you over, or something."

Although still annoyed, I'm also slightly touched that he was worried enough to come and find me. I calm down and offer half an apology for snapping at him.

"I suppose it wasn't entirely your fault. But to make up for the bit that was your fault, you can help me get into that garage up there."

We get to the door, which, as expected, is locked, and I tell Darren to go back to the car to see if there are any tools in the boot, or something else we can use to pick the lock.

Ignoring my request, he fishes around in his pockets and produces a set of assorted keys and picks. "No need for all that nonsense, Sean. I never leave home without these babies."

By now, I really shouldn't be surprised by anything about Darren, but in 1983 he is still a school kid and I shake my head in disbelief. "You really are a thieving little fucker, aren't you, Phillips? Well, go on then. Don't just stand there like an idiot.

Wipe that smug grin off your chops and get to work on that lock before someone sees us."

Less than thirty seconds later, there is a satisfying click as the lock turns and the door opens. Darren is about to step inside, but I stop him and tell him to wait outside.

"This is police business and you are more involved than I would like already. Wait here and shout out if you see anyone."

He reluctantly does as he is told, and I go in and turn on the light. Unsurprisingly, the inside of the garage consists solely of a single room with a bare concrete floor. The room is far from empty though. On a table in front of me, there is an elaborate model of a place that I recognize instantly. The model is a perfect representation of the Heathrow Trading Estate and has sticky notes attached to all of the gates and checkpoints that detail the numbers of police and security personnel expected to be on duty on December 24th.

Under the table there are two cardboard boxes, which I carefully open. Inside I find the Securicor uniforms and the ID badges for George John Benson and Peter Edwin Lane. With this latest discovery I am now convinced that the driver of the Ford Sierra must be "T". If this is true, it would also mean that Paddy was lying after his arrest about never meeting "T" or knowing who he was. The absence of a third ID card tonight confirms that Stuart Goldsmith is the security guard that my interference has put in the firing line. I resolve to do something about that as soon as possible.

Satisfied that there is nothing else to find, I return the boxes to the same place under the table and I switch off the light and go outside. Darren is leaning against the wall smoking and he asks me if I found what I was looking for.

I nod. "Yes, you could say that. Now put your fag out and make sure the door is properly locked again. It's time we were going."

■ ■ ■ ■ ■ ■ ■ ■

A few minutes later we get back to the car and I tell Darren to drive back towards Fulham.

"Yes, sir. Any part of Fulham in particular?" he asks me sarcastically."

"Yep, you can drop me off where I met you today near the market."

My plan to get home tonight is to meet up with the dossers again for a glug of their vodka and an ice-cold step to sleep on. Freezing to death really wasn't that bad compared to some of the ways I have topped myself in the past. And, to be honest, I can't be arsed to hang around looking for anything more inventive tonight.

Darren pulls away and then asks me what he should do with the car afterwards.

"It seems a shame to have to dump it, Sean. It's a lovely motor."

"It is a lovely motor," I tell him. "It's also a stolen motor and by now its owner will have reported it missing. As soon as you drop me off, take it somewhere and torch it. I don't want any forensics left. You understand?"

He nods and then for effect says, "Yes, sir! Understood, loud and clear, sir!"

"Good, now shut your cake hole and keep your eyes on the road and your speed within the limit. I don't want us getting pulled over."

Darren is about to say something when he looks away and checks his rear-view mirror. "I think it might be too late for that, Sean. I think we've been spotted."

I look over my shoulder, just as the blue lights come on and the patrol car flashes its headlights at us.

"Fuck, that's all I need. Put your bloody foot down, Darren."

Confused as to why I would want to get away from the police, Darren hesitates, "But, I thought you were a co—"

"I am a cop, but this investigation is not exactly official, if you know what I mean. So, unless you want to be spending the next couple of years in a young offenders' institution for breaking and entering and car theft, I suggest you stop asking stupid questions and see exactly what this beauty can do."

Not needing to be told twice, Darren floors the accelerator and the patrol car is left for dead as the XR3i rapidly picks up speed.

"What now, boss? They are not going to give up and they've probably called for backup by now. I can take us somewhere to lie low until the heat dies down, if you want?"

"No, just keep going," I tell him. "I need you to get as far ahead as you can, then make a turn and stop. As soon as you can, get out and disappear. I'll take care of the car."

"You sure? I can lose them no problem in this."

"Just get as far ahead as you can, then get ready to get out."

Darren looks back to the road and as soon as the gap between us and our pursuer is big enough, I shout, "Now, Darren, turn here!"

He jerks the wheel and the tires screech horribly as we make the turn. A split second later he slams on the brakes and I'm already sliding across to the driver's seat before Darren has had the chance to fully get out.

I push him towards the door and shout, "Come on, get a bloody move on, Phillips!"

He tumbles out of the car, and I pull the door shut and drop the window to tell him that I might be in touch again.

Whether he hears me or not, I have no idea. Darren is already back on his feet and running. The last I see of him is the back of his jacket as he sprints down one of the side streets and disappears into the shadows.

I hit the gas and, as I pull away, the patrol car makes the turn and continues the chase. My destination is the M25 London Orbital Motorway. I know that If I can make it there without being intercepted, I will be able to find what I am looking for and get up enough speed to get myself home.

Ten minutes into the pursuit, a second and a third patrol car join the chase, but they are too late. I pass the sign for the M25 on-ramp and a few seconds later I merge onto the motorway, which, given the time of night, is moving freely.

Thankful in the end that Darren stole something decent, I push the engine to the max and I'm soon topping out the speed. My pursuers are also pushing their motors hard and one of them seems to be gaining ground on me, but it's all going to be to no avail.

I've been looking for an articulated lorry and up ahead I see the taillights of one plodding along at no more than fifty miles per hour on the inside lane. I switch lanes and with the accelerator pushed down as far as it can go, I ignore everything else and focus solely on the rear wheels of the lorry. At 115 mph, the result is an almost forgone conclusion and the ground between my vehicle and the lorry is eaten up in seconds.

The rear end of the lorry is at the perfect height to allow the front of my car to slide perfectly under and between the huge wheels. A split second later the windscreen strikes the rear bumper of the lorry and the canopy of this beautiful car is sheared entirely off … along with my head and a good portion of my upper body.

Present Day – Tuesday, May 1st, 2018

I sleep through until my alarm wakes me at just after 7:30. I fumble around trying to turn it off, then I reach for my cellphone to check for missed calls or messages. There are no missed calls, but there are two messages. The first is from Cath and was sent at 1:04 a.m.

Mate, I was right about the ink. The forensic boys reckon it is no more than a month old. No luck yet on the names or service numbers. I've left them at it and am heading home now to sleep. Will follow up again in the morning.

The second message is from DCI Morgan and was sent less than an hour ago.

Come to my office for 8.30 and bring DC Swain with you.

No prizes for guessing what he wants, and the curtness of his message suggests that he is pissed with me for not updating him yesterday.

I forward the message to Catherine and an hour later I meet her outside Morgan's office where she wastes no time in laying into me.

"You bloody told me that you were going to call him. Christ, you even fake dialed him in front of me. I could bloody swing for you sometimes, Sean."

I'm about to apologize when the office door opens and Kevin Morgan shouts across the room to invite us in. "No need to swing for Sergeant McMillan just yet, DC Swain. In you come please."

We take our seats and DI Gray closes the door behind us, before she takes her seat and starts the meeting. "If I didn't know better, I would think that you were both trying to avoid us. What happened to the update yesterday, DS McMillan?"

"Um yes. I'm sorry about that, ma'am. We were following up on a couple of important leads and the time just ran away with us. It won't happen again."

"Damn right it won't," Morgan says. "Go on then, tell us about these leads and your visit to Thierry Pinois yesterday. What happened?"

"Yes, sir, well, first off, the visit to Thierry was a non-starter."

"And why was that?" DI Gray asks.

"Because he has been dead since 1979," Cath replies. "He was shot dead by an armed response unit, supposedly on his way to an armed robbery."

Morgan sits up straight and asks, "Supposedly, DC Swain?"

"Yes, sir. His teenage daughter was also in the car at the time. So, I think it's highly unlikely that he was on the way to a robbery. And there was no weapon found in his vehicle."

"Yes, well, that's not for us to speculate on," Morgan responds. "Either way it rules out this Pinois fella as the brains of the operation."

"It rules Thierry out as the brains. But I still think there could be a connection, sir."

"And how is that, DS McMillan?" Morgan asks.

"I don't know yet, sir. Just a gut feeling. Although Clive Douglas didn't initially suggest the name Thierry, he was the one that put us onto the Pinois connection, and he is desperate to get his move to Cat C. It makes no sense for him to send us on a complete wild goose chase. He knows that if we come up empty, he gets nothing."

Sarah Gray clears her throat and says, "You need to be careful about putting too much faith in that man, Sean."

"Yes, ma'am. I know that. But we know beyond doubt that the case is real and I'm certain that if we remain patient, we can find out exactly what Douglas is playing at."

Morgan leans back in his chair and asks, "What about the third blagger? Any luck with finding a name for him?"

Catherine shows the three ID card copies. "Unfortunately, no luck with the name, sir. But we do have the identities of the three guards scheduled for the pickup on the day of the robbery."

"Great, speak to them as soon as you can," DI Gray says.

Catherine's face gives her away and Morgan shakes his head. "We don't know where any of them are, do we DC Swain?"

"No, sir. It appears that all three disappeared after the robbery. We think there could be a possibility that they were murdered and disposed of to keep them quiet."

Morgan now looks incredulous. "This just gets better and better. Give me some good news, please. Tell me that you have located the one suspect that we do know about. Tell me that at least, DS McMillan."

"Uhm, not exactly, sir. We're hoping to locate him this morning. It's pension day."

"What? Bloody pension day!" Morgan exclaims. "It will be pension day for the pair of you if you don't stop pissing around with this investigation and start making some progress. Have you made any progress in the last few days?"

I wait for him to finish speaking and then I say, "Actually, sir. Yes, we have, I believe we have made a significant breakthrough. Cath, the inquest notes please."

Catherine takes out a copy of the notes and I point out the areas that have been redacted. "Sir, these are copies, but the originals are with the forensic boys. Both the inquest notes and the investigation into the killing of Thierry Pinois have had the names and badge numbers of the firearms officers redacted."

"Okay, you have our attention," Morgan says.

"Well, sir, these documents are from 1979 and the redactions were made by hand, with a black marker or some other kind of black ink."

Fool's Gold

"That's very unusual," Sarah Gray comments.

"Yes, ma'am. That's not the real clincher though."

Morgan is starting to look impatient and tells me to get to the point.

"Yes, sir. It was DC Swain that picked up on it. I'll let her explain."

"I wish somebody bloody would. Get on with it please, if you would, DC Swain."

"Yes, sir. Sorry. When I was looking through the notes, I thought I could smell the ink. So I took them to the boys in the lab. They estimate the redactions to be no more than a month old and possibly as fresh as a week."

Morgan looks at Gray and nods, then he makes a note on a Post-it and asks, "And what about the names and badge numbers? We need those."

"Nothing yet, sir," I say. "The lab boys are still working on those. I think you're right, though. If we can get those names, we might be able to work out what the hell is going on. Is this enough for us to get this case officially reopened? We need to be able to interview our suspects under caution."

Sarah Gray stands up and joins Morgan behind his desk. He turns his chair to face the wall and they talk quietly for a few minutes so that they can't be overheard. Cath and I sit in uncomfortable silence until they finish, then Morgan turns his chair back around to face us.

"DS McMillan, DC Swain, from this point on we need to assume that Clive Douglas is somehow trying to set you up for something. I don't know why, what, or how, but it seems probable that he is being assisted by someone on the inside. Until we know what is happening, this investigation needs to stay off the books and it must remain between the four of us in this room. Clear?"

We both nod and I say, "Yes, sir. What do you suggest next?"

"You carry on as before," DS Gray responds. "You don't give Douglas any reason to think that he is under suspicion in any way. Continue as planned today with trying to locate Patrick Newman and follow up as planned with forensics. As soon as they have anything, you call right away, but get everything back from them. We don't want any of them talking about this investigation outside of school. In parallel, I'm going to make some calls to see if we can get our hands on unredacted copies of the inquest and investigation notes."

"Thank you, ma'am. Anything else?"

Morgan says, "Yes, one last thing, DS McMillan. No need to attend the morning briefings for the next few days. I want you and DC Swain to give this investigation your full attention. Okay, carry on."

We stand up to leave and Sarah Gray shows us to the door. "Don't be a stranger, DS McMillan," she says.

"Sorry, ma'am?"

"You know what I mean, Sean. Keep in touch and keep us updated."

■ ■ ■ ■ ■ ■ ■

The door to the elevator closes and Catherine nudges me and raises her eyebrows. "I think that Sarah Gray has the hots for you, mate."

"What? No, she doesn't," I say uncomfortably. "What makes you say that?"

"Female instinct, Sean. Her body language was all over the place. And that don't be a stranger comment, there was a hidden meaning in there somewhere. Is there something I should know about?"

To hide my blushes, I laugh and call Catherine an idiot. "I think deep down, you might have a bit of a crush on me yourself and you try to hide it by making up all these other fictitious romances for me to take the heat off yourself."

"Like Maria Pinto?" Catherine asks with a smirk.

Just in time, the elevator door opens at our floor and I say, "Ooops, saved by the bell. Come on we have work to do. Grab your car keys, you're driving, Cath."

"Yeh, whatever. To be continued, mate."

■ ■ ■ ■ ■ ■ ■ ■

An hour later we are sitting at a table in the window of a café opposite the central post office on Fulham high street.

"So, we're supposed to just wait here until Patrick deigns to show up? If, of course, he deigns to show up at all."

"Unless you have a better idea for finding him, Cath?"

"No, but it's not even ten yet and the post office is open until five-thirty. We could be in for a long wait."

I smirk and say, "So, check your selfies on Facebook or something. Or read one of the gossip magazines by the counter."

"Thanks, that's very helpful and very sexist. Not all women spend all day taking selfies and flicking through glossy magazines, you know."

Our banter is interrupted by the waitress bringing our drinks and a couple of egg and bacon toasties. She leaves and I ask Catherine to pass the ketchup.

"Right, stop your bleeding moaning and get that down you. You're always grumpy when you're hungry," I tell her.

■ ■ ■ ■ ■ ■ ■ ■

Nearly two hours pass, and the waitress is growing increasingly irritated at how long we have been hogging one of her best tables. She sarcastically asks for a third time if we will be ordering anything else and I'm just about to order another tea when Catherine stops me.

"Hang on, boss. Is that him?"

A shabby looking old guy in a battered gray overcoat and a black woolen cap is crossing the street heading towards the post office. He has his back to us and is walking with a stoop, but his bulk is hard to miss.

"He's a big lad, whoever he is. You think that could be our boy?"

I'm already on my feet.

"Yeh, I think it might be. Come on, let's go and find out."

■ ■ ■ ■ ■ ■ ■ ■

Our target is third in line to be served and I hand Catherine a passport application form. "Here, take this. Let's pretend to fill it in at the counter so that we can get a look at his face."

Catherine gets to work on filling in the form and I casually turn around to face the queue. The last thirty-five years have not been kind to Patrick. Despite his size, he now looks frail and resigned to living out his remaining years eking out a meagre existence on a basic state pension. I almost feel sorry that we are going to be questioning him about a crime that technically he has already paid for through twenty-two years of hard time in a Cat A prison. Then I remind myself that we might now be looking for three other bodies and I refocus. I turn back to Catherine.

"That's our boy alright. Let's wait outside for him."

■ ■ ■ ■ ■ ■ ■ ■

Patrick emerges from the post office just as the heavens open, and he ducks back into the doorway next to us. He checks the time and then grumbles something about the British weather.

Taking this as an opportunity to introduce ourselves, I ask if we can give him a lift to the pub.

Taken aback by my offer, Patrick leans closer and asks, "What was that, fella?"

"I said, unless you don't mind getting soaked, we can give you a lift to the pub, if you want. Our car is just over there, Patrick. It is, Patrick, yes? Patrick Newman? Or do you prefer to be called Paddy?"

My mention of his name causes him to move away and he looks us both over with suspicion. "I knew you were coppers as soon as I saw you playing happy families at the counter. Even after so long, I can smell bacon from a mile away."

He turns to leave, and Cath boldly places herself in front of him. "Just hang on please. We're not here for you, but we do need to speak to you about the Heathrow robbery and the murder you went down for."

He thinks about it for a few seconds and then says, "That was a long time ago. I've done my time and I've got nothing else to say about it. I just want to be left alone."

He tries again to get past, but, despite his size, Cath stands her ground and tells him to stay where he is. "Listen, Patrick, we understand that you've done your time and kept your nose clean since your release from prison, but we do need to speak to you. So, we can either treat you to a couple of pints while we talk, or we can make it official and pull you in for questioning. All we want is thirty minutes of your time and then we can let you get on with the rest of your day."

"Do I have a bloody choice?" Patrick grumbles.

"Come on, our car is just over there," I say. "Once we are done, we can leave you or drop you off wherever you need to go."

Paddy points to Cath's handbag. "I want to see your badges before I go anywhere."

We take them out and Cath formally introduces us. "I'm DC Swain and this is my partner, DS McMillan. We work on the cold case squad based at Blackwell Station."

"Did they re-open the case?" Paddy asks. "What for? Mike is dead and I already did my ti—" He stops mid-sentence and then says, "You must be after the others, or the gold. It's the gold, isn't it? After this long, I doubt whether anybody gives a fuck about the others. But the gold, now that's a different story. I think I will have that drink with you after all."

■ ■ ■ ■ ■ ■ ■ ■

While Catherine gets the drinks, I ask why we are in the Wheatsheaf and not the Bluebell. "Wasn't that Davies and your favorite haunt back then?"

"Yes, it was, but it was demolished sometime in the early nineties. Besides, if it was still open, I doubt whether I would be welcome back. Not after I splattered Mike's brains all over the bar." At the end of that comment, I'm stunned when Paddy laughs and adds, "That kind of thing doesn't tend to be forgotten too easily."

He might appear old and frail, but it's obvious that the years in prison have done nothing to change him as a person. Making a mental note not to underestimate him, I join Cath at the bar to help her carry the drinks.

"Let's tread carefully, Cath. I don't think Paddy is as old and decrepit as he wants us to think. He just made light of murdering his best friend."

Cath shakes her head and as we walk back to the table, she quietly says, "Once a psycho always a psycho."

I hand Paddy his pint and he turns up his nose when he sees our drinks. "Soda and lime. What is this? Are you both teetotal or something?"

"No, but we're both on duty and I'm driving," Cath says.

"That never used to stop the coppers in my day," Paddy responds. "Those hypocritical bastards used to be half-cut all bloody day long. Anyway, suit yourself."

He takes a long gulp from his pint and then places the glass back down. "I take it you want to know who the other players were?"

Cath already has her pocketbook out and leans forward expectantly. "Yes, that would be very helpful, Patrick."

Paddy leans across the table and points to the pocketbook. "Okay, make sure that you get this, because I'm only going to say it once."

"Yes, go ahead, I'm ready," Catherine says.

"Good, because I don't want anyone to get the wrong idea. So, open you ears and write this down exactly as I say it."

He takes a deep breath and then clearly and calmly says, "Patrick Newman is not, never was, and never will be a bloody grass. So, go fuck yourselves. Next question please?"

Catherine looks like she is about to explode. Before she does, I reach for her arm. "No, that's okay, DC Swain. I can see that Patrick here is a man of honor." Then turning back to him, I ask, "What do you know about a blagger called Thierry Pinois? He was active around the same period as you and Davies."

"Until he was gunned down by you lot," Paddy says.

"So, you knew him?" Catherine asks.

"I knew of him."

"You would have moved in the same circles," I suggest.

"Our paths crossed once or twice, if that's what you mean, sergeant."

Catherine asks if they ever worked together. "Did you ever pull a job together or discuss hitting the Heathrow Trading Estate?"

Patrick takes another long gulp of his beer and then says, "No and no. Until Brinks Mat, I had no idea that the Heathrow Trading Estate even existed. And by then, Pinois was long since rotting in his box."

"So, who put you onto the job then, Paddy? This was too big for you and Michael. You were purely small time until then."

Paddy sneers at me. "You should be careful, sergeant. You're in danger of hurting my feelings saying things like that. We might have been small time to you, but the job wasn't and if things hadn't gotten so messed up, we would be living it up on the Costa Del Sol to this very day."

Realizing that he is not going to give away anything about the other accomplices, I change direction and ask about his partner in crime. "When you say getting messed up, you're talking about killing Michael, aren't you?"

My question hits a nerve and after finishing his drink he ignores me and angrily slides the glass across the table towards Catherine. "My mouth is dry. I don't think so clearly when my mouth is dry."

I nod to Cath and she takes the glass to the bar for a refill. I check that she is looking the other way and then, taking my chance, I ask, "Did Thierry Pinois ever own a lockup garage or a white Ford Sierra?"

I've barely finished asking the question when the color drains completely from Paddy's face. 'Wait ... I mean, no. How could you possibly know that?"

Before I can say anything else, Catherine heads back to rejoin us. I've confirmed what I suspected anyway, so to Patrick's obvious confusion, I tell him to keep quiet.

Catherine asks if she has missed anything and Patrick tries to speak, but I interrupt and talk over him.

"No. Nothing, DC Swain, but Patrick was just about to tell me why he killed his partner, weren't you, Patrick?"

"Was, I?" he asks suspiciously.

"Yes, you were. So, go on then," I prompt. "Did you have a falling out over the loot? Is that why you killed him?"

Paddy laughs and says, "Michael was my best mate from when we were in short trousers and there was more than enough from the robbery to keep everyone happy for the rest of our lives. It was never about the money, sergeant."

"So, tell us. What was it about?" I ask. "You don't just walk into a pub in broad daylight and shoot your best friend in the face for no reason."

"I had a bloody reason. A bloody good reason," Patrick barks and slams his fist down on the table. "It's between me and Michael, though."

Cath says to herself, "It was a woman." And then to Patrick, "You fell out over a woman, didn't you?"

Ignoring the question, he takes a drink and then says, "I told you already, it's personal. I want to go home now."

"Not yet," I say. "You need to answer DC Swain's question. Did you kill Michael over a woman?"

Patrick shakes his head. "Don't make me laugh. Me and Mike were best mates. It took a damn site more than a bit of skirt for us to fall out over anything." He then puts on his cap and says, "Can I go now?"

"Just one more question and then you can leave. Did you ever hear of any other big players that might have been referred to simply as 'T'?"

Cath gives me a sideways glance, but although Patrick is staring directly at me to try to understand how I knew about "T", his face remains perfectly calm as he says, "I've no idea what you're talking about, DS McMillan."

"Yes, you do," I say. "And somebody else has confirmed that recently," I lie.

Patrick smiles and shakes his head. "So now we get to the truth of it. Some old lag has sold you a fairy story about a crock of gold in return for an early release and the great detective duo McMillan and Swain swallowed the bait in the hope of getting another gold star."

We are momentarily stunned into silence, until Patrick chuckles to himself and says, "Don't look so bloody surprised. I can read, and you pair were all over the news after that police corruption case. Such a shame, though, that you've fallen for such an obvious scam. It's actually a little bit pathetic and quite frankly it's all a little bit tragic, if you ask me."

He's now gloating at our expense and I lose patience.

"Yes, well we didn't ask you, did we? You can make your own way home, Newman. It looks like the rain has stopped anyway."

Paddy nonchalantly shrugs and says, "Of course, I wouldn't want to put you both to any trouble anyway." And then with no small hint of sarcasm, "Not when you are working on such an important case."

He gets up to leave and Catherine asks him where he lives.

"Just in case we need to talk to you again before the next pension day," she explains.

She makes a note of the address and then asks if it's his own house.

"Yeh, it's the one just opposite Buckingham Palace, love." he replies sarcastically. "Do I look like I own my own house? It's a residential home for the over sixties. Feel free to check if you want."

"Don't worry, I will." Catherine responds.

■ ■ ■ ■ ■ ■ ■ ■

"Better or worse than you were expecting that to go?" Catherine asks once Paddy is gone.

In answer to the question, I call to the barman and ask for a double Jameson and a glass of red wine.

"Yeh, that's what I thought," Catherine says. "Did we get anything out of that, Sean?"

I certainly did, but for obvious reasons I can't tell Catherine what I have just found out. I now know that the lockup and the white Sierra probably did belong to "T", but I still have no idea what the connection is. Apart from that, Paddy didn't give us anything new and on the face of it, he doesn't appear to be related in any way to the current events.

In fact, the only thing that seemed to rattle him was my questioning him about the murder of Michael Davies and Cath's suggestion that it was over a woman. I look back over my own notes and then suggest to Cath that we should look further into Paddy's and Michael's personal lives for any girlfriend or female acquaintances.

"You think I was right?"

"I think you hit a nerve, Cath. And guys can do some dumb shit when a pretty face is involved."

"And what about his comment about the old lag selling us a fairytale. I couldn't have put that better myself, Sean. You still think that Douglas is worth the effort of all this?"

I take a sip of my drink and then say, "Yes, I do. This case has more to it than first meets the eye, and the redactions prove that Douglas isn't the only player on the board. There's no way we can drop it now, Cath. The game's just getting interesting. Right, finish your drink and then drop me back to the station to get my car."

"You're going somewhere?" Cath asks.

"Yes, I've got a couple of missed calls from Clive Douglas. I may head across to see him and then I'm going to grab an early finish to run a couple of personal errands."

"Okay, and what about me?"

"Get back over to forensics to see if they've managed to find out the names of those firearms officers, then get onto the girlfriend connection for Paddy and Michael."

■ ■ ■ ■ ■ ■ ■

Catherine stops at the entrance gate to Blackwell Station and before I get out she asks if I want to grab a drink later to compare notes.

"Uh, yeh, possibly. I'll call you and let you know, Cath."

"Which means that you won't," she mutters.

"What was that?" I ask.

Catherine shakes her head and frowns. "Nothing, boss. I'll talk to you later."

I watch to make sure she has left, then I head down to collect my own vehicle. After a quick google search for the address, I edge my way into the early afternoon traffic and steer a course for Angels fancy dress shop on Shaftesbury Avenue.

If I'm going to get away with witnessing the murder of Michael Davies two months after when I think I'm going to be murdered myself, then I need a decent disguise and I remember a colleague telling me how good the gear is in Angels.

I arrive forty minutes later, and unable to find any public parking nearby, I park on the double yellow lines outside the store and leave my blue lights flashing to keep the traffic wardens at bay. The teenage girl behind the counter looks alarmed at my arrival, but she visibly relaxes when I smile and ask her where the wigs are.

"Not your shitty cheap ones, though. I'm looking for something realistic. And show me what costumes you have from the eighties as well, please."

With no one else in the store, she comes from behind the counter and helpfully shows me around. She guides me towards the racks of costumes and makes a couple of suggestions.

"The 80s hip-hop is good, or what about Mr. T? That one is always popular. Don't black up your face, though. People get upset about that kind of thing these days."

I frown and say, "Yes, I can imagine. Let's forget about Mr. T. I'm actually looking for something a bit more regular. Something a regular guy would have worn in the eighties."

The young girl smirks and says, "Oh, something boring you mean?"

Before I can answer, she reaches to the back of one of the rails and hands me a realistic looking, but obviously fake and far from regular, white Armani suit and a pastel pink t-shirt.

"What about this? It's Miami Vice. It comes with the white loafers and sunglasses and I can find you a suitable wig to match."

The costume is actually so bad that it's good. I try it on and whilst I look like an absolute tool, I also look nothing like Sean McMillan in 1983, 2018, or any other year for that matter.

I pay for my items and ten minutes later I am heading out of central London and on my way home. By 3 p.m., I have changed into my costume. I spend a final few seconds making sure that my Sonny Crockett blonde wig is on straight. Happy that even my own mother wouldn't recognize me, I finish by putting on my sunglasses and then I call Catherine to check in.

"Hey, boss. What's up?"

"Nothing, Cath. I was just calling to see if the boys at the lab managed to make any progress with those names."

"Not a thing," Catherine replies. "They seem to think that whoever made the redactions deliberately let the ink soak right in to make it difficult."

"Okay, that's not good news. And what about Michael and Paddy? Any luck turning up a girlfriend for either of them?"

"Absolute zilch, Sean. I'm still working on it, though. What about you? Did you speak to Douglas?"

"I called twice, but no answer," I lie.

"Maybe he is out at his country club or playing a round of golf," Cath quips.

"Yeh, probably. Whatever he is doing, he'll call back. You can be sure of it."

Catherine starts to say something else, but I pretend not to hear and cut off the call.

"Okay, thanks, Cath. I'll call you later."

Knowing that I only have a maximum window of a few hours to travel before Cath or anyone else calls or comes looking for me, I check myself one last time in the mirror before reaching for a bottle of whisky. Recently, I've been trying to rely on alcohol less and less to travel, but it's mid-afternoon and I am wide awake.

Reluctantly, I unscrew the lid and lift the bottle to my lips. I swallow nearly a quarter of the bottle and the neat alcohol burns as it hits the back of my throat. The desired result is achieved, though, and after a few minutes I start to feel unsteady on my feet. I lie down on my bed and picture the outside of the Bluebell Pub in February of 1984.

The Past – Saturday, February 4th, 1984

"Oy, cloth ears! Are you getting on or what?"

The voice reminds me of my uncle, but the bus conductor looking down on me is at least ten years older than my uncle was when he passed away.

Confused, I look around and then ask the conductor where I am. Amused at my question, he turns to the bus driver and raises his eyebrows, "Here we go, another one on drugs." Then turning back to me, he says, "If you took those bloody ridiculous glasses off, you might be able to see where you are going, son. Now, are you getting on or not? We've got a schedule to keep."

Not knowing where I am and with no other choice, I get on the bus and ask the conductor where it is going. "I need to get to Fulham High Street. Is this going anywhere near there?"

The conductor smiles and says, "Luckily for you, yes, it is, young man. Single or return?"

I hand him the money for a single and he hands me my ticket. "We won't get to Fulham High Street for another ten minutes. You might as well take a seat."

The lower level of the bus is almost completely full, so I make my way to the upper deck and find a seat next to an elderly Sikh gentleman, who politely nods as I sit down.

A few minutes later we arrive at the next stop and there is a short commotion on the lower level before the bus continues its journey. A few seconds later, three teenage boys wearing Chelsea colors appear at the top of the stairs. One of them is chanting something about up the blues, and all three are swigging from cans of Tennent's extra strength lager. Spotting an opening, they stagger down the aisle and to my dismay sit down in the row of seats directly behind me. Barely thirty seconds pass before the expected torrent of abuse starts.

"Hey, how do you stop a Paki from drowning?" one of the teenagers shouts loudly enough for the whole top deck to hear.

"Take yer foot off his head," another of them shouts to the amusement of his mates. Then he adds, "What about this one? Why do Pakis smell?"

When his friends don't answer, he bursts out laughing and answers for them, "So the blind can hate them too."

The old Sikh gentleman is doing his best to ignore the jibes, but when one of the boys leans forward and whispers, "Smelly Paki fuck" in his ear, he turns around to face his abuser.

"I am Indian, not Pakistani, you ignorant fool. India and Pakistan are two completely different countries."

As expected, his reprimand does nothing to diffuse the situation. Instead I can feel the atmosphere get noticeably more tense and I know that I need to step in. Forgetting for a moment that I am wearing shades and a white Armani suit, I turn around to warn the boys off. Instead of looking worried, they look at me with amusement. The ringleader sizes me up and then says, "What's up with you, bender? Is this Paki your boyfriend then?"

"Just leave the man alone," I reply. "He's not bothering you, so why don't you and your mates do yourselves a favor and just leave him alone?"

"Actually, gay boy, he is bothering us," one of them responds. "It bothers us that him and his Paki mates come over here and take all our jobs."

"Oh yeh, and what jobs are those?" I ask. "You lot don't look like you've done a hard day's work in your life."

My question throws them for a second and then the ringleader smiles and says, "Alright smart guy, see if you can answer this question." The Indian guy has already turned back around to face the front of the bus, and the bully pokes him hard in the shoulder. "You too, Gupta. Pay attention."

The old man turns back around, and the thug leans forward and looks directly at him as he asks the question.

"Okay, here we go. Why do Pakis have a red spot in the middle of their head?"

I already know the answer to this one and I tell him not to do it. "I'm giving you fair warning, mate. Do not do it, or there will be consequences."

Already committed in front of his mates, the young thug ignores me.

"Well then, what's the answer, Gandhi? Why do Pakis have a red spot in the middle of their forehead?"

The old man obviously knows the real cultural significance of the marking, but he knows that it is not the answer that his abuser is looking for. He shakes his head and with a satisfied sneer the teenager predictably raises his hand and pokes him repeatedly in the forehead while saying, "No, no, no, no, you can't have another corner shop, you dirty Paki bastard."

Losing patience, I lunge for the boy's hand and viciously drag his arm through the gap between the top of the chair and the handrail. The other two boys jump to their feet ready to fight, but the howls from their friend as I painfully twist his arm are enough to make them sit quickly back down.

Despite his apology and pained whimpering, I hold him like this for the rest of our journey. At Fulham, I allow the Indian gentleman to get off the bus first and then, once he has had enough time to leave, I release my victim and he falls into the gap between our seats. I get off the bus myself to a round of applause from the rest of the passengers and I even get something of a compliment from the conductor.

"You handle yourself well for a poofta. Well done, lad."

■　■　■　■　■　■　■　■

For the third time in as many days, I navigate my way through the market and make my way to the Bluebell Pub. I get there at just after two in the afternoon and if my memory serves me correctly, Michael was shot dead by Paddy at around 2:45. I pause to check my reflection in one of the glass-door panels and, satisfied with my appearance, I push open the door to go inside, but am nearly knocked over by two tipsy young couples coming out.

As they pass me, one of the girls drunkenly slurs something about my sunglasses that I can't quite make out, but it soon becomes apparent when I get inside. The combination of my dark glasses and the gloomy interior makes it difficult to see properly and after nearly tripping on the way to the bar, I wonder whether it might be better to take them off.

I lift them slightly off my nose to survey the room, but I drop them straight back down when I see that Michael Davies is already here. The change in his appearance from when I last saw him is striking. He is holding court at the end of the bar with three attractive young women hanging off his every word and his expensive clothes and watch are no doubt part of the attraction. He barely gives me a second glance, but I decide it is too risky to take the glasses off.

The landlord, Maurice Stevens, has been hovering patiently at the bar and when I turn around to order a drink, he stares at me open-mouthed for a few seconds before turning to his wife and laughing.

"I was right, Annie. It's Stevie Wonder's white cousin. What can I get you, Stevie Blunder?"

Annoyingly, his comment is loud enough for everyone else to hear and suddenly all eyes in the room turn in my direction. It takes all my nerve not to make eye contact with Michael and to keep facing forward. But I do just that. I laugh off the comment and order myself a pint. With nothing to see, I'm soon forgotten, and Michael turns away and resumes his conversation with his young female companions. I pay for my drink and take a seat in one of the booths where I can keep a discreet eye on them.

I watch for thirty minutes trying to work out if any of the girls might be a girlfriend, but it soon becomes obvious that it could be any one of them. As the drinks flow, Michael is generous with his cash and the girls are happy to play up to his flirting and hands-on affection. Another round of shots is delivered by Annie and Michael gets unsteadily to his feet to make a toast. Before he can start, he is interrupted by the phone ringing behind the bar.

Maurice takes the call and Michael looks away to carry on with his toast. He is drunk and slurring his words, but I make out, "Fuck the police." The girls laugh and repeat the words before knocking back their shots.

Shortly afterwards, Maurice brings the telephone to the end of the bar and taps one of the girls on the shoulder.

"It's Paddy on the phone for you, Teresa."

At the mention of Paddy's name, Michael asks what he wants. "Did he say he was coming?"

"He didn't say anything," Maurice replies. "He just said he wanted to speak to Teresa."

Michael watches as the young woman talks for a few seconds and then she places the handset back onto the receiver and smiles.

"Well, what did he say?" Michael asks. "Is he coming?"

Teresa smiles again and then stands up. "Yes, Mike. He said he would be here in a few minutes and to get him a drink in." She then turns to her companions. "Come on, girls, let's get freshened up."

The girls pick up their handbags and as Michael orders a pint for Paddy, I watch as they walk towards the bathrooms. Michael is too drunk to notice, but I'm not.

Checking that he is not watching, Teresa deftly steers her friends back towards the front door and they quietly leave. I'm pondering whether Teresa could have been Patrick's girlfriend, when the door opens and the man himself slowly walks towards the bar. He doesn't look to me like a man about to commit a premeditated murder, but he does look annoyed. Unlike Michael, he is dressed simply, and he certainly doesn't have the air of a man that has recently come into a large amount of cash.

He gets to the bar and Michael is quick to comment that he doesn't look happy. "What the fuck is wrong with you, big fella? You've got a face on you like a slapped arse. Cheer up and live a little, for fuck's sake."

Paddy knocks back half of his pint and then angrily slams the glass down on the bar. "What did we say about taking things slow, you flash cunt?"

Michael looks confused at the outburst and, worried that they can be overheard, he tells Paddy to keep his voice down. Paddy ignores him and points to his clothes. "Look at you, you stupid fuck. You're poncing around like Prince bloody Charles in your flash new clothes and I bet that new red BMW outside is yours as well."

The expression on Michael's face tells Paddy all he needs to know, and he shakes his head. "I knew it. For God's sake, Michael, you're meant to be the smart one. This is exactly how lags like us get caught. What the hell were you thinking?"

Michael starts to bluster an apology, but then he stops himself. "Listen, I was just letting off a bit of steam. I was going stir crazy lying low for so long. There's no harm done. Come on, mate, let's get some more drinks in. The girls should be back in a minute."

"No, they won't," Paddy says.

"What? No, they will. They're in the bathroom. They should be—"

In a dramatic escalation, Michael is stopped mid-sentence as Paddy takes a small revolver from his pocket and points it at his face. At sight of the gun, Maurice quickly pulls Annie into the backroom and half of the pub customers rush for the door. The other half fall silent and are too afraid to move as Michael struggles to understand what is happening. "Jesus Christ, Paddy. There is no need for that. I said I was sorry. If you feel that strongly about it, I'll take the car back. Now put the gun away, you silly bastard."

"This is not about the car or your poncey clothes," Paddy barks. He pushes the gun closer to his friend's face and his own face looks strained with emotion.

"So, what is it about then?" Michael asks more cautiously. "Because I've got no bloody idea why you're pointing a gun in my face. Come on, mate, tell me what's bothering you."

From where I'm sitting, I can see that Paddy's hand is shaking. For a few seconds, he struggles to find the words, but then he screams, "You're a fucking rat, Mike!"

Realizing now that Paddy isn't messing around, Michael straightens up and tries to reason with his friend. "Paddy, you're my oldest friend. What are you're talking about? I'd never rat on anybo—"

"Liar!" Paddy screams. "You set him up and the police killed him. Why, Mick? What did they have on you? Please don't tell me it was just for the money."

"Mate, I have no bloody idea what you are talking about. Who's been talki—"

Out of nowhere, Paddy lashes out and pistol whips Michael across the top of his head with the butt of his revolver and screams again for him to keep quiet. "You're a bloody liar. I'm warning you, Mick. If I hear one more lie come out of your mouth, I will shoot you in the fucking face."

Michael is stunned into silence at the ferocity of the attack, and as he slowly lifts his head and takes his hand away, I can see blood oozing from a large gash on his forehead. Instead of looking scared, though, he now looks defiant. Deliberately ignoring the trail of blood slowly snaking down the side of his head, he leans forward and snarls, "You've been listening to that stupid bitch of yours, haven't you, Paddy? And what else has she been filling your head with?"

Paddy shakes his head in disgust. "So, it's true then. You ratted him out? Are you planning on doing the same to me?"

"Don't be a fucking idiot," Michael says. "It was different with him. I didn't know him that well. You're my best friend, and whatever that bitch has told you, I would never do the dirty on you. She's using you to get back at me. Can't you see that?"

Paddy raises his weapon again and pushes it back in Michael's face. "All I can see is a bloody rat."

Michael raises his hand to push the gun away from his face and a split second later a hollow-point bullet shatters the back of his skull. His lifeless body falls from the barstool and a few seconds later Paddy calmly stands up and spits on it. He then turns towards the bar and shouts for Maurice to come out from where he is hiding.

"Get out here, Stevens. Don't worry, I've done what I came to do."

Telling Annie to stay where she is, Maurice cautiously comes into the bar and rather bizarrely, Paddy apologizes for the mess. He then says, "The police are going to come soon. Say whatever you have to say. You have nothing to worry about from me. You have my word on that."

Then turning to the rest of the witnesses, "That goes for you lot as well. I'm sorry you had to see this, but it had to be done."

He then kneels next to Michael's body and rummages through his pockets. Finding the keys to the BMW, he gets back

up and turns towards the bar. "I guess this is it then. I don't
expect that I will be seeing you again. Take care, Maurice."

A few seconds later he is gone. I also get up to leave along
with some of the other customers who until now have been too
terrified to move. Annie joins Maurice at the bar, but they are
both clearly in shock and have no idea what to do next. Feeling
slightly sorry for them, I go behind the bar and pass them the
telephone.

"I think you should call the police. Tell them what you have
just seen and tell them to go to the Fox and Hounds on Maxwell
Street."

Maurice looks at me in confusion and I repeat myself, "Tell
the police to go to the Fox and Hounds. That's where they will
find him." I flash my warrant card and say, "Trust me. I'm with
Miami Vice."

Before either of them can say anything, I turn to leave and
as I get to the door, I hear Annie say, "Is that the new American
police program on the BBC?"

■ ■ ■ ■ ■ ■ ■ ■

My taxi takes me to Goodison Park, and I arrive just in time
to catch the fans emerging from the stadium following today's
second division match between Chelsea and Huddersfield.

As always, there are police and marshals around the
stadium to keep the opposing fans apart, but there are never
enough of them to fully contain the hardcore element that come
to the matches determined to make trouble.

Today it is the Huddersfield fans that start the aggro. A
bottle is thrown across the police lines and it strikes a middle-
aged Chelsea fan on the back of his head. This is more than
enough provocation for trouble to kick off in earnest and within

seconds there are two angry mobs hurling missiles and abuse at each other in a tense and angry standoff.

The police quickly draft in reinforcements and with the help of attack dogs and a mounted police contingent, the opposing groups are gradually surrounded and marshalled away from the genuine fans and the general public towards a row of back-to-back terraced houses.

This is a well-rehearsed tactic and, confident that the only damage they can do now is to themselves, the police gladly hold back and watch on as the opposing fans trade kicks and punches.

With my colleagues distracted, I take the opportunity to slip past the cordon and into a narrow passage that leads into an alley at the rear of the terraces. I move from yard to yard and on the third attempt I find an unlocked rear door. With no obvious sign that anybody is home, I cautiously climb the stairs to the top floor. The bedroom facing the stadium is empty and after some effort, I force open the sash window and climb out onto the ledge.

Below me, the opposing fans are completely oblivious to my presence, but I am quickly spotted by one of the officers in the cordon and he wastes no time in shouting a warning on his megaphone.

"Oy, get back inside, you silly bastard!"

Slowly but surely, the intensity of the fighting dies down as more and more of the fans look up to see what I am doing. With the fighting completely at a standstill, a Chelsea boy points up at me and shouts, "Look at the clobber on that fucking mincer. He must be one of you northern monkeys."

This, of course, is met by a barrage of abuse from the Huddersfield fans who vehemently deny that I am one of them. One individual puts his point across very eloquently.

"Fuck that, ya soft southern shites. That poof's not bloody with us." Then to howls of laughter from his mates, "That's the Chelsea away kit, isn't it?"

This is more than enough for the fists and boots to start flying again. I raise my arms and at the top of my voice, I shout my own insult using my best scouse accent, "Oyyyy! You'se lot. You're all a bunch of fucking maggots. I'm from Liverpool and I'll kick the living shit out of all of you'se soft bastards."

I let go of the ledge and am halfway through a beautiful swallow dive before the unfortunates directly below me have enough time to react. They partially break my fall, but I still hit the ground hard enough to be incapacitated and I'm quickly engulfed in the throng as both sets of fans try desperately to get to me first. The first and second kicks to my head are excruciating, the third is a blur and the fourth … well, the fourth, thankfully, I don't remember the fourth.

Present Day – Tuesday, May 1st, 2018

The violent slamming of a door in the corridor is more than enough to jolt me awake, but the effect of the earlier alcohol has left me disorientated. For a few seconds, I stare aimlessly out of my bedroom window trying to understand whether the graying skies are an indication of early evening or early morning. Unable to decide which one it is and panicking that I may have slept completely through the night, I desperately fumble around for my cellphone.

I eventually find it at the end of my bed. After rubbing the sleep from my eyes, I relax and slump back down as the time and date slowly come into focus. To my great relief, I've only slept for four hours. But just as importantly, I haven't missed any calls or messages from Cath, DI Gray, or DCI Morgan.

I remain there for a few minutes more with my eyes closed and then, conscious that one of them is likely to call me soon, I force myself off the bed and into the bathroom.

Without waiting for the shower to warm up, I step under and let the cold water cascade across my head and shoulders. For the first few seconds, I feel like I have fallen through a hole in the ice, but this is exactly what I need right now to fully wake myself up. As my head starts to clear, I gradually turn up the heat. I use the rest of my time in the shower reflecting on what I have just witnessed in 1984.

The murder of Michael Davies by Patrick Newman was common knowledge, of course, but I now have a motive other than a falling out over the robbery proceeds or a falling out over a woman. Paddy called Michael a rat and Michael more or less confirmed that he was. But who did he rat out? What was it that Paddy had said? He said, "You set him up and the police killed him."

This must then be Thierry Pinois he was talking about. But what's the connection between them and why set him up to be killed? I know already that Thierry was dead long before the robbery, but the lockup garage and the white Ford Sierra are somehow connected to him. I'm missing something obvious; I know it.

And what about the girl, Teresa, and why did she leave with the other girls just before Paddy arrived? Did she know what Paddy was going to do? Did she set Michael up for Paddy to kill him? Was she the one that Michael was referring to when he said, "You've been listening to that bitch, haven't you, Paddy?"

If it was her, then what is her connection to Thierry Pinois and the interest in how he died? As always, I have more questions than answers, but at least now I have another line of enquiry to follow up on.

More than likely, Cath will have already knocked off for the day, but I'm in no mood for putting my feet up. I finish dressing, then I call and tell her to pick me up outside my apartment block in thirty minutes.

■ ■ ■ ■ ■ ■ ■

When I reach the lobby, Catherine is already waiting outside in her car. She finishes touching up her makeup in the mirror before asking what the panic is.

"I hope it's good, boss, because I'm meant to be meeting the man of my dreams tonight."

"Is he on Tinder?" I ask with a smirk.

"Maybe not, but the woman of your dreams is," Catherine replies sarcastically. "It's just such a shame that you're so far out of my league. Now, where are we going?"

I tell her to turn left at the end of the road and then say, "Were going to pay a visit to Patrick Newman."

"And I'm guessing it's not a social call?"

"Nope. I spoke to Clive Douglas and he has given me some new information about the robbery. Or, more specifically, he has given me more information on why Paddy killed Michael."

"Go on then," Catherine urges me, "don't keep me in suspense. What has he told you?"

"It looks like you might have been half-right, Cath. About it being something to do with a woman. But Douglas also told me that Michael may have been the one that told the cops that Thierry Pinois was on the way to a robbery."

"He was a grass?" Cath exclaims.

"Yes, it seems that way," I reply.

Cath nods and says, "That would be reason enough for Paddy to kill him, I guess. But where does the woman come into it? Who was she?"

"That's what I'm hoping to find out from Paddy. As always, Douglas wasn't particularly forthcoming with the details. All he would say is that Paddy killed Michael for being an informer and that somehow it was also connected to a young woman called Teresa."

"Just Teresa?" Cath asks me.

"That's right. Douglas said that he didn't know the surname, and I actually believe him."

Catherine turns to me and shakes her head. "So, what we have, boss, is another bloody needle in a haystack. There must be thousands of Teresa's in London."

Not waiting for a response, she turns back to face the road and then says, "Do you think that if this Teresa exists that she could be 'T'?"

Until now the thought hadn't even crossed my mind. The girl that I saw in the pub couldn't have been more than twenty-five years old and she certainly didn't come across as a master criminal. But it would certainly fit with the name originally given to us by Clive Douglas. Terry could as easily be short for Teresa as Terence, Teddy, or Theodore.

"Jesus, Cath. That would be embarrassing if it turns out we have been searching for a guy when we should have been searching for a girl. Let's see what Paddy has to say about it. How far away are we?"

Catherine checks the GPS and then smiles. "Another twenty minutes should do it, boss. We should be there well before the old folks get tucked in with their bedtime cocoa."

■ ■ ■ ■ ■ ■ ■

We pull up outside a sprawling red-brick bungalow complex and Catherine points to a white sign with hand-painted black lettering. "This is it, mate, Sunnydale House."

"It looks nice enough," I comment. "But is it me, or do all these places have the word sunny in the name?"

Catherine laughs and says, "Yeh, I think they do. It must be to mask the impending sense of doom that arises from the fact that most of their guests arrive here with a one-way ticket to the grave."

I mock shudder and say, "Shoot me if I ever need putting in a home, Cath."

"You don't need to worry about that," Catherine says with a chuckle. "I'm pretty sure I will have shot you long before then."

■ ■ ■ ■ ■ ■ ■

We are met at the reception by a stern-looking middle-aged woman wearing standard-issue nurse's whites and a graying pair of white Croc's. Clearly irritated at our arrival, she checks the time on the wall clock behind her and then begrudgingly asks how she can help us.

Catherine shows her warrant card and tells her we are here to speak to Patrick Newman. "This is the address he gave us," she says, "Does he live here?"

The sight of the warrant card does nothing to change her attitude. Instead of answering the question, she proceeds to berate us for coming outside of the acceptable visiting hours.

"We don't allow visitors after 8 p.m. on weekdays. This is for the safety and comfort of all of our residents. This is quite clear in our terms and conditions of residency and we don't make exceptions unless there is an emergency." She then glares at us in expectation. "Well, is there an emergency?"

"No emergency," I tell her. "But we do need to speak to Mr. Newman. Which bungalow is his?"

"This is most irregular," she snaps. "I must insist that you come back tomorrow during visiting hours. Patrick is an old man and—"

Losing patience, Catherine leans over and snatches the residents' register off the counter. Ignoring the protests of the nurse, she flicks through the pages until she finds Patrick's details. "Here we go. Patrick Newman. Bungalow Seven."

Catherine then hands back the register and asks, "Will you be pointing us in the right direction for number seven, or would you like us to arrest you for obstruction?"

Obviously no fan of the police, she screws up her face and says, "We all know about Patrick's past, but he has paid his debt to society. As far as we are concerned, he is just another resident and, as residents go, he is one of our better ones. We don't get any trouble from Patrick."

"We get it. He's done his time and now he's up for a sainthood," Catherine says. "He won't mind us talking to him then. Now, which direction for number seven?"

Resigned to the fact that we are not going to leave, the nurse reluctantly points to a glass door that leads out onto a landscaped courtyard.

"Through that door and it's the fourth building on the left."

■ ■ ■ ■ ■ ■ ■ ■

A group of elderly men and women are enjoying the relatively mild spring evening by relaxing in the courtyard. Some are playing chess, some are chatting, and some are simply enjoying a beer or a glass of wine. Confirming that Patrick is not with them, we keep walking and Catherine rings the bell at number seven. Behind us a female voice shouts that he is not home.

"You've just missed him, but if you're quick you might be able to catch him before he leaves."

"Sorry, what was that?" Catherine asks.

The woman stands up and points to the rear of the bungalow. "You've literally just missed him. Patrick keeps his car parked on the road behind his house."

"Car. What car? What make and color is it?" I shout.

Raising my voice is a mistake. It scares the old woman and she stumbles over her response, "It's a ... I mean, it's a red Ford, or perhaps a Chevrolet. I'm not sure."

"It's a blue 2016 Mercedes convertible," one of her male companions helpfully offers. "You had better get moving, though, if you want to catch up with him. That thing moves like shit through a goose."

I thank them, then I grab Catherine's arm. "Come on, back to the car, Cath. That road leads back around to where we are parked."

■ ■ ■ ■ ■ ■ ■ ■

We burst out of the reception, just in time to see Patrick in the driver's seat as the Mercedes passes by. I call out to him, and Cath runs into the road and frantically waves her arms. Whether he saw us or not is debatable, but regardless he keeps going and we take up the chase.

Less than a minute later, we catch sight of the Mercedes up ahead and I tell Cath to hold back a bit.

"You don't want to pull him over?" Cath asks.

"For what?" I reply. "He's not speeding and that's his own car as far as we know. We've no reason to pull him over."

"So, what then? We just follow him?"

"Yeh, for now, Cath. I want to see where he is going."

Catherine nods and then says, "And I'd like to know where he got the money for that motor. I can't afford a car like that on my salary, so how can he afford it if all he has got is his pension? And that residential home was no slum either. They're not bloody cheap you know."

I smile and say, "Did you notice what he was wearing, Cath? He was clean shaven, his hair was slicked back, and from what I could see that was a pretty nice suit he had on. A bit different from the destitute pensioner look we saw earlier today."

"This is absolute bollocks," Cath says with frustration. "We know that Douglas is playing us, but are we really so stupid that between us we can't put the pieces together?"

I'm about to say something, when Paddy indicates to take the ramp onto the M25. We follow him for another fifteen minutes and when he indicates to take the lane for Enfield, Catherine who is always at least ten seconds ahead of me turns and smiles. "Fuck, Sean. He's going to Ponders End. He's going to see Rosemary Pinois."

If he is going to see Rosemary, that would go some way towards explaining a few things. If Paddy is linked to Rosemary, then this would explain the link between Paddy and Thierry.

Taking that a step further, perhaps Rosemary was one of the girls I saw with Teresa and if somehow she had discovered that Michael was responsible for the death of her father, it's feasible that she could have manipulated Paddy into killing him. If this is true, then we have as much to worry about from Rosemary as we have from Paddy.

I nod and tell Cath to keep her eyes on the road. "This case suddenly just got interesting again, DC Swain. Let's not lose sight of him please."

When Paddy passes the Ponders End Lock and takes the turn into Rosemary's street, I tell Catherine to slow down. "Give him enough time to park and go inside, then drive slowly past the front of the house."

"We're not going to go in?"

"No, no point letting them know we are on to them just yet. Let's just make sure Paddy is there and then you can drop me home and get on with your search for Mr. Perfect."

■ ■ ■ ■ ■ ■ ■ ■

We hold back for just over a minute and then I give Cath the nod.

"Go on then, that should be long enough."

Catherine switches off her headlights and we slowly cruise past the front of Rosemary's house. If we were in any doubt before about the extent of their relationship, we are left in no doubt now by the sight of them embracing in the doorway.

Concerned that they will turn around and see us, Cath speeds up and we watch in the rear-view mirror as they both go inside. Catherine turns her lights back on, then she playfully squeezes my leg and smiles.

"You were right, boss. This case has suddenly just got very interesting. Very bloody interesting indeed."

161

■ ■ ■ ■ ■ ■ ■ ■

On the drive home, we recap what we know so far and we discuss our next steps.

"Well, that was a bloody turn up for the books, Cath, but it confirms Paddy's connection to Thierry."

"Do you think that Rosemary could have known that Michael was the grass that set her father up?"

"Yes, it looks that way, and if Paddy and Rosemary were as loved up back then as they appeared to be tonight, then she could have used that relationship to settle the score."

"So, what about this Teresa then? Another red herring, boss?"

I shake my head. "I've no idea, but I want to see Douglas again first thing in the morning. I'm pretty sure that he knows exactly who all the players are in this game. I'll ask him about Thierry, Teresa, Rosemary, and Paddy. After that, I think we should have another chat with Rosemary. I'll meet you back at the station once I'm done with Douglas and we can head over to her place together."

"I'm not coming with you to the prison?" Catherine asks.

"No, I want you to get back over to Securicor and have another go at the archives."

"Okay, but I went through everything with a fine-tooth comb already. I'm not sure what you thi—"

"Yes, I know, Cath. But you never know. Now that we have a few more pieces of the puzzle, you may see something that didn't mean anything before. Once you're done there, I want you to unearth as much information as you can on Rosemary Pinois. She is an integral part of this case. I'm sure of it. And have a go at this Teresa as well. I know it's not much to go on but try anyway."

Catherine nods and then says, "And Patrick Newman, what about him?"

I think about the question for a few seconds.

"Let's see what we get tomorrow. Hopefully, we can get enough for Morgan to agree to make this case official. If we can, then we can pull all the players in for questioning officially, including Paddy Newman."

We arrive at my apartment block and I thank Catherine for her help. "I hope I haven't totally ruined your evening though. Do you think your date will still be waiting for you? It's still relatively early."

Cath tells me not to worry. She grins and points to herself. "Look at me, Sean. You'd wait, wouldn't you?"

Much as I hate to admit it, she is right. If I wasn't deep in the friendzone and she wasn't my partner, I'd definitely tap that. I laugh and nod. "Yeh, I think I probably would, Cath. Go on, go and enjoy the rest of your night.

■　■　■　■　■　■　■

My second trip of the day will hopefully be a short one. And where I'm going I'm not overly concerned about looking out of place or being recognized. With this in mind, I keep my suit on and pour myself a drink. I take the ID card copy of Stuart Goldsmith from my jacket pocket and then I sit down to enjoy my drink. Since discovering that I may be responsible for his death, it's been weighing heavily on my mind. Tonight, I'm hoping to put that situation right.

I decide once more to take my warrant card on this trip. It might be needed.

I finish my drink and then I retrieve a shoe box from under my bed. Inside it there is a less-than-official handgun that I confiscated from a suspect in a previous case. I check that the safety catch is on before stuffing it into my waistband and lying down on my bed. My intended destination is the home of Stuart Goldsmith on the day before the robbery. I don't know the address, but his face is clear in my mind. I start my chant and the light comes quickly and pulls me in.

The Past – Friday, December 23rd, 1983

Okay, so coming without an actual address probably wasn't my best idea ever, but at least I know where I am. The sign at the top of the wall on the first house in the street says, Berwick Place, NW3, The London Borough of Islington.

It's a random location to say the least, but I'm desperately hoping that I've come to the right place, for two very good reasons. Firstly, the hassle and wasted time in trying again is a major pain in the ass that I can well do without. Secondly, I've arrived early in the morning and it's absolutely bloody freezing. I'm willing to wait around and freeze my nuts off to get a result but freezing my nuts off without getting one is another thing entirely.

Deciding to give it thirty minutes, I huddle into a doorway and watch as the milkman wends his way slowly down the street on his cart making his deliveries.

Every now and then a door opens and someone comes out to bring in the milk or to pay their bill, but frustratingly I don't see any sign of my target. I'm frozen stiff and almost resigned to giving up when a door opens on the other side of the street and a middle-aged man comes out onto his doorstep. I push myself further into my hiding place and watch as he flags down the milk cart that is making its way back towards us. When it draws level, the cart stops and the driver gets out.

"Good morning, Mr. Goldsmith. Did you want something extra today? I've got a lovely bit of bacon in my chiller."

Clearly worried about something, Stuart nervously looks from side to side and then says, "No thanks, Trevor. I just need to pay my bill, and I wanted to let you know that I will be going away for a while. I need to cancel my regular delivery, if that's okay?"

"Yes, of course," the milk man replies. "Going somewhere nice, I hope?"

"Um, just away to visit my family," Stuart says. "I'm not sure how long I will be gone for. I'll let you know when I'm back."

He hands over some cash and the milkman tucks it away in a brown leather satchel hanging by his side, "Right you are, Mr. Goldsmith. Have a good trip then."

The milk cart pulls away and, with a final nervous look up and down the street, Stuart picks up his milk and goes back inside. I take the automatic pistol out of my waistband and double check that the safety catch is still on. I've only brought it along for dramatic effect, and the last thing I want is any accidents. I check that the coast is clear, then I cross the street and ring the doorbell.

■　■　■　■　■　■　■　■

Behind the door, I hear the faint sound of the security chain being pulled into place, but the door doesn't open. I wait for a couple of seconds and when nothing happens, I lean forward and press my face against the spyhole.

"I know that you are in there, Mr. Goldsmith. I'm a detective sergeant with the flying squad and you need to open the door please."

When there is still no answer, I take out my badge and hold it up for him to see. "Stuart, you need to listen very carefully please. I know what is planned to happen tomorrow and I know how you are involved."

From behind the door, a muffled voice says, "Go away please. I don't know who you are, and I don't know what you are talking about. Please, just go away."

I put away my badge.

"The people that have got you mixed up in this robbery are not your friends, Stuart. I don't know how much cash or what else they have offered you to disappear, but you need to believe me when I say that they have no intention of letting you walk away from this. I'm here to help you, Stuart. Open the door, so that we can talk face to face please."

For a few seconds nothing happens, then I hear the lock turning. The door opens a few inches but stops dead as the security chain engages. Stuart peers nervously around the edge of the door and I move as close as I can before he tells me to stop.

"That's far enough. Just stay where you are now, or I'll close the door again."

I raise my hands and smile. "All good, Stuart. I'm not here to hurt you. I'm here to warn you about Patrick Newman and Michael Davies. They have no intention of letting you—"

Stuart stands up straight and interrupts me, "Wait. I don't know who those people are. I've never heard of either of them."

"Maybe they've used different names," I say. "I really need to come in, though. Your life is in danger. Please, open the door and let me in."

I carefully try to edge closer and Stuart reacts by trying to slam the door in my face, but he is too slow. I push against the door and wedge my leg into the gap as Stuart ducks out of reach.

"Stuart, if I were here to harm you, I wouldn't have wasted my time knocking on the door, would I? I am a police officer, and I am here to help you." I take out my warrant card and hold it out to him. "Here, take the card and check for yourself."

He shakes his head and shuffles further backwards. At risk of losing him completely, I take a gamble.

"Stuart, wait, please. If you don't believe me take the card and call 999. Give them my badge number and ask to be connected to Detective Chief Inspector Montgomery at New Scotland Yard. He can verify who I am."

If he does call my bluff and call 999, then my story will quickly unravel. I'm banking on the fact that he doesn't want to speak to the police any more than I want him to. Either way, he still needs my warrant card and that's when I will make my move. Caught between a rock and a hard place, he shakes his head unsure of what to do. I hold up my card again and quietly say, "Just take the card. There is no harm in just taking the card is there?"

With no other option he reluctantly comes forward and reaches for the card. At the very last second, I allow it to fall from my hand and Stuart watches it fall to the floor. This is all the distraction I need, and I push against the door just hard enough to give me a few more inches of reach. My right hand drags him face first towards the door and my left hand pushes my pistol under his chin.

"I'm sorry to have to take such drastic action, Stuart, but we don't have time to fuck around and I'm freezing my testicles off out here. Now open the door please, before I'm forced to do the job I came here to stop."

Trembling, he reaches up to slide across the security chain and I release my grip and let him fall to the floor. I pull him by his scruff into the hallway and then I kick the door shut behind us and push him into the kitchen.

"Now sit the fuck down and wake the fuck up. I'm here to bloody help you, asshole."

He is shaking so badly with fear that I doubt he is hearing anything I'm saying and the gun in my hand is probably not helping. I tuck it back into my waistband and sit down opposite him.

"There, is that better, Stuart? If I were here to kill you, I would have done it already."

"So, why are you here?" he asks.

"I've told you already. I'm here about the robbery you've got yourself mixed up in, and the trip that you think you're taking."

Unbelievably, he still tries to feign ignorance.

"What trip? What are you talking about? I don't know these—"

"For fuck's sake, man, I've just bloody dragged you past three suitcases in the hallway. Do not sit there all innocent and try to tell me that you're not planning on disappearing today, Stuart." I reach for my gun again and this is enough for him to finally see sense.

"Wait, no. Okay, okay. I am leaving today. But if I speak to you, I'm a dead man."

"You're a dead man if you don't speak to me, Stuart. I'm here to warn you that if you don't leave town immediately it's highly likely that Newman and Davies will kill you."

Stuart shakes his head. "Those names again. I don't know who they are. I'll admit I know about the robbery and that I'm getting paid to stay away from work and disappear, but I don't know anyone by those names."

"But you've met a couple of fellas," I say. "One of them is a big lad that you wouldn't easily forget."

"No. I've never met anyone other than … well, what I mean is, I don't know who is behind the robbery. I probably shouldn't say anything else."

I take out the gun and pull back the slide to feed a round into the chamber.

"Actually, I think you should say something else. In fact, I insist on it. If you've never had any contact with anyone called Newman or Davies, then who has put you up to this?"

Stuart starts to tremble again. "Please, you have to understand, she told us that these blokes were dangerous, but if we did exactly what they said, then none of us would get hurt."

"She? Who is she?" I ask. "And who else are you talking about? Who else wouldn't get hurt?"

Desperate to be anywhere but here, Stuart looks down to the floor and I am forced to point the pistol at his head to get his attention back. "Stuart! Look at me, please. I don't want to do this, but I will if you don't start talking. I need to know who you are talking about, and I need to know now."

He looks up and finally blurts out, "It was Teresa. She told us that we had all been targeted, but if we did exactly as we were told, then we would all be alright."

Hearing the name Teresa sets my heart racing, but it's not enough. "Teresa who? Give me a surname."

"I can't. She said that they would kill us all if we spoke to the police. Please, just let me go, or take me in and I will tell you everything," Stuart begs.

"No, I want to know who Teresa is and who else is involved Give me that and then I can protect you."

Before he can say anything else, we are interrupted by the doorbell ringing and I tell him to keep quiet. "Are you expecting anyone else today?"

He shakes his head and I pull him to his feet and jab my gun into his ribs. "Go and find out who it is, but don't let them know you are here."

I push him slowly forward and then I watch from a short distance as he leans towards the spyhole. He turns back around to face me and mouths, "It's her. It's Teresa."

I pull him away from the door and take a look for myself. It's definitely the same girl I saw on the night of Michael's murder, but now there is something vaguely familiar about her that I can't quite place.

I curse under my breath and then quietly say, "Find out what she wants, but don't let her in."

Stuart looks sheepish and says, "I already know why she is here."

"What? You said you weren't expecting anyone. You fu—"

"I know, I'm sorry, I panicked. She's here to take me to meet the others."

"You mean George Benson and Peter Lane?" I ask.

He nods and I shake my head. "You could have made this a lot bloody easier for us, Stuart."

I'm no longer bothering to keep my voice down and from outside, Teresa rings the bell again and follows up by tapping on the door with her car keys. "Stuart is that you in there? We need to get going," she calls.

I push him towards the cases in the hallway. "Choose one and get the hell out of here."

He hesitates and looks towards the front door. "I don't have any money. Teresa was going to give us the money. I need the—"

"What you need is to get the fuck out of here. Teresa is not here to give you any money, Stuart. She is here to take you where you really don't want to go."

I pick up one of the suitcases and force it into his arms. The bell rings again and Teresa hammers on the door.

"Stuart, who are you talking to in there? You need to open the door now!"

I gesture towards the back door with my gun and urge him to get going. When he still hesitates, I drag him towards the lounge window. I carefully pull back the lace curtains just enough for us to see Teresa with her ear pressed against the door. She has a silenced pistol held low against her side, but we can both see it clearly enough. I pull Stuart away from the window and shove him roughly back towards the kitchen.

"Now do you understand what I am saying? Teresa is not your bloody friend. Now get the hell out of here before she calls for reinforcements."

He picks up his suitcase and asks, "What about George and Peter? Will you warn them as well?"

I assure him that I will, and then I push him out of the back door. "Just keep running and don't ever come back. I'll keep Teresa busy."

Realizing that I still don't have her surname, I call out to him, "Hang on. I need her surname. What is Teresa's surname?"

Fear is a great motivator, though, and Stuart has taken me at my word. He keeps running and he doesn't look back.

I lock the back door and walk to the front door. I take off the safety catch and lightly tap on the door with the butt of my pistol. There is a short pause and then Teresa asks, "Stuart, is that you? Is there someone in there with you?"

Trying hard not to snigger, I put on a girly voice and say, "I'm sorry, Stuart has been a bad boy and is not allowed out today. Come back tomorrow."

The next sound I hear is unmistakable. Teresa has just cocked her own weapon and is now probably pointing it at the door. A few more seconds pass and then she says, "Let's stop fucking around, shall we? Who the hell is in there with you, Stuart?"

I reset the safety and tuck my pistol back into my waistband, and then I position myself directly behind the door. I take a deep breath and in the same girly voice say, "It's Nunna." And then in my own voice before she can respond, "It's Nunna. Nunna your fucking business, Teresa!"

The first shot smashes through the door and drags splinters of wood through my lungs. The second shot tears a path through my intestines and out my lower back. The third pierces my heart and I am dead before I hit the floor.

Present Day – Wednesday, May 2nd, 2018

I'm on the road well before 8 a.m. and I'm feeling confident that today is going to be a good day. Since last speaking to Douglas, we have confirmed a link between Thierry Pinois and Patrick Newman through Rosemary, and I am certain now that the mysterious "T" is a woman called Teresa. What's more, I'm convinced that Douglas knows all of this and more. In fact, it wouldn't surprise me at all, if Patrick, Rosemary, and Teresa were all old acquaintances of that shady bastard. The time for beating around the bush is over and I make up my mind to ask him directly about each of them.

I park my car in the visitor's area and open the glove box to take out the small plastic bag I have brought with me. Senior Officer Patrick Bayliss meets me at the reception area and leads me towards one of the interview rooms. Outside the room he stops me to give me a heads-up, "He's not in the best of moods this morning, Sean. Getting processed for this visit meant that he missed his breakfast."

I peer through the small window in the door.

"He looks like he could lose a few pounds anyway. You lot are feeding him too well. I need him to cooperate, though. Would you mind sorting out a cup of tea for him?"

Bayliss nods. "Of course, I'll get right onto it. Officer Knight will be outside if you need anything."

He leaves to arrange the tea and I go inside the interview room. Douglas doesn't bother to stand up. Instead he gives me a dismissive look and shrugs his shoulders.

"Good morning, DS McMillan. I would say it's nice to see you, but that would be a lie. I was hoping that your lovely partner would be with you, but it would appear that my day is going to be full of disappointments."

173

He then nods towards the bag I am holding. "I missed breakfast because of you. So I hope that's what I think it is. Or is that going to be the third disappointment of the day?"

I smile and pass him the bag. "There is a cup of tea on the way, with two sugars and a splash of milk, just the way you like it."

Clive looks inside the bag and nods appreciatively. "Two packets of milk chocolate digestives. My day has just got better, Sergeant McMillan."

Just then Senior Officer Bayliss returns with the tea. He places it down in front of Douglas and leaves to join his colleague in the corridor. Douglas takes a sip from his tea and I gesture towards the biscuits.

"Help yourself. You can eat while we talk."

He pushes the bag away and shakes his head.

"No, thanks. I've never really been that keen on digestives. I just wanted to see how far I could push my luck."

Annoyed, I move forward to grab the bag, but Douglas pulls it away and laughs.

"I'm just messing with you. I'll save them for later, if that's okay?"

I ignore the question and take out my pocketbook.

"I'd like to ask you some more questions about the robbery, Clive. Your transfer is in process, but I need your help to clear up a few things."

"All in good time, Sean. Tell me about my transfer. Where am I going and when?"

I shake my head. "That hasn't been decided yet. Your crimes are serious, and your move needs to be approved by the Home Office. These things take time."

Douglas leans across the table and scowls. "And that's why I've been helping you out. The information I have been giving you has been to grease the wheels to make them move faster."

I shrug and point to my pocketbook. "To be honest, Clive, you really haven't given us that much. You've told us about a robbery where the only real suspect has already done time, and you've given me a couple of tenuous leads regarding the ringleader. If we were to measure that information in terms of grease, then I'd say you've given us about a teaspoonful. Hardly surprising things are moving slower than you would like."

Douglas thinks about what I have just said and then he opens one of the packets of biscuits.

"I think I might have a couple of these after all. Go on then, Sean. I'm all ears."

"Okay, let's start by talking about Thierry Pinois. When I spoke to you last, I asked whether we should be looking for Thierry instead of Terry. Do you remember?"

"Yes, I remember," Clive replies. "I passed comment that you had made some progress."

"No, you actually said that we had had some luck," I correct him. "Why did you say that when you knew full well that Thierry had been shot dead by an armed response unit more than four years before the robbery?"

Douglas leans back in his chair and stretches his neck from side to side. "His daughter still lives in his house. I knew that it wouldn't take you long to find out he was dead. But my comment still stands. Thierry is the key to breaking this case."

"Do you know Rosemary Pinois personally?" I ask.

"Our paths have crossed," Clive concedes.

I point to my notes and say, "That's funny. Someone else used that exact same expression recently. What about Patrick Newman? Do you also know him personally?"

That question elicits a smirk and Douglas raises his hands. "What can I say? Our paths may also have crossed. I'm a popular guy."

175

"I'm assuming that you also knew that Rosemary was in the car when Thierry was killed?" I ask him.

"Oooh, yes. That was a nasty business and it must have been devastating for her. Seeing something like that must have been very traumatic and not something she would easily be able to forget. Or indeed to forgive."

I shake my head. "Having Patrick as a shoulder to cry on must have been a comfort though?"

Douglas chuckles and then slowly claps his hands. "You have been a busy little bee, haven't you, Detective Sergeant McMillan? Just a few more pieces of the puzzle to put together and then you might be able to shove your nose even further up your boss's ass. And that reminds me, Sean. Be sure to pass DCI Morgan my best wishes next time you see him."

"You can count on it. He's always asking how you are doing. Tell me about your other friend, Teresa. Or would you prefer it if I just called her 'T'?"

Clive laughs. "What is this? Who the hell is 'T'? That sounds like a character from the latest James Bond movie."

"Do you know who Teres—"

"I know who she is," Douglas snarls. "She doesn't have a license to kill, but you should still be careful all the same."

"You've been playing with us right from the start," I say. "This is one big game to you, isn't it?"

"Everything's a bloody game," Douglas snaps. "We're just playing for different prizes, Sean. You're playing for glory and recognition and I'm playing for a better life. Is that so hard to understand?"

I shake my head. "No, I'm not buying that rubbish anymore. You're not going through this charade just for a move to a Cat C prison. You've got another agenda entirely."

"Maybe I have," Clive says with a nonchalant shrug of his shoulders, "but show me someone that doesn't have a hidden agenda."

Our conversation is interrupted by Senior Officer Bayliss coming into the room.

"Sorry to break up the party, DS McMillan. Your partner has left a couple of messages asking you to get back to Blackwell Station urgently."

I thank him for the message and then tell him that I am nearly done anyway. "I've just a few more questions, Officer Bayliss, then you can take him back to his cell."

Bayliss leaves and I turn back to Douglas who is now sporting a fake frown on his face. "Aww, what's up, Sean? Is Catherine getting lonely without you?"

I ignore the obvious attempt to wind me up and instead bombard Douglas with a barrage of questions.

"Who is Teresa? What's her surname? Is she the brains of the robbery operation? Is she 'T'? Is she another personal friend of yours?"

My onslaught causes Clive to sit back in his chair and exclaim, "Whoa! Just hold your horses there, Billy the Kid. One question at a time please."

"Sure," I say. "How about giving me something real to work with that I don't already know? Give me Teresa's surname."

He thinks about if for a second. Then he shakes his head and frowns. "No, I don't think so. That would be making things too easy for you. Ask me another question but make it a good one. Because after that, we are done for the day."

I know Clive well enough to know that when he says he is done, he is done. I look carefully through my notes and then I ask, "Who have you still got on the inside working for you?"

He shakes his head and looks at me questioningly. "I'm not following you, sergeant."

I say to him, "Let me put it a different way then. Who do you have on the inside that would have access to the case files for the robbery and the inquest into the death of Thierry Pinois?"

This time he smirks and leans back in his chair again.

"Very good, Sean. That's the second time you've impressed me today. You are so close to the truth you could almost touch it. Unfortunately, I'm going to have to respectfully decline to answer that question too."

"Who redacted the notes?" I persist.

Clive shakes his head. "No comment."

"Why the need for the redactions? What are they hiding?"

Douglas stands up and says, "And again, no comment."

He reaches for the plastic bag containing his biscuits and I put my hand across it.

"Who were the firearms officers involved in the death of Thierry Pinois?"

Douglas pulls the bag out from under my hand. "You don't need anything else from me, Sean. You have most of the pieces you need already. You just need to be smart enough to put them all together."

He then turns towards the door and shouts, "I'm done here, Bayliss. Take me back to my cell please."

■ · ■ · ■ · ■ · ■ · ■ · ■

I get back to my car and for a few minutes try to make sense of Clive Douglas's last statement. I had suspected already that the pieces were falling into place, but Douglas himself has just more or less confirmed it. I still don't know who Teresa is, though, and I still don't know who is responsible for the redactions and why they were needed. The way Clive was talking, the answers to these questions are probably staring me in the face, but I just can't see them. I'm in the middle of mentally beating myself up when my phone rings. I answer and Catherine immediately asks me if I got her messages.

"Yes, I did. I've just finished with Douglas now. I asked him abo—"

"Save that for now," Catherine interrupts me. "Just get yourself back here as fast as you can. I've already spoken with DI Gray. She's going to be waiting for us with DCI Morgan. There have been som—"

Now it's my turn to interrupt, "Cath, slow down. What the hell has happened?"

"Better that I tell you when you get back here, boss. But, put it this way, it's a major breakthrough and it's going to blow your socks off. Get back here asap, mate."

Before I can say anything else, Catherine hangs up and leaves me hanging on the line and muttering to myself, "Thanks, Cath, I love going into these meetings completely blind."

■ ■ ■ ■ ■ ■ ■

It goes without saying that my drive back to Blackwell was something of a speed record and was aided in no small part by the liberal use of my strobes and sirens to clear the traffic. On arrival, I leave my car in front of the station entrance and head into the reception, reaching into my jacket pocket for my station access pass. I keep the pass in the same holder as my warrant card, but neither is in any of my pockets. For a moment I think that I may have left them in my car, but then I go cold when I get a flashback to dropping my warrant card in Stuart Goldsmith's hallway in 1983 in order to distract him. "Fuck, that's not good," I mutter as I realize that I was the one to get distracted — I had never picked it up again.

The sergeant on duty at reception looks up from his paperwork.

"Is there anything I can help you with, Sean?"

"Yes, buzz me in please, Ted. I've left my access card at home and the boss is waiting for me for an urgent meeting."

He presses a button behind the desk and the automatic barrier opens to let me pass through. A couple of minutes later, I step out of the lift and meet Catherine who is waiting outside DCI Morgan's office.

"Any chance of filling me in before we go into the lion's den, Cath?"

I am so keen to get some answers from her that I fail to pick up on the subtle warning signals she's trying to send. When I do finally get the message, it is too late. I turn around and almost bump into Kevin Morgan and Sarah Gray, who have both just come out of Sarah's office.

Morgan smirks at me and says, "I was wondering what you lot called my office. The lion's den, eh? I think I like that. In you come please."

■　■　■　■　■　■　■　■

We take our seats and Morgan holds up a brown padded envelope. "This is the unredacted copy of the inquest notes. Hopefully, they should shed some light on why someone felt the need for the redactions in the first place. First things first, though. DC Swain, you told DI Gray that you've had a major breakthrough."

Morgan puts down the envelope and I can see that it hasn't been opened yet. I'm curious to know what is hiding under the redactions, but, like Morgan, I'm more curious to know what Catherine has discovered. All eyes are on Cath as she takes a deep breath.

"As you know, sir, we have been following up on the information initially given to us by former Detective Superintendent Clive Douglas pertaining to a Brinks Mat style robbery in December of 1983. We were initially given a suspect named Terry Pinois, but we later discovered that this could in fact have been Thierry Pinois. We followed up this lead by meeting with his daughter Rosemary, only to discover that Thierry had been killed in May of 1979."

Knowing how impatient Kevin Morgan is, I gesture for her to skip what they already know and get to the point.

"Well, sir, since our last update to you and DI Gray we've been able to establish a clear link between Rosemary Pinois and Patrick Newman."

"They appear to be lovers," I chip in.

"We also believe we know why Patrick killed his partner Michael Davies," Catherine continues.

"Michael was a rat," I interrupt her again. "It appears that Michael was the informant that put Thierry Pinois in the firing line, sir."

"That would be enough motive, I guess," Morgan says. "So, DC Swain, you believe that Rosemary Pinois could have persuaded Patrick Newman to kill Michael?"

Cath nods. "Yes, sir. We do."

"And could she also be connected to the robbery?" DI Gray asks.

I lean forward to say, "No, ma'am. Douglas has recently given us information on a new suspect possibly named Teresa."

I'm about to say more when Catherine stops me and then turns back to face Morgan. "I'm sorry, sir. Unfortunately, DS McMillan was busy with interviewing Clive Douglas again and I haven't briefed him on the new developments yet."

Catherine then turns back to face me and says, "You were right, boss. I went back to the Securicor archives this morning. At first I thought I was wasting my time, but then I found this."

She hands me a dog-eared file and points to the name on the cover. "It's the employment record of Teresa Pinois. She was an admin clerk at the Securicor head office from August of 1983 until May of 1984."

I shake my head, "Okay, that would explain a lot of things. But who is she, Cath? Is she a niece or another relation of Thierry's?"

To the amazement of us all, Catherine shakes her head and says, "She's his daughter, boss."

"But Thierry only had one daughter," I say. "What are you talking about?

Catherine opens the file and takes out a copy of Teresa's birth certificate, and points to the name. "She joined Securicor as Teresa Pinois, but her full name is Rosemary Teresa Pinois."

To confirm what we are all thinking but afraid to say, Cath nods and then says, "Yep, Rosemary and Teresa are one and the same, which must mean that she was the one that set up the robbery. As a clerk at Securicor, I imagine that she would have had full access to schedules, employee records, security arrangements, and anything else that a team of blaggers would have needed to pull this job off. It's also likely now that she already knew Davies and Newman through her father."

"And as a young woman beyond suspicion, she would have been able to destroy any records or interview notes and quietly resign as soon as the heat died down," DI Gray suggests.

DCI Morgan looks confused. "So, why leave the employment record for us to find? That would have been the first thing that I would have destroyed."

"I think I can answer that question, sir," I respond.

Morgan nods at me. "Go on, Sean. What are you thinking?"

"They wanted us to find it, sir. As we suspected, this whole thing has been a set up right from the start. Douglas more or less admitted it this morning."

"You said they wanted us to find it. Who is 'they'?" DI Gray asks me.

"Clive Douglas, Rosemary Pinois, and Patrick Newman, ma'am. I believe that Douglas knows Pinois and Newman personally and that they are all working together. I still don't know what they are up to, but I'm convinced that the three of them are in bed together. Sir, if we can make this investigation official, then we can interview all of them under caution. Surely we have enough justification to—"

DCI Morgan holds up his hand to stop me. "I need something else if I'm going to convince the Home Office to move quickly on this. What else have you got, Sean?"

I have nothing else to give, but Catherine does. She smiles at me and then turns towards Morgan and Gray.

"Yes, sir, we do. And this one is an absolute corker. After discovering what I did in the Securicor archive, I came straight back here and did a little more digging around on Rosemary. I was particularly interested in finding out what she had been doing since leaving Securicor, but I was unable to find any further work history for the next thirty years."

"Living off her share of the takings, I assume," Morgan interjects.

"I think that's likely," Catherine replies. "Either way, it wasn't until November of 2017 that she resurfaced on the job market as a clerk at ..."

We all wait with bated breath for her to finish the sentence.

"... the Metropolitan Police Central records office, and her primary reference was from none other than former Detective Superintendent Clive Douglas."

We take a moment to let the news sink in, then we all turn towards Morgan who looks like he is about to explode.

"I can't bloody believe it! This has been going on right under our noses and well before Douglas was arrested for corruption. This must be about something else and I want to know what that is."

Turning to me, Morgan adds, "Sean, I want you and DC Swain to pull Rosemary Pinois and Patrick Newman in for questioning immediately."

"What about the Home Office?" I ask.

"Don't worry about the Home Office, son. Let me worry about them. Christ, the bloody arrogance of the pair! Start with Pinois. Get over to Central Records and drag her out by her hair if you have to."

I'm about to stand up when Catherine says, "I've checked already. She's not there, sir. She hasn't been in the office for the last couple of days. Flu apparently. We can be at her home address in less than an hour, though, if we make a move now."

Morgan gestures for us to get going, but then he remembers the envelope. "Hold on, in all the excitement we nearly forgot about this. Before you go, let's find out what these bastards have been so keen to hide from us."

We sit back down, and Morgan tears open the envelope. He carefully lifts out the inquest notes and we wait patiently as he reads them line by line. More than once, it looks like he has seen something significant, but then his face suddenly flushes red and he abruptly stuffs the notes back into the envelope and stands up. DI Gray asks if everything is okay, but Morgan ignores her. When he gets to the door, he stops and tells DI Gray to carry on.

Sarah Gray is as mystified as we are.

"Was there something in the notes, sir? Are you sure you're okay? You don't look well."

Morgan shakes his head. "Uhm, no. I'm fine. I need to speak to the Home Office. You take it from here please, Sarah."

Without another word he leaves with the envelope and we are left staring at each other. Catherine is the first to speak.

"What the hell just happened, ma'am? The boss looked like he had seen a ghost."

DI Gray shakes her head, as shocked as we are. "I have no idea, DC Swain. But whatever it is, I'm sure the boss will have had his reasons for not telling us what was in those notes."

"So, what now?" I ask.

"You heard DCI Morgan. Get after Rosemary Pinois and then come back here for some backup to bring Newman in."

"And what about the boss?"

"I'll try calling him in an hour or so and I'll be in touch if there is anything to worry about," she says.

On the way out of the office, Gray tells us to be careful, before adding, "Not a word of this to anyone, you understand? This never happened."

■ ■ ■ ■ ■ ■ ■ ■

On the drive to Ponders End, we struggle to make sense of what has just happened.

"I'm worried, Sean. I've never seen Morgan react like that to anything. He looked dreadful."

"Yes, he did. Something in those inquest notes has rattled him and we need to know what the hell it was."

"You don't think, the boss is—"

I cut Cath off and say, "No, no way. I know what you're thinking, Cath, but don't even say it. There is no way that Kevin Morgan is mixed up in this. He's the straightest copper I know."

Catherine apologizes, but then adds, "It doesn't make any sense, though. If he found something significant, then why not tell us what it was? If not us, he could have at least told Sarah Gray."

"I don't know. Like she said, though, I'm sure the boss had his reasons. Let's just forget about it for now and concentrate on what we do know."

185

Cath nods and opens her pocketbook. "Okay, so what we have so far is three of the four perpetrators positively identified. The possible ringleader is Rosemary Teresa 'T' Pinois. Number Two is almost certainly the lover of Rosemary, Patrick 'Paddy' Newman. Number Three is Michael Davies, who we know was killed by Paddy Newman on 4th February 1984, almost certainly for being the informant involved in the death of Rosemary's father, Thierry Pinois. And then we have suspect number four, still unidentified and still at large."

Because of my interference in the timelines, suspect number four is none other than my good self. I shrug it off and say, "He's not a priority. Our focus for now needs to be on our star-crossed lovers and their connection to Clive Douglas."

"Agreed," Catherine says. "What we also know is that Rosemary was most likely responsible for disposing of any records of the robbery in the Securicor archives."

"And the redaction of the files in the central records office," I add. "But why just redact them? Why not get rid of them completely?"

"For the same reason she didn't get rid of her employee record, boss. They wanted us to find them. There is something in those files that they wanted us to see."

"Not us," I say. "I think they wanted Morgan to find something."

"But you said—"

"I know what I said, Cath. Fuck! I don't know what I'm saying. There is no way Douglas is just doing this for a bloody move to Cat C and if Paddy and Rosemary still have the gold stashed somewhere, then what the hell are they still doing here? Paddy was released in 2007, and with that much gold they could go anywhere they want."

Cath checks her notes again. "Yep, I think you're right. The move to Cat C is total bullshit. Douglas wasn't arrested until

February of this year, but he gave the reference for Rosemary in October of last year. Whatever he is up to, it has nothing at all to do with serving out his sentence in a cushy nick."

We pass Ponders End lock and I smile as we pull up outside Rosemary's house. "I'll let you do the honors, Cath. I'm in the mood for a bit of girl-on-girl action today."

Catherine shakes her head and smirks. "For a moment there, I thought I'd been transported back to the 1970s. You do know it's 2018, don't you, Sean?"

Without waiting for an answer, she shakes her head again and then asks, "What's the charge?"

"Good question. You can take your pick between conspiracy to commit robbery, incitement to murder, or conspiracy to pervert the course of justice."

Cath laughs. "Wow, so many wonderful options. Let's start with robbery, shall we?"

I raise my eyebrows and in my best French waiter accent, I say, "An excellent choice, madam. And perhaps a side portion of perjury to accompany your entrée?"

"Thank you. That will be perfect. Now, let's go and get the bitch."

■ ■ ■ ■ ■ ■ ■

Catherine is about to ring the doorbell when I stop her.

"No, let's not give her any chance to slip away."

"I doubt she knows that we're coming." Cath says.

"I wouldn't be so sure about that. After this morning, Douglas knows that we know about their lovely threesome. I would be surprised if he didn't make a few calls after I left him. Come on, let's try around the back."

The garden is empty, but there is a rake leaning against a tree on the lawn and a short distance away there is a pile of leaves and grass cuttings.

I sniff the air. "She's home. I can smell that grass from here. It's been cut this morning."

I carefully turn the handle on the back door. It is unlocked and we can hear a radio quietly playing somewhere in the house. I turn to Cath and tell her to go back to the front of the house.

"Make sure that she doesn't try to leave by the front door. Go on, I'll give you thirty seconds to get there before I go in."

Once Cath has had enough time to get into position, I open the door and announce my arrival.

"Hello, Rosemary. This is Detective Sergeant McMillan. I need to speak to you again please."

There is no response, but a few seconds later I'm surprised to hear the volume of the radio increase to the point that I can clearly make out the words to The House of the Rising Sun, by Eric Burdon and the Animals. I step into the kitchen and open the door to the hallway. The music appears to be coming from one of the rooms upstairs, so I cautiously peer around the edge of the doorway towards the stairs.

When our eyes meet, it is too late for me to avoid the shovel-sized fist that slams into my face. For an old guy, Paddy Newman is surprisingly agile, and he throws his full weight onto me before I can recover fully from his punch. His massive hands find my throat and it is all I can do to call Cath for help before he starts to squeeze. I desperately jab punches into his ribs, but my strength is fading fast as he presses down on my windpipe like some deranged human Anaconda.

I fumble for my Taser, but my arms now hang limply by my sides as my body succumbs to a lack of oxygen and my brain begins the inevitable process of shutting down.

Through bulging eyes, I see an explosion of color and an image of Catherine flying through the air that is so real I can almost touch it.

Suddenly, the crushing weight is gone from my chest and my lungs rejoice at the taste of fresh sweet air. Catherine has come to my rescue and her drop kick has put Paddy on his back, but she is now in her own desperate fight for survival. Her Taser is pressed against his chest, but he is a big man and appears to be completely impervious to the electricity coursing through his body.

He swats Cath away with the back of his hand and her head hits the wall with a sickening thud. Paddy quickly gets back to his feet and comes for me again. Still weakened by my earlier beating, I try to crawl away, but he grabs one of my legs and pulls me back across the tiled floor.

"Where do you think you're bloody going? I'm not finished yet."

He turns me over and is about to finish what he started when Catherine's extendable baton crashes down on his shoulders and she throws herself onto his back. In an attempt to dislodge her, Paddy thrashes from side to side, but Cath stubbornly clings on.

In desperation, he throws himself backwards onto the floor and with the wind knocked out of her, the baton drops from Cath's hand. She is far from done, though, and with nothing else to hand, she opens her mouth and bites down on Paddy's cheek as hard as she can. When she pulls away, she takes a good sized chunk of flesh with her. Paddy screams in pain, but he refuses to give up and jerks his head backwards again and again trying to butt Cath in the face. Knowing that sooner or later he is going to score a hit, I shakily push myself up onto my knees and grab for my own baton.

My first strike connects with his shins and is enough to divert his attention away from Catherine. I'm poised for a second strike, when a shot rings out and dislodges a chunk of plaster in the wall behind me. In an instant we all freeze and turn towards the source of the firing.

"I wouldn't if I were you, Sergeant McMillan. Put down the baton."

Rosemary is slowly descending the stairs, clutching a pistol in one hand. She swings it around to level at Catherine. "And you. Let go of him right now."

Reluctant to release her grip, Catherine holds on and Rosemary moves closer and presses the gun against Cath's forehead. "Don't test me, DC Swain. Let go or I will kill you."

Cath looks to me for guidance and I nod. "Do as she says, Cath."

She releases her hold and Paddy gets to his feet and turns to Rosemary. "What should we do with them? We can't let them go."

Picking up on his meaning, Rosemary shakes her head. "No, that's not part of the plan. Cuff them to one of the radiators and then put the cases in the car."

"You're going somewhere?" Cath asks sarcastically. "We could give you a lift?"

Ignoring her, Rosemary holds her gun to Catherine's face while frisking through her pockets for her cuffs and radio.

"Patrick, get his and then get them both into the laundry room," she orders. "The radiator in there is cast iron. Cuff them to the brackets either side of it."

Newman searches me but I've left my cuffs in the car. "He doesn't have any. What now?"

Rosemary gestures to the laundry room door. "Get them in there."

Paddy roughly pushes us inside and Rosemary keeps her weapon pointed at my face, while Paddy cuffs Cath to the radiator. While I'm wondering what they are going to do with me, Rosemary orders me to face the wall. She steps forward and pushes the barrel of her pistol against the back of my head. Fearing that I am about to be executed, Catherine tries to stand up. She pleads with Rosemary, "Please, no! This doesn't have to end like this."

Rosemary swings the pistol towards Catherine. "Sit down, Swain. I'm not going to kill him."

Catherine reluctantly backs away, but then tries to shout a warning. At the exact same moment something hits me hard on the back of my head and my face slams into the wall.

■ ■ ■ ■ ■ ■ ■

I'm not sure how long I was out for, but by the time I regain consciousness, the blood around my nose has already dried up. Catherine is leaning over me shaking my shoulders and behind her I can see three or four uniformed police officers.

"Come on, mate, wake up. The paramedics are on the way. They should be here in a few minutes."

A nasty bruise is starting to grow on the side of Catherine's head and there is still blood around her mouth from where she took a bite out of Paddy's cheek.

Through a groggy head, I force a smile and say, "I think your makeup could do with a bit of a touch up, Cath. You look like an extra from the bride of Dracula."

Indignant, Catherine takes her hand off my shoulder. "Asshole, I thought you were badly hurt. You're not looking so good yourself, Rocky."

I'm helped to my feet by two of the uniformed officers and they take us both into the living room and tell us to sit down. While they leave us to check where the paramedics are, I ask Catherine how long I was unconscious for.

"Around ten minutes or so. For a minute, I really thought that Newman had killed you. He hit you with a bar stool."

191

I carefully rub the back of my head. "Yeh, I was wondering what that was. I've got a lump the size of a bloody ostrich egg. How did the cavalry get here so fast?"

"I managed to call it in before I got to you, and after they left, I called 999. Rosemary took my radio, but in the panic she missed my cellphone."

"We need to find them, Cath. And we need to let Morgan and Gray know what is happening." I reach for my own cellphone, but Catherine stops me.

"Already done. The boys in blue have Newman's plate number and address. Unlikely that they will be there, but a couple of squad cars are already on the way to Sunnydale House."

"And what about Morgan and Gray?"

"I called both of them. DCI Morgan's phone went to voicemail, but I managed to speak to Sarah Gray. She wants us back at the station as soon as the paramedics have checked us over."

I nod my head. "Good. That's good work. And thanks."

Catherine looks puzzled. "For what?"

"For getting stuck in like that. That's another one I owe you, mate. I really thought I was a goner this time."

Ever modest, Cath brushes off her heroics as nothing more than what she is paid to do. In danger of showing more emotion than either of us would like, we breathe a sigh of relief at the arrival of the paramedics. They get to work straightaway and, after a quick checkup, give us the all clear, but the senior paramedic advises us both to take the next couple of days off.

"Particularly you, Sergeant McMillan. If you really were unconscious for as long as your partner said you were, then you should take it easy for the next forty-eight hours. And if you start getting headaches or generally feeling unwell, you should get straight to a hospital. That goes for you as well, DC Swain."

We thank her for the advice and then I tell Cath that we need to get going. A young constable who until now has been standing quietly by the door asks me if I need to get anything from my car. Confused as to why I would need to, I raise my hands and shrug. "I know that I'm probably concussed, but am I missing something here, constable?"

The young officer grimaces and then gestures towards Catherine. "I'll let you give DS McMillan the good news."

I turn to face Catherine and say, "Well?"

"Yeh, about that, boss. Bonny and Clyde must have been worried that you would wake up and give chase before they could get away. So, they …"

She pauses and I snap, "What? What have they done? Please tell me they didn't torch my car."

Catherine shakes her head and then screws up her face. "No, but they did slash your tires."

Hearing this, I relax slightly and say, "Okay, it could have been worse, I suppose."

Anticipating my reaction, Cath then carefully adds, "And … they put a cast-iron garden chair through your windscreen for good measure."

"They bloody did what?" I shout. "Now, that's just … Oh, for fuck's sake, there was no need for that. Constable, get us back to Blackwell please."

■ ■ ■ ■ ■ ■ ■ ■

Sarah Gray is in the middle of a telephone call, but when she sees us coming, she immediately ends it and stands up.

"Oh my God, Catherine, you didn't tell me that you'd both just gone ten rounds with Mike Tyson. You should both be at home resting."

"Honestly, ma'am, it's okay, we're both fine," I say as I sit down. "Unfortunately, I can't say the same about Paddy Newman."

"He's injured?" Gray asks.

I gesture towards Catherine. "Yes, you could say that, ma'am. Hannibal Lector here took a bite out of his face."

For a second DI Gray is unsure of whether I am joking or not. When Cath shrugs her shoulders and smirks, Gray nods with satisfaction. "Okay, good. Admittedly, its unorthodox, but looking at what he did to you both, I'm sure the bastard had it coming."

In unison, we both nod and say, "Yes, he did."

I then ask if there has been any luck finding either of our suspects.

"Unfortunately not, Sean. They haven't gone to Newman's address and I doubt whether they will risk going into a hospital to get his face looked at. My guess is that they will have gone to ground somewhere or will be trying to get out of the country. You're sure that they were already leaving before you got there, Catherine?"

"Yes, ma'am. Rosemary told Newman to cuff us and then to put the cases in the car. They were definitely already planning to leave."

"Okay. Well, we've circulated the names and descriptions to all the ports, airports, and train stations, so unless they had another way out, it's more likely that they are holed up somewhere waiting for the heat to die down."

"Or waiting for Clive Douglas to make his next move," I remark. "They wouldn't just leave, ma'am. This has been part of a bigger game right from the start and, apart from us showing up unannounced at Rosemary's house, I think that so far everything has played out exactly as they planned."

"And what do you think the next move is?" Gray asks me.

"I don't know, ma'am. I'm still trying to figure that out, but if we could get a look at that unredacted inquest report, I've a feeling that we might get a clue as to what it is."

My question is a leading one and DI Gray looks reluctant to say anything.

Catherine breaks the silence. "I called DCI Morgan, ma'am, to let him know what had happened to us, but his phone went straight to voicemail. Have you managed to spea—?"

"No, DC Swain. I haven't managed to speak to him yet. I'm sure he will call when he has something to share with us."

"What about getting another copy of the report?" I suggest.

"I've already requested one," she replies. "But I don't think it's going to be that easy. The boss had to call in a lot of favors to get a copy, and I think that door might have closed again."

Catherine looks at me and I have a feeling that we are both thinking the same thing. I know what the answer to my next question will be, but I ask it anyway.

"Ma'am, I hope that you don't take this the wrong way, but do you think that DCI Morgan might be in trouble, or—?"

"Or involved somehow in this case?" Gray interrupts. "I'd be lying if I said it hadn't crossed my mind after the way he left yesterday, but no. I can't explain why he left the way he did and why he hasn't contacted us since, but I'm sure that DCI Morgan has valid reasons that he will share in due course. You both agree?"

Again, we answer in unison, "Yes, ma'am."

Then I add, "I'm sorry for asking. It's just not like the boss to keep us out of the loop on something that could be so crucial to a case. We were just worried about him."

"That's okay, Sean. If he hasn't called by five, I'll try calling him again. In the meantime, I want you both to take the rest of the day off. I think tomorrow is going to be an interesting day and I need you both as rested as possible."

I try to protest, but DI Gray holds up her hand to stop me. "Sean, I don't pull rank very often, but that wasn't a request. It was an order. I wasn't joking when I said that you both looked like you had gone ten rounds with Mike Tyson. It will do you both good to get an early night. If there are any developments, I will call you. Understood?"

Sarah is right, and even if she wasn't, I don't have the energy or the will to fight with her anyway. The effects of my run-in with Paddy are starting to kick in. I suddenly feel very tired and Catherine is probably feeling the same way. We both thank DI Gray and gratefully take our leave.

Outside the office, Catherine offers me a lift, but I suggest that we should both take a taxi. "You look as worn out as I feel, mate. Grab an Uber just to be on the safe side. Your car will be okay here in the station car park until tomorrow."

Catherine's cab arrives first, and I wish her a safe trip home and a good night's sleep. While I wait for my cab I check my phone to see if there are any messages from Kevin Morgan.

Disappointingly, there aren't any messages from the boss, but I smile when I see a message from Maria.

Hi, Sean. I just wanted to thank you again for Saturday. The whole evening was perfect. Are you busy this weekend? I would like to thank you properly.

On any other day, I would already be reading more into that than I probably should, but today I'm too exhausted to even think about sex. Instead I type a short reply to answer the question, without getting into a long exchange of messages.

Hi, Maria. That sounds great. I'm not sure if I am free yet but will let you know as soon as I can.

■ ■ ■ ■ ■ ■ ■

It's rare that I take a bath, but today it is exactly what I need. Tonight, I'm planning to travel back to the day of the robbery, but I'm feeling like I've been hit by a bus and the thought of soaking in a hot bath somehow makes me feel better. I also want to use the time to figure out how to explain my injuries to Paddy and Michael.

While I wait for the tub to fill, I stand in front of the mirror to assess how much of the damage that 2018 Paddy has done to me will be visible to 1983 Paddy. The lump on the back of my head is mostly hidden by my hair, but there is a small gash on my forehead and some heavy bruising around my eyes and nose. With my history, I can probably get away with saying these were from a recent bar fight, but the horrific bruises and hand marks around my neck are a different thing entirely. For a moment, I shut my eyes and picture Paddy trying to choke me to death. I've been through a lot of "deaths", but the thought of how close I was to dying for real makes me shudder and I open my eyes to look at myself again. I wipe away the condensation from the mirror and shake my head. "Fuck him, Sean. You're one of the good guys and the good guys always win."

With the bath full, I turn off the taps, strip off, and climb carefully in. The water is hotter than I am used to, but I force myself to lie down fully to let the warmth of the water do its work. The soothing effect on my aching muscles is almost instantaneous. It also reminds me just how tired I am and for a few minutes I allow myself to close my eyes to think about how to explain my injuries to Paddy and Michael. When I wake up, it is completely dark, and the water is freezing.

The Past – Friday, December 23rd, 1983

My head breaks the surface and I gasp for breath, frantically treading water as I try to work out where the hell I am. The last time something like this happened was when I inadvertently woke up in the river next to Assistant Chief Constable Maurice Butterfield's home in Cobham.

On that occasion, however, I had been fully clothed and equipped and, despite ending up in the river, I had at least gone through the motions of my dream-travel ritual. Tonight is a complete first for me. I have traveled without trying and, to make matters worse, I am treading water, stark bollock naked in a freezing river in the middle of winter.

I look in all directions and then say to myself, "Absolutely fucking wonderful. You've outdone yourself this time, Sean."

Above me is the base of a bridge and in the distance to my right I can clearly see the lights and distinctive outline of another one. Thankfully, London Bridge is a clear enough indicator to know that I am in the River Thames somewhere, and Blackfriars Bridge to my left confirms that I am bobbing around underneath Southwark Bridge.

I now have a choice. Find a way to die quickly and travel as planned tonight or take my chances that I have ended up more or less where and when I need to be. Worried that I may have already slept for most of the night, I take my chances and wearily kick off for the north bank of the Thames. The effort of the swim warms me up, but by the time I reach the muddy bank, I am almost totally exhausted. I use my remaining energy to crawl the last few yards through the mud and then I drop down besides the embankment wall to catch my breath.

The cold soon overtakes me again and I stand up on my tiptoes to cautiously peer over the wall.

In the distance, I can see the spire of Southwark Cathedral. To my great relief, the few cars passing by are consistent with those from the eighties. I'm also pleased to see that the ninety-five-story Shard Skyscraper is missing from the skyline. When you consider that they didn't start construction of it until 2009, if it had been there, I would have been better off saving my energy and drowning.

For now, though, drowning is the furthest thing from my mind. If I don't find some clothes or shelter soon, I am at serious risk of freezing to death.

I wait for a bus to pass and with no other cars in sight and the road seemingly empty, I climb over the wall and make a dash for a dustbin next to the bus shelter on the opposite side of the road. Desperately cold, I pull at the black refuse sack lining the bin until it comes loose and then I duck inside the shelter to inspect my prize.

Against all the odds, the refuse sack is empty. The bus shelter, however, is not. Sitting quietly at the opposite end of the shelter and obviously in shock at the sight of a half-frozen naked guy clutching a refuse sack are a middle-aged woman and two young girls. For a second, I am frozen to the spot, then I slowly move the bag to protect my modesty before trying to offer an explanation.

"Um, sorry about this, love. I'm meant to be getting married tomorrow, but my best man is a prankster. Just give me a second and I'll be on my way."

Unconvinced by my explanation, the woman pulls the girls closer towards her and, with nothing to lose, I turn my back to them and punch holes in the top and sides of the refuse sack for my head and arms. I pull the sack over my head before turning around and walking towards them. They look terrified and when I reach forward to pull the woman's woolly bobble hat off her head, she looks like she might faint.

"I'm sorry, love, but right now, my need is greater than yours. Oh, and I'll be needing your boots as well, if you don't mind?"

Her black Pixie boots look to be around a size seven and I'm a size nine but looking like a twat in ill-fitting footwear is preferable right now to frozen feet. When she doesn't say anything, I help myself and tug the boots off the end of her feet.

Before leaving, I offer another apology. Then, looking like an escapee from a fetish club, I set off at a painful trot in search of a telephone box.

I find one within a few minutes and, thankful to be out of the wind again, I rack my brains for the number before making a reverse-charge call to the only person I know in 1983.

■ ■ ■ ■ ■ ■ ■

The voice on the other end of the line is cultured and polite. The complete opposite to what I had been expecting to hear.

"Hello, Phillips household, Janice speaking. How may I help you?"

"Um, I'd like to speak to Darren please, if he's home."

"Yes, he's watching TV. May I ask who's calling please?"

In the background I hear Darren call, "Who is it, Mum? If it's Kelly, tell her I'm not here."

"It's not Kelly," she replies to him. "It's a man."

"What man? Tell him I'm not here."

"Hang on, I'll ask hi—"

"Tell him, it's his friend, Sean," I interrupt her. "Tell Darren we met a couple of weeks ago and went for a drive together."

There is a short pause and then I hear her say, "Somebody called Sean. You went for a drive together."

Next, I hear what sounds like a short scuffle and then Darren's voice much closer saying, "Mum, give me the phone please. Never mind who he is. He's just a mate. Ta. Now, how about a nice cup of tea? I won't be long."

I hear a door shut and then Darren comes onto the line.

"Sean. Sorry about that, mate. That was just my mum. I wasn't sure if I was gonna hear from you again. What are you up to?"

"Shut up and listen, Darren. I have another bit of work for you. I need you—"

"Cool. What is it?"

"If you shut up, I'll tell you. I need you to come and pick me up and take me to Fulham. Can you get your hands on a car?"

"Course I can. Piece of cake, Sean. When do you need this doing?"

"Now," I say. "And the quicker the better. I'm in a phone box on the North Bank Road in Southwark. It's opposite a newsagent."

"What? Right now?" Darren exclaims. It's nearly midnight, mate. And what the fuck are you doing in a phone box in Southwark?"

"Listen, I don't have time to explain. But get here as fast as you can and bring a spare set of clothes. I'll make it worth your while. Bring whatever is the baggiest on you. Oh, and some socks and shoes as well."

Darren chuckles to himself and then says, "Are you having a fucking laugh, mate? Is this a wind-up or something?"

Irritated by the constant questions, I snap, "I don't do wind-ups, Darren. Oh, and one last thing — buy a jerrican of petrol on the way. Okay? Get here within the hour and there will be five hundred quid waiting for you."

For a second there is silence and then Darren says, "For five hundred quid, I'll be there in thirty minutes. See you soon, partner."

■ ■ ■ ■ ■ ■ ■

True to his word and almost exactly thirty minutes later, the early morning silence is shattered by the sound of screeching tires as Darren takes the corner and lurches to a halt outside the telephone box in a small canary yellow Ford Fiesta. I step outside to meet him.

Darren winds down the window and immediately bursts out laughing. "What the fuck have you got on? You look like a right bloody bellend."

I nod my head and smirk. "Yeh, thanks. Tell me something I don't already know. Now unlock the back door and let me in. I'm freezing my knackers off out here."

He unlocks the door and I climb in the back. Before he can say anything else or ask me what I have been doing, I ask him if he brought the clothes and shoes, and the petrol. In response he indicates a jerrican on the floor and passes me a small black holdall.

"This is my loosest stuff, but I reckon they'll be tight on you. I'm a lot skinnier than you, but the shoes shouldn't be too bad. We've got about the same sized feet, I reckon."

Inside the bag, there is a shiny silver Fila tracksuit, a white t-shirt and a scruffy-looking pair of blue Adidas training shoes, size 9 I'm pleased to see. I tell Darren to face the front, and he laughs and turns away.

"With pleasure, mate. I have absolutely no inclination to get a gander at your bleeding wrinkly old knob."

I lift the black refuse sack over my head and, when Darren sees in the rear-view mirror that I am completely naked, he pretends to retch.

"Jesus Christ, Sean, this is my mum's car. I hope your ass is bloody clean. She'll go bonkers if you get skid marks all over the upholstery."

I pull on the tracksuit bottoms and poke Darren in the shoulder blades. "Shut up and drive, moron. And if I were you, I'd be more concerned about my balls rubbing on these lovely trackies of yours. It's been a helluva sweaty night, you know."

He pulls away, talking nonstop.

"I want another hundred for the clothes, Sean. There is no fucking way I'm taking them back when you're done with them."

"Shut up and take me to the Clem Atlee Council Estate in Fulham. You know it?"

"I know it. But why do you want to go there? It's a shithole."

"Just drive, Darren. It's police business. What day is it by the way?"

"What? It's Friday. No, I mean it's Saturday. What have you been smoking?"

"It's Christmas Eve?" I ask.

Darren checks his watch. "Yeh, for the last twenty-five minutes. What's this about?"

I breathe a sigh of relief and say, "Thank fuck for that."

Confused, Darren asks, "Thank fuck for what? You're not making any sense."

"Like I said, it's police business. Just keep your eyes on the road."

I finish dressing and climb into the front passenger seat.

Darren turns to me and says, "Did you hear what I said? I want six hundred quid, not five."

"I heard you, Philips. Don't worry you'll be happy enough tonight."

He shakes his head. "I hope so. Because I don't see a wallet and I'm not taking cash that's been anywhere near your ass, pal."

I ignore the comment and tell him to take the next right turn "The entrance to the estate is just up here on the left."

We take the turn and Darren asks again, "What are we doing here, Sean? Has this got something to do with that pair of old benders we followed last time?"

I ignore him again and direct him towards the block of garages where I have hidden Paddy's Cortina.

"Wait here and keep a lookout for anyone coming. I won't be long."

Inside the garage, I'm relieved to find the car exactly as I left it a couple of weeks ago. I retrieve the Securicor uniform from the boot and put it on over the tracksuit. Everything fits exactly as it did before and, apart from one small but important detail, I look and feel every inch the security guard.

The small but important detail are the scruffy Adidas shoes on my feet. They are a dead giveaway, but there isn't much I can do about them now. Darren is also wearing trainers so I will just have to plead ignorance with Paddy and Michael when I meet them.

I toss the helmet and baton onto the backseat of the Cortina, pour the petrol into the tank, and then go outside to speak to Darren. He is leaning on the bonnet of the Fiesta smoking a cigarette, which he quickly snuffs out when he sees me coming. He looks me up and down and nods approvingly.

"Fuck me. You're going to rob a security van. Is that it? That is some serious shit, Sean. Either you're deep undercover or you've been pulling my pisser all along about being a cop."

I nod my head. "I am a cop, Darren. I can assure you of that. I need you to go home now and you need to forget what you've seen tonight. You understand me?"

Confused, he shakes his head. "But I can help you, Sean. Just tell me what you want me to do. I might only be a kid, but I'm not afraid of anyth—"

"Darren, stop. This is where things get dangerous. I appreciate what you've done for me tonight, but this is as far as we go."

He reluctantly nods his head and says, "Yeh, okay. What about my money though?"

I point to the garage and say, "That car there is a 1982 Ford Cortina Mark V, and it's got less than two thousand miles on the clock. It's worth at least a couple of grand and it's yours to do whatever you want with, after I've finished with it."

He now looks more confused than ever, so I explain further, "At 11 a.m. tomorrow morning, that car will be parked outside the Bluebell Pub."

"The one where we gave those fellas a pasting?"

"That's right. The car actually belongs to one of those blokes, but you can trust me when I say he won't be making a fuss if it goes missing. It's yours to do with as you please."

Happy with the arrangement, Darren smiles and says, "Cool. Eleven o'clock tomorrow. I'll be there."

I nod and say, "Good. I'll leave the keys under the driver's side wheel arch for you."

Before Darren leaves, and worried about his safety, I remind him again not to be late. The robbery is due to go down at just after 11 a.m., so I know it will be safe for Darren to take the car at that time. Any time after that and the risk of him being caught by Paddy or Michael increases exponentially by the hour.

This is a scenario that I don't even want to contemplate, but Darren assures me he will be there on time and I watch until the Ford Fiesta disappears out of sight.

■ ■ ■ ■ ■ ■ ■

I get back into the Cortina to keep warm and to get some sleep. Then just before 9 a.m. on the morning of Saturday 24th

December 1983 I pull up and park opposite the entrance to the Bluebell Pub in Fulham. Checking that no one is watching me, and as promised to Darren, I stash the keys under the driver's side wheel arch, before walking towards the pub door.

I'm less than two feet away when the door opens, and Paddy's huge right arm drags me inside.

"For God's sake, get inside, you bleedin' Muppet! And what the fuck has happened to your face?" He pushes me against the wall and closes the front door. Michael is also there, and he looks me up and down in disbelief.

"Please don't tell me you've been cruising around in Paddy's car dressed in that uniform and looking like you've been in a bloody car crash? For pity's sake, Sean. You could have got ready here."

I try to explain myself, but he holds up his hand to stop me. He leans forward to inspect my injuries more closely and grimaces when he sees the marks on my throat.

"Wow, you really pissed someone off, didn't you?"

I'm saved from answering for a second time when he looks down at my feet. "And what in the name of Christ are those supposed to be?"

Paddy turns to Michael and shakes his head. "I told you that he was a bloody liability, Mick. Let's just do—"

With my fate already determined, Michael cuts him off and in a softer tone says, "No. It's okay. It's not Sean's fault. We should have explained that he needed to wear black shoes to go with the uniform. I'll go and see if Maurice has got a pair he can borrow."

Paddy is about to say something else, but he stops when Michael shakes his head. "Okay. I suppose so," he mutters.

He then turns back to me and holds out his hand.

"Give?"

When I look confused, he shakes his hand and says, "My car keys, asshole. Hand them over."

I make a pretense of trying to look for them and then I raise my hands and shrug. "I must have dropped them outside somewhere." Given that we're dressed like Securicor security guards, I know that he won't want either of us stepping back out into the street.

He looks like he is about ready to punch me in the face, but before he can decide what to do, Michael returns with a shiny pair of black brogues.

"Here, put these on, Sean. And get a move on, our ride will be here in a few minutes."

The shoes are a good fit and Paddy begrudgingly grumbles a mild acceptance. "At least now you don't look like a complete bloody amateur. You sure you're up for this, Sean?"

"He's up for it," Michael says. "Stick your head out the door, Paddy, and see if the car is here."

Paddy does as he's told and then turns back to us and nods. "Grab your shit, boys. It's showtime."

I slip my baton into its holder and pick up my helmet. Paddy and Michael do the same and then Michael picks up a brown-leather tool bag and hands it to me. "Hold on to this, Sean."

The bag is heavy, and I ask what it is.

Paddy smirks and says, "Nothing for you to worry about." And then in a sarcastic reference to his missing car keys, "Just try not to lose it between here and the car please."

Waiting outside, there is a black Range Rover with heavily tinted windows. Checking that the coast is clear, Michael is the first to leave the pub. He climbs into the back seat and beckons for me to join him with Paddy closely following behind. As soon as the door is closed, the car pulls away.

Whoever is driving says nothing and the hood of the parka he's wearing completely hides his identity from behind.

207

The driver remains facing forward and with Paddy and Michael boxing me in on either side, I have no chance of getting a clue from the rear-view mirror either. Confident that I know who it is, anyway, I settle back and ask Michael where we are going.

"Just going for a little drive, Sean."

He takes the bag from me and pulls the zipper across. He then takes out two sawn-off shotguns and hands one to Paddy. Seeing the look on my face he smiles and says, "Nothing to worry about. Just for insurance, that's all."

I shrug my shoulders and cockily say, "I'm not worried. I can handle a gun. Is there one in there for me?"

Michael rummages in the bag and takes out a small black revolver. I hold out my hand to take it, but Michael stuffs it into his waistband. "If the time comes when we need to start shooting, you can have it then. Okay?"

I nod and Michael zips up the bag and drops it in the seat well. "Right, get ready, we should be there soon."

■ ■ ■ ■ ■ ■ ■ ■

Ten minutes later we take the M4 exit towards Brentford and then pick up the A4 to Stanwell where we stop at the edge of a park shielded by high conifer trees. The driver remains facing forward, but Paddy turns to me and tells me to put my helmet on.

"This is it, fella. Too late to back out now."

We get out and walk towards the waiting Securicor armored car. The doors open and two uniformed guards get out and walk towards us. George Benson and Peter Lane have clearly been given explicit instructions not to speak to us. They walk past without making eye contact and I watch as they climb into the back of the Range Rover. Paddy jabs me in the shoulder with the barrel of his shotgun.

"Oy, don't worry about them. You just concentrate on not messing up. Get in the driver's seat."

I climb into the driver's seat and Michael takes the passenger seat. Paddy gets into the back of the van and I hear the door lock from the inside. A few seconds later, a grille slides across and Paddy says, "Good to go, Mick."

Michael pats me on the leg. "Keep your speed under the limit and keep a cool head. If all goes to plan, in a couple of hours, you're going to have a very merry Christmas."

I pull away and Michael tells me to follow the signs for the Heathrow Airport Trading Estate. Despite their outwardly calm exterior, I know that Michael's and Paddy's hearts will be racing because mine is too, even though I know that the heist goes off without a hitch.

To break the tension and to maintain my ignorant persona, I turn to Michael and state the obvious.

"Isn't that the place that got done over recently? The place that lost all the gold?"

Michael turns to me and smiles. "That's right. Which makes it perfect."

"I don't understand. Won't there be more security now?"

Behind me, Paddy laughs and presses his face to the grille. "No, boy. It's Christmas Eve and that thing with the IRA last week was the best bloody Christmas present ever."

"Best present ever, until today," Michael says.

"Yeh, that was what I meant," Paddy chuckles again.

I'm still looking confused, so Michael screws up his face and says, "Bloody hell, Sean. Have you been living under a rock since we last saw you? How can you not know about the IRA car bomb outside Harrods last week? It killed six people and wounded another ninety."

"And three of those killed were coppers," Paddy adds. "It should have been more of the bastards for my liking, but it was enough to put every bobby in London onto the manhunt. They might as well have left the door wide open for us."

So, now I know how it was so easy for them to get in and out unmolested. Not only did they have the advantage of Rosemary's insider knowledge, but the fate handed them an unexpected boost in the guise of an IRA attack on Harrods Department Store just a week before the planned date of the robbery.

I feign realization and then say, "So that means …?"

Michael smiles. "It means, that there shouldn't be many coppers on duty today. If any at all. In fact, if our intelligence is right, it should just be the regular security fellas today."

Paddy interrupts us and slips his ID card through the security grille. "Face front, boys. This is it."

Ahead of me is the first of the security checkpoints. The gatehouse is manned by two security officers and there are two more behind the barrier post. On the opposite side of the road, I can see a police patrol car, but Michael tells me not to worry about it.

"Just keep facing forward, Sean. That's just a token presence to deter the amateurs. Trust me, there won't be any coppers inside."

I drop the window and hand over the ID cards and our collection manifest. The young guard on duty compares our photographs and signatures to a list on a clipboard. Then, after a cursory look at our faces, he hands back the cards. I'm about to continue, when my heart sinks as he shouts for me to stop.

"Hey, you forgot your collection note. You won't get very far without that."

Underneath my helmet, I'm sweating like a blind lesbian at a fish market and for a second I think he may be about to say something else, but then he smiles and hands over the manifest. "Your pickup is ready at dock number four."

The barrier lifts and the two security officers on the road step aside to let us pass. I slowly pull forward and Michael pats me on the leg again.

"What did I say, Sean? A piece of fucking cake. There are two more gates, but they won't check our IDs again. They're just to make it harder for blaggers to get out if there's a robbery."

Michael is right. We pass through the next two gates without stopping. After the third gate we are directed towards dock number four and, after checking our manifest, the security supervisor helps to marshal me backwards towards a hydraulic ramp. I apply the handbrake and Michael hands me his shotgun and tucks his handgun out of sight.

"Keep hold of this. I don't think it's going to be needed. You stay here and keep the engine running."

Behind me, I hear Paddy opening the back doors. Michael gets out to join him and I watch in the wing mirror as a steel roller shutter door slowly opens.

I'm not sure what I was expecting to see, but the sight of twenty million in gold, two million in cash, and three million in gems is a little underwhelming when it's loaded onto a single pallet in nondescript wooden crates. At more than five hundred kilograms, though, it still needs a forklift truck to move it and the rear of the van lowers dramatically as the end of the pallet touches down. The forklift driver pushes the pallet as far into the van as its reach will allow and then it disappears back into the depot and the roller shutter starts to drop.

A few minutes later, I hear the back door of the van close and the inner lock click into place. Michael is still chatting with the security supervisor, though, and I whisper through the grille to Paddy.

"What's going on? What's he talking about?"

"Don't panic, boy. They're talking about the previous robbery and about the IRA bombing. Mick knows what he's doing."

"But we should get out of here," I say. "Before somebody works out who we—"

"You just keep bloody cool. You're about to be rich."

In the mirror, I see Michael shake the supervisor's hand, then he turns and walks towards the steps. He takes his seat next to me and puts on his seat belt. Then out of the corner of his mouth, he says, "Nice and steady now, Sean. We're nearly home free."

In a reversal of our arrival, the first two gates open to allow us out without needing to stop. At the final gate, our ID cards are given a cursory check again by the same security officer and a copy is made of the collection note. Satisfied that all is in order, he smiles, and hands back our documents.

"Okay, that all seems to be complete. Merry Christmas, lads."

■ ■ ■ ■ ■ ■ ■

With what I know already, I really shouldn't be surprised, but even so, I'm still gobsmacked at just how easy it was for us to get in and out of the depot. Despite the significance of the IRA attack last week and the reassignment of resources to the manhunt, the Metropolitan Police and politicians have clearly learnt nothing from the lessons of Brinks Mat. It's no wonder they were so keen to keep this second robbery under wraps.

Well clear of Heathrow, I turn to Michael. "Where to now, boss?"

He points the way and less than ten minutes later he directs me down a dirt track into Ashdown Forest. Ahead I see the black Range Rover and Michael tells me to park behind it.

"This is it, Sean. This is where we offload and part company."

And by that what he really means is, this is where Sean gets his head blown off.

I get out of the van and if I needed any more confirmation of my fate, the sight of Paddy pointing his shotgun at me is it. I turn to Michael who shrugs and points his handgun at me.

"It's nothing personal, you understand. You were just along for the ride as extra insurance. But now you're no use to us."

He points towards a wooded area and tells me to take off my helmet and follow Paddy.

"And don't try making a run for it. If you cooperate, I'll make it quick and painless. If you run … well, let's just say, you don't want to run, Sean. That won't be pleasant at all."

I turn to follow Paddy into the woods and after two hundred yards, I see Rosemary "T" Pinois standing next to a freshly dug pit. She comes over to join us and when she sees me there is an instant spark of recognition.

"Well, well, this is a turn up for the books."

"You know him, T?" Paddy asks.

Rosemary reaches into her pocket and takes out my warrant card and hands it over.

"Yeh, you could say that, Mick. We've never actually met face to face, but this is the fella that was at Stuart Goldsmith's home yesterday. He left his ID behind."

Paddy hands the card to Michael and, in a panic, he says, "Fuck, Mick. He's a bloody copper. They must have been onto us from the start."

Michael inspects my card and then hands it back to Rosemary. "No, I don't think so. If the cops were onto us, they would have taken us down in the depot. No, I think this chump is on his own." He points the barrel of his shotgun under my chin and asks, "Is that it, Sean? Are you doing a bit of freelance work? Is that even your real name? That card looks like it came out of a bloody cornflakes box."

I ignore the questions and tilt my head towards Rosemary. "So, you're T. I've been looking forward to meeting you."

Rosemary laughs and points to my face. "Where did he get the bruises from? Was that you pair?"

Michael shakes his head. "Not us. He showed up at the pub like this."

Rosemary thinks it over for a second and then points towards the pit. "Whatever. Take him over there."

Paddy jabs the barrel of his shotgun between my shoulder blades and pushes me forward to the edge of the pit. "On your knees, boy."

As I'm understandably somewhat reluctant to comply, he lands a perfectly placed kick behind my knees and I drop to the ground. The pit is easily eight feet deep and at the bottom I can see the bodies of George Benson and Peter Lane. Both are face down in the dirt and each have a neat bullet hole through the skull. I know I'm about to die, but I still need answers. I turn to face Rosemary and ask what this was all about.

She looks at Paddy and Michael and then says to me, "Money, you fucking moron. What else would it be about?"

"The death of your father," I say.

Shocked at the mention of her father, Rosemary takes the handgun out of Michael's waistband and pushes it into my face. "What the hell do you know about that?"

"Enough," I say. "But you should ask Michael if you really want to know what happened."

She turns to face Michael and spits at him, "What's he talking about?"

Michael is clearly flustered but he doesn't falter. "Ignore him. He's just trying to save himself. He doesn't know anything. Shoot him, Paddy."

Fool's Gold

Paddy pushes the shotgun against the back of my head and is about to shoot when Rosemary stops him and lifts my chin with the revolver.

"Stop. I want to know what happened to Goldsmith. Where is he, McMillan?"

After all the trouble I went to helping Stuart get away, there is no way I am going to help Rosemary find him. I smile and shake my head. "He's long gone, and you will never find him."

In response, Rosemary shrugs and says, "So be it. Have a safe trip, Sean, or whatever your real name is."

She nods to Paddy and I brace myself for my head to be ripped apart by the shotgun pellets, but the big lad has something far more sadistic in mind for me. Something hard cracks the back of my skull and I topple forward into the pit onto the bodies of Peter and George.

For a few moments, I don't realize what is happening, but when the third clod of earth lands on my back, I force myself to roll over. Paddy smiles at me and waves. Then he scoops up another load of earth with his shovel and continues to bury me alive.

Michael and Rosemary also pick up shovels and I'm quickly covered completely. Of all the ways to go, this is possibly the worst so far. The weight of the soil on my chest is crushing and any small pockets of air in the dirt are quickly exhausted. I'm literally seconds from death when another huge weight crashes down onto the soil above my chest and shocks me back to life. A few more seconds pass and the soil crushes down onto me once again. My scrambled brain struggles to make sense of what is happening, but then I find the answer.

Content that I now know what they did with the gold, I relax, smile and exhale my final breath.

Present Day – Thursday, May 3rd, 2018

I'm being pulled upwards, and as my head breaks the surface, the sudden intensity of the light in my eyes is blinding.

Catherine drags me bodily over the edge of the bathtub and unceremoniously dumps me onto the tiled floor where I proceed to cough my guts up. Exhausted by the effort of lifting the deadweight of my body, Catherine slumps down next to me to catch her breath. She lets me finish the worst of my retching before she opens up on me.

"What the hell, Sean! How long have you been in there?"

Still slightly disorientated but now more than a little confused and conscious of my nudity, I reach for a towel to cover myself.

"I've no idea, Cath. What time is it?"

"It's just after 7:30. What the fuck, Sean! Who the hell takes a bath this early in the morning? You've got some bloody explaining to do … again!"

Realizing that I have been in the bath for nearly twelve hours, I shudder and then lie about how long I have been in there.

"I'm sorry, Cath. I was still feeling rough this morning, so I got up for a hot soak around seven and must have fallen asleep."

"Bloody seven," Cath exclaims. "So, you were in there asleep for thirty minutes. What the hell would have happened if I hadn't got your caretaker to let me in?"

"Happened?" I ask.

"Sean, you were bloody unconscious. If I hadn't come in and found you, you would be bloody dead by now. What the fuck …"

Her words trail off and tears start to well in the corners of her eyes. "For Christ's sake, Sean, what the hell were you thinking?"

216

I pull her towards me.

"I'm sorry. I must have been more tired than I thought. I'm okay, though. Thanks to you again, mate."

Realizing that there must be a reason why she has come looking for me so early, I take the opportunity to change the subject.

"Why are you here so early, Cath? Has something happened?"

Wiping her eyes with a tissue I've handed her, Catherine frowns and says, "It's Kevin Morgan. His wife phoned Sarah Gray to say that he didn't come home last night."

"Maybe he stayed with friends," I suggest unconvincingly.

"Maybe. But he hasn't showed up for work yet today either. You know Morgan as well as I do. He's normally one of the first in the office and one of the last to leave. DI Gray wants us to go to his home and wait there to see if he shows up."

I hand Cath a towel to dry herself off and then I leave her and go to my bedroom to get dressed. Five minutes later I join her in the living room where she has just finished a call.

"Change of plan. Uniform have found the boss's car abandoned in Epping Forest."

"And the boss?" I ask her.

"No. No sign of him. Local PD have the area cordoned off. DI Gray has told them to back off until we get there."

I pick up my jacket and move towards the door, but instead of moving with me, Catherine raises her eyebrows and says, "One of these days, I'm going to figure out what goes on in that head of yours, Sean."

I nod my head and say, "Yep, I'm sure you will, Cath. And when you do, let me know what you find. For now, though, the boss is out there somewhere, and he needs our help."

■　■　■　■　■　■　■

We get to Epping Forest at just before nine in the morning and a patrol car from Essex Constabulary meets us at the south gate to guide us to the location of DCI Morgan's car. The forest itself covers an area of nearly six thousand acres and contains numerous lakes and secluded areas that would be perfect for hiding a body, or even a car for that matter.

Morgan's vehicle, however, is parked next to a well-used footpath and there has been no attempt to conceal it. Uniform have set up a fifty-yard perimeter and we join the group of officers manning the cordon. The senior officer introduces himself and I ask if there were any witnesses to the arrival of the car.

"Nothing at the moment, DS McMillan. It was reported by a young couple out walking their dogs at just after six this morning."

Catherine asks if there was any reason why they would have reported it. "It looks okay from here. It could have just been someone else walking their dog."

Inspector Harrington nods and then says, "You can't see from here, but you'll see when you get closer. The driver's side window is smashed and there are small traces of blood on the seat and dashboard."

Cath turns towards me and our shared look of concern for Kevin Morgan's well-being is obvious. For a moment, Inspector Harrington looks uncomfortable, but then he lightly touches Catherine on the shoulder.

"Please don't worry, DC Swain," he says. "If DCI Morgan is out there somewhere, we will find him. Some of my lads are already combing the surrounding area and I've requested for some additional units and search teams to be on standby if needed."

He then refers to his pocketbook and looks uncomfortable again. "Listen, I'm sorry to ask you both but is there anything we should know that might help us find him or that might shed any light on what this could be about. Is DCI Morgan in any kind of trouble that you kno—?"

Despite Harrington's seniority, I stop him dead. "No, sir. This is nothing to do with DCI Morgan personally. We're currently working a high-profile case and it looks like the boss may have inadvertently stirred up a hornet's nest. Can we take a look at the scene please?"

Without waiting for permission, I lift the barrier tape and usher Catherine through the cordon. Harrington follows us, but he tells his officers to wait where they are. We carefully approach Morgan's silver Jaguar and I peer through the broken window.

The driver's seat and the floor are littered with small pieces of glass and I can see a smear of dried blood on the leather headrest and a bloody handprint on the dashboard. To nobody in particular, I nod and say, "Looks like he was hit over the head with something."

"What was that?" Harrington asks.

"Most of the blood is on the headrest, sir. With this window broken it's likely he was struck on the side or back of his head by something. The natural inclination then is to put your hand on the injury, which would explain the handprint on the dashboard."

I tell Catherine to go to the other side. "Have a look on the passenger side and on the back seat. See if you can see any more blood."

Catherine puts her search gloves on and opens the passenger side door. In the back there are more small pieces of glass, but no apparent signs of any more blood.

"Check the glove box, Cath. It's a long shot, but maybe his phone is in there. If it is, we can try and pinpoint his movements for the last twenty-four hours."

Catherine opens the drawer and carefully lifts out the contents. Along with the usual registration and insurance documents you would expect to find, there is a small white envelope. Cath turns to face me and nervously says, "It's addressed to you, Sean."

The handwriting is neat, clear, and far too formal for the circumstances: For the attention of Detective Sergeant Sean McMillan.

Fearing the worst, neither of us speak until Catherine tells me to put my gloves on, then she hands me the letter.

I carefully check the edges of the envelope before slipping out the neatly folded sheet of paper inside. There are just three words on the paper: Call Clive Douglas. Unable to believe what I am seeing, I read them twice more before holding the letter up for Catherine to see the message.

Like me, she is momentarily shocked. Then the anger kicks in. "Call Clive Douglas? I'll bloody well do more than that, Sean! If that bastard has hurt the boss, I swear I'll bloody swing for him."

Inspector Harrington moves closer.

"You found something significant, DC Swain?"

While his eyes are focused on Catherine, I tuck the letter into my jacket pocket and out of sight.

"Yes, sir, we did. But I'm not at liberty to tell you what it is due to its sensitivity and relevance to our current investigation."

Harrington looks slightly annoyed, but he is an experienced enough officer to know when not to overstep the mark. He reluctantly nods and then says, "Okay, I understand, sergeant. May I be permitted to know, though, if what you found has any bearing on the disappearance or possible whereabouts of DCI Morgan?"

"Yes, sir. I believe so. And I think it's safe to assume that we won't find him here in Epping Forest."

"I can stand down my officers?" Harrington asks.

"Yes, sir. And if I'm wrong, I will take full responsibility for my decision."

Relieved that I have taken it upon myself to shoulder the operational burden of finding DCI Morgan, Harrison instructs his officers to remove the cordon and then he hands me his business card.

"I'm on duty until five this afternoon, but you can get me on this number twenty-four seven if you do get any new information or need the assistance of Essex Constabulary. Good luck, Sergeant McMillan."

I wait for him to get out of earshot and then I turn to Catherine. "I'll call Clive from your car and put him on speakerphone. Don't let on you are with me but record the conversation on your phone. We need to capture every word of that conversation."

Catherine shakes her head. "Actually, mate. I think we should wait until we get back to the station to speak to—"

"What? No! Every minute we waste could be putting the boss in more danger. We need to speak to him now, Cath."

I'm already walking towards the car and Catherine pulls me back.

"Sean, wait please. I'm as keen as you are to hear what Clive Douglas has to say for himself, but this is getting way to personal now. Douglas has addressed that letter to you because he knows it will push your buttons."

I nod and point out, "And yours too, Cath."

"Yes, and mine, Sean. Which is exactly why we shouldn't speak to him alone. He's looking for some kind of reaction and we are both too involved with him to stay impartial. If he does know anything about what has happened to the boss and we go blundering in, we could make things a whole lot worse for him."

"So, what are you suggesting?" I ask her.

"I'm suggesting that we get straight back to Blackwell and make the call in the presence of DI Gray. She needs to know about the letter anyway."

Part of me still wants to make the call now, but Catherine is yet again making perfect sense. Sensing, though, that I am still undecided, Cath deftly sums up the situation with a few final words.

"Sean, if we don't involve Sarah Gray in this and the shit hits the fan, then we can both say goodbye to our careers in the Met." She adds, "Worse still and God forbid, we could also get the boss killed or seriously hurt. We need backup on this, mate. Please, Sean?"

I'm frustrated, but I can't argue with her logic.

"You're right, Cath. But, God, that bastard gets right under my skin."

"You and me both. Come on, if we put the lights on, we can be there in thirty minutes. You can brief Sarah on the way."

■ ■ ■ ■ ■ ■ ■

DI Gray is waiting for us in her office, but she is not alone.

"DS McMillan, DC Swain, I'd like to introduce you to Inspector Mike Thurgood from Hostage Rescue and Negotiation."

Thurgood stands up and I shake his hand. "Very good to meet you, sir."

"Pleased to meet you too. But no need for the sir with me, Sean. Call me Mike please. All my friends do."

Thurgood is a good-looking giant of a man with a full head of jet-black hair, a boxer's nose, and an impressive Tom Selleck-style moustache. It would be easy to imagine him kicking down doors to rescue hostages single-handed, and the way Cath's tongue is hanging out, it's not hard to guess who she would like to rescue her the next time she is in trouble.

Stifling my natural urge to say something to her, I hide my smirk and look towards Sarah Gray. "You've fully briefed Inspector Thurgood, ma'am?"

"I have, Sean. I think it's best that we keep all our options open. I've asked him to sit in on the call. He won't participate, but his advice could be useful in determining our next steps."

The second stranger in the room has civilian written all over her and my suspicion that she is a civil servant is confirmed when she introduces herself.

"Good morning, Sergeant McMillan. My name is Samantha Hope-Stanton. I'm a senior legal counsel with the Home Office."

Under the circumstances, the presence of Inspector Thurgood makes perfect sense, but I have no idea why someone from the Home Office needs to be present. Confused, I turn back to Sarah Gray.

"Ma'am?"

"Our commanding officer is missing, Sean. I thought it best that we had someone in the room from the Home Office to listen first-hand to what Clive Douglas has to say."

"For what purpose, ma'am?"

"For the purpose of making a quick decision if we need it. Ms. Hope-Stanton has the authority of the Home Secretary to authorize operations up to and including the use of firearms, if required."

I nod my agreement. "Understood, ma'am. That makes perfect sense."

Sarah gets up to close her office door.

"Good. Now if we are all ready," she says as she returns to her desk, "let's get down to the business of getting the boss back."

Catherine adjusts the speakers and I punch in the number for Clive's pay-as-you-go cellphone. The call connects and I cue Cath to start recording.

"In three, two, one ... and go."

■ ■ ■ ■ ■ ■ ■ ■

After three rings the call is answered, but there is silence for a few more seconds until Clive Douglas finally speaks.

"You're calling from a landline number, Sean. I assume then you have the whole team with you listening in. Am I right?"

"Not a team," I say. "Just myself, DC Swain, and Detective Inspector Sarah Gray."

I hear Douglas chuckle to himself and then he says, "Somehow, I think that's unlikely, Sean, but have it your way."

I'm about to ask something, but Douglas cuts in to congratulate Sarah Gray on her recent promotion.

"I did hear something on the grapevine about it, but I didn't believe it, of course."

"And why would that be?" Sarah asks him.

Douglas pauses before answering and knowing him as well as we do, Catherine and I are braced to hear something sarcastic.

"Well, because you ... well, what I mean, DI Gray, is that I heard you were always something of an under-achiever. I suppose Morgan must have seen something in you though."

Then to me, "Is she a looker, Sean?"

Although none of us would blame her if she lost her cool, Sarah grits her teeth and stays silent. We let Clive laugh for another few seconds and then I ask him about the letter.

"Let's not waste time on these infantile jibes, Douglas. You obviously know something about what has happened to DCI

Morgan, so why don't you just save us all a lot of time and tell us what you want and what you know?"

We can hear him tutting and then he says, "Sean, my boy, no need for the hostility. I told you what I want days ago. I want a move to a nice Category C facility, and I want it right now."

Sarah Gray leans closer to the telephone.

"Clive, if that's really still what you want, then you need to help us locate Kevin Morgan. Help us get him back safely and you have my personal guarantee of an immediate move. If you want to play games, though, and any harm comes to him, I can assure you that there will be no deal of any kind."

Our friend from the Home Office frowns and makes some notes, but Sarah ignores her and carries on. "How does that sound to you? You help us, we help you."

"That sounds wonderful, Sarah. But I'm sure you've already worked out by now that I've been helping myself from the start."

"What does that mean?" I ask.

"It means, Sean, that I can give you Kevin Morgan, but I can also give you the missing gold from the second Heathrow robbery."

With his connection to Paddy Newman and Rosemary Pinois, it's likely that he can give us the gold, but there is no reason why he would without some other benefit to himself.

"That's bullshit, Douglas. If Newman and Rosemary Pinois still have the gold, why would they allow you to turn it over to us? And why would you want to anyway? You will get your move to Cat C if you help us locate DCI Morgan unharmed. Why would you—?"

"Because I also want more than just a move to Cat C. I also want a significant reduction in my final sentence, Sean. And by my reckoning two hundred million in gold bullion would go a long way to convincing the Home Office to grant that reduction."

At the mention of the Home Office, Ms. Hope-Stanton shuffles uncomfortably in her chair, but she doesn't say anything. We take a moment to digest what we have just heard and then DI Gray takes the lead again.

"Okay, Clive. That request will be relayed to the Home Office, but we need to know now about DCI Morgan. Like I just said, if any harm comes to him, you can kiss goodbye to any deal. For us to help you, you need to tell us right now what you know."

There is a short pause and then Clive says, "Okay. I'm ready."

Sarah looks at me unsure of what he means. "Ready. Ready for what, Clive?"

"Ready to take DS McMillan and DC Swain to where Morgan is. How long will you be, Sean?"

Sarah Gray loses her cool and bangs her fist on the table, "No. No way. That's not going to happen, Clive. You need to wise up and start cooperating or the deal is off the table right now."

Clive laughs. "I think those under-achiever rumors might possibly have had some truth behind them. If I were in your position, I wouldn't be so hasty to cut me off, DI Gray."

"Really, and what is my position?" Gray snaps. "I'm not the one facing the prospect of life behind bars."

"No, but you are the one that can make the difference between whether DCI Morgan lives or dies, Sarah. Has the mail arrived yet today, by the way?"

We all look at each other and shake our heads. Then Sarah Gray whispers, "What the hell is he talking about? What mail?"

Inspector Thurgood gestures towards the phone and whispers for her to keep Douglas talking.

She takes a deep breath and asks, "You need to explain what you mean, Clive. What mail are you talking about?"

"Now, now. Don't go all coy on me, Sarah. A package was sent to your office and was signed for just over an hour ago. Go and check in your pigeonhole."

Catherine is already on her feet and Sarah nods her agreement for her to leave the room.

"Okay, DC Swain has gone to check. Can you tell me what's in the package, Clive?"

"I could, but that would ruin the surprise. Don't panic, though, it's not a bomb or anything designed to hurt you."

"We have your word on that?" Sarah asks.

"You do, DI Gray. It's not in my interests to hurt any of you. I need your help, don't I?"

I lean closer to the phone. "Yes, you do. So, make damn sure that the same principle applies to Kevin Morgan as well. If anything, happ—"

Annoyed at my outburst, Douglas loses his temper and raises his voice, "If anything happens to Kevin Morgan, it will be because of your lack of action. It won't be down to me, Sean. Just you bloody remember that."

Then to Sarah, "Put your mongrel on a leash, DI Gray."

At that same moment, Catherine returns carrying a brown padded envelope. She hands it to DI Gray and quietly says, "Be careful, ma'am, it's heavy."

Her words are loud enough for Clive Douglas to hear and he says, "It sounds like my gift has arrived. Don't be shy, Sarah. Open the envelope. There are two items inside but unwrap the bigger one first."

Despite Clive's assurance, DI Gray still inspects the package carefully before cautiously cutting off the end of the envelope. The first item she takes out is a small cardboard box neatly tied up with a red silk bow. She briefly inspects the box before placing it back down on the table.

Although the second item is wrapped in brown paper, the sender has made no attempt to disguise its shape and its obvious weight in Sarah's hands is a dead giveaway. She carefully removes the wrapping paper and places the gold bar down next to the box.

The sound of it being placed on the table is clear enough for Douglas to hear and he pipes up once again.

"It might not look much, but that is one kilogram of 99.9 percent pure, 24 karat gold. The approximate value today is around forty thousand pounds. Consider it a gift from me to you, DI Gray. A show of faith, if you will."

"A show of faith in what?" Sarah asks.

"A show of faith in my ability to take you to the gold, of course. This is one of the bars from the robbery. Feel free to run a search on the serial number."

Ahead of all of us as usual, Catherine has already noted the serial number and sent a picture to another of our team to check it out. Like all of us, though, Sarah is less interested in recovering the gold than she is in recovering the boss.

"Thank you, Clive. We're happy to take your word that this is one of the bars from the robbery, but how about a show of faith now regarding Kevin Morgan?"

"Of course, Sarah. You have the small box in front of you?"

"Yes, I do. Can I open it?"

"Be my guest, Sarah. The box is for you."

She unravels the bow and carefully starts to lift off the lid before thinking better of it. She places the box down onto the table and whispers to Catherine.

"Make a recording on your phone. Just in case it is a bomb or there are any other nasty surprises."

When Catherine indicates that she is ready, Gray leans over and removes the lid. Whatever is inside has been covered with a small silk handkerchief. Using a pair of tweezers, she carefully lifts the handkerchief, then she leans closer in to look inside. What we see is shocking even by the standards of Clive Douglas. Sarah Gray immediately recoils and drops the tweezers. Catherine looks like she is going to scream, or cry, and Ms. Hope-Stanton turns away and violently empties the contents of her stomach onto the floor.

I am momentarily left speechless and in shock. The only person seemingly unaffected by the sight of the bloodied finger in the box is Inspector Thurgood. Taking control, he replaces the lid on the box and helps Ms. Hope Stanton out of the room. As the door closes, Clive speaks again, but his attitude now is of a man who is firmly in control.

"I'm sorry that you had to see that. But it was important for you to understand just how serious the situation is. So now that I have your attention, let's stop messing around and get down to business."

Cath, who until now has been sitting quietly, pulls the phone towards her and exclaims, "Fuck you, Douglas! You are finished and if that is Kevin Morgan's finger in the box, I will personally see to it that you spend the rest of your miserable existence in fear of your life."

Both Gray and I gesture to Catherine to keep quiet.

Realizing that she has finished her rant, Douglas responds, "That was an understandable reaction, Catherine, and believe me, I'm sincerely sorry that I have had to resort to such barbaric measures to get my point across. The finger does indeed belong to Kevin Morgan. If you don't believe me, bring his wife in. I'm quite sure she will recognize his wedding ring."

For the second time, Catherine looks like she is about to cry, but she holds it in and retains her composure.

"So, what now?" I ask him.

"The what now, Sean, is that you come and collect me from this hole, and I take you first to the gold and then to Kevin

Morgan. Before I go anywhere, though, I want to see a letter signed by the Home Secretary guaranteeing me a move to a Category C prison and an automatic seventy-five percent reduction in my final sentence."

Sarah Gray grimaces. "We're going to need some time for that, Clive."

"You don't bloody have time!" Clive snaps. "If McMillan and Swain are not here with that letter by 3 p.m., the postman is going to be working overtime today. I'm sure I don't need to spell out to you what I mean by that."

We all understand completely what he means, but Sarah Gray is now caught between a rock and a hard place.

"Okay, none of us want that. But you need to be reasonable. A request of that kind will take time to get approval and it's already nearly eleven."

"Well, I suggest you stop wasting time then and get whatever desk Johnny you have with you from the Home Office to start earning their pay. If I'm not out of here by 3 p.m. exactly, you are going to be receiving more than just a bloody finger."

Ms. Hope-Stanton had returned to the room just a few seconds earlier and at mention of the finger, she turns a ghostly shade of gray. DI Thurgood hands her a glass of water and tries to console her, as Gray continues.

"Okay, Clive. We're already onto that, but you mentioned earlier that you want DS McMillan and DC Swain to come to collect you. That's not the usual protocol. If we do get approval to take you out of prison it will be under armed escort."

"Fuck your protocol!" Clive shouts. "It's McMillan and Swain or nothing. And if I see another copper within five miles the deal is off and Morgan dies. I'm warning you, Gray. Don't test me. I'm a man that has lost everything, so I have nothing left to lose."

"Okay, Clive. It will just be DS McMillan and DC Swain," Gray says in a placating voice.

"And no weapons, no wires or radios and definitely no helicopters or bloody drones following us. You understand me, Gray?"

"Yes, I understand, Clive. Now what about an assurance that, apart from a missing finger, Kevin Morgan is safe and being looked after?"

"He's alive. That's all you need to know right now. Call me when you have that letter. My battery is low and until you have that letter there is nothing else to say."

Before Sarah can say anything more the line goes dead and we are left staring at each other. We then all turn to our friend from the Home Office, but it is Cath who speaks. Her abrupt tone leaves Ms. Hope-Stanton in no doubt as to the urgency of the request.

"Well, you heard the man. We need that letter and we need it now. Go and earn your pay, Samantha."

Worried that she has taken offence, I lean forward and offer a smile. "What DC Swain means to say is Kevin Morgan is not only a highly respected serving police officer and our boss, he is also a very good friend and we are running out of time. We need you to relay what you have heard here with the utmost seriousness and urgency to the Home Secretary and get us that letter as quickly as you can. A man's life depends on it."

She stands up to leave. "Thank you, DS McMillan. I'll do everything I can to help."

■ ■ ■ ■ ■ ■ ■

As soon as she is gone, Inspector Thurgood says, "I hope you were just playing along with him when you said that Sean and Catherine would be doing this on their own, Sarah."

Sarah nods. "Of course I was — but whatever backup we do assign will need to stay well out of sight. Let's not forget that

Clive Douglas not only knows every trick in the book. He was the one who invented most of them."

We all nod, and Sarah adds, "Good. Mike, I suggest you go and brief your team and anyone else you think might be useful. Sean, Catherine, I suggest you go and grab some lunch. It's going to be a long day and you might not get another chance. Go on, I'll call you as soon as there is any word from Samantha."

■ ■ ■ ■ ■ ■ ■ ■

I go with Catherine to the station canteen, but neither of us is in the mood to eat. Cath is also still visibly upset, and I try to reassure her that everything will be okay even though I need reassurance myself.

"We're going to get the boss back, mate. Douglas is desperate, but even he is not stupid enough to kill a senior police officer. We just need to let him think he is in control until we've got—"

Catherine looks up and angrily interrupts me.

"Sean, he is bloody in control. Can't you see that? He's been pulling the strings from day one. The only progress we have made on this case is the progress that he has allowed us to make. He's smarter than us and he knows it."

I let her finish and, with the rant over, Cath's tone softens. She wipes away a teardrop from the corner of her eye.

"I'm scared, Sean. For all we know the boss could be dead already and this could be a setup to get to us."

I take her hand. "No, Cath. You can't think like that. The boss is alive, and we are going to get him back. You're right, Douglas is smart, but so are we. We can beat him, Cath."

Cath shakes her head. "I don't know, Sean. I've got a bad feeling about this."

She looks down at the table and I squeeze her hand. "Look at me. We can beat him. Say it, Cath. Say we can beat him."

Catherine wipes her eyes again and then takes a deep breath and composes herself. "Yes. Fuck it. Yes, we can beat him."

"Atta-girl, Cath. We've beaten that fucker once before and we can beat him again. Now sit tight there. I'll get us something light to eat and something to drink."

■ ■ ■ ■ ■ ■ ■

I leave Catherine at the table and join the queue at the hotplate. When she's not looking, I take out my phone to make a call. The person on the other end of the line is pleased to hear from me but is taken by surprise when I explain what I want.

"This sounds a bit dodgy, Sean. Are you sure this is above board?"

"It is, but I don't have time to explain. Time is running out and you're the only one I can rely on. I don't know when we will be leaving, but I need you to get to the station now. Are you in or not?"

"Yeh, yeh. Of course I am. Who's this fella you want me to call?"

Catherine looks towards me and I smile at her and nod. "I'll text you his name and number now. I've got to go. Just get here and do exactly what I've told you. Clear?"

"Yeh, yeh. Clear."

Catherine joins me at the hotplate, and I end the call.

"Everything okay, mate? Who was that on the phone?"

"All good, Cath. That was my mum. I just wanted to give her a quick call before ... well, you know what I mean."

Catherine smiles and says, "Yep, I know what you mean. I should probably call my mum. Just in case."

■ ■ ■ ■ ■ ■ ■ ■

With Clive's deadline fast approaching, we are relieved to be finally called back to DI Gray's office at just after 2 p.m. Inspector Thurgood is wearing his full tactical uniform and is armed with a Heckler & Kock MP5 silenced submachine gun and a SIG Sauer P226 automatic pistol. Samantha Stanton is sitting next to him with a white A4 envelope in front of her. Sarah Gray takes the envelope and hands it to me.

"Is this it, ma'am? Is the deal on?"

DI Gray nods, "Yes, it's on." Then looking at Catherine, she adds, "Ms. Hope-Stanton has earned her pay today. This letter is from the Home Secretary and gives approval for both of Douglas's demands. Don't make yourselves comfortable, though, you need to leave now."

"What about backup, ma'am?" I ask.

Thurgood stands up. "My men will have you in sight at all times, Sean. We've also put a GPS tracker on DC Swain's car, just in case we do lose visual at any time."

"You'd better not lose us," Catherine says. "And if Douglas takes me hostage, you have my permission to take the shot, DI Thurgood."

Catherine is clearly worked up, and Thurgood tactfully touches her arm to reassure her. "Well, let's hope that's not necessary, Catherine. But if it is, I promise you, I will make that shot personally."

His smile seems to calm her down and she nods and takes a deep breath. "Thank you. Okay, let's go and get the boss back."

■ ■ ■ ■ ■ ■ ■ ■

We make the drive in silence and by the time we get to Meerholt prison, Ms. Hope Stanton has already spoken with the

Governor and faxed him a copy of the release order to save time.

As we pull into the prison yard, Clive Douglas is escorted outside to meet us. His hands are cuffed, and he is flanked on all sides by four burly prison officers, but he is grinning and clearly feeling pleased with himself.

The Deputy Governor asks me to sign for his release and then she tells her officers to bring him over.

"He's all yours now, Sergeant McMillan. Is there anything else we can assist with?"

I point to the handcuffs. "Yes, take these off please."

The cuffs are removed, and Douglas rubs his wrists. "That's better. Until my current situation, I never realized just how uncomfortable those things were."

"Enough of your bullshit," Catherine snaps. "Let's go."

"Tut-tut, Catherine, not so fast please. Are you both clean? No wires, no weapons, no radios or cellphones?"

"We're clean," I say.

Douglas nods and raises his eyebrows. "Well, call me a doubting Thomas, but I'll check for myself, if you don't mind. Both of you get your arms up."

To the obvious bewilderment of the prison staff, I raise my arms to let Douglas frisk me. When he gets to my crotch area, he winks and says, "I hope that's not a couple of hand grenades in there, Sean. Those could be dangerous."

Satisfied that I am clean, he turns his attention to Catherine. She looks to me and I nod. "Go on, Cath. Get it over with, so that we can get the boss back."

She reluctantly raises her arms and Clive starts his search. In the same way that he searched me, he pats and rolls every inch of her clothing, but his hands linger longer around her crotch than is necessary. When he cups his hands below her breasts he leers directly into her eyes, but Cath remains stony-faced.

Clearly uncomfortable with what she is seeing, the Deputy Governor tries to intervene, but I tell her to stay where she is. Failing to get any reaction from Catherine, Douglas unbuttons her blouse to check for wires. In a final attempt to provoke a reaction, he licks his lips and says, "Nice underwear, princess. Is that bra from Victoria's Secret?"

Catherine buttons up her blouse. "Are we done?" she says.

Ignoring the question, Douglas turns towards the Deputy Governor and holds out his hand to her. "I guess this is goodbye, Miss Campbell. I don't expect we will be meeting again."

She, of course, refuses to shake his hand and he angrily brushes her off. "Suit your bloody self, Billie Jean King." Then to us, "All the same, those dykes. No bloody sense of humor. Get me out of here, McMillan."

■ ■ ■ ■ ■ ■ ■ ■

Catherine takes the driver's seat and I get into the back with Douglas.

"Okay, what now? Where are we going?" I ask.

Clive ignores me and inhales deeply. "Is that Chanel, Catherine? It's very nice. It's been a long time since I smelled something other than my cellmates' BO and farts. Remind me to buy you a new bottle when all of this is over. It suits you."

Catherine remains facing forward, but she shakes her head. "Don't go to any trouble, Clive. When this is over you are going back to prison, so I'd get used to the smell of farts and BO if I were you."

Douglas chuckles to himself. "Beautiful and funny. I'm liking you more and more, DC Swain." Then to me, "Kings Cross Station and get a move on. In thirty minutes, Morgan loses another finger, if I don't make my train on time."

Without waiting for me to say anything, Catherine lights us up and sets course for Kings Cross Station. As we weave through the traffic with our blues and twos clearing a path, Clive is in his element.

"This is just like old times, Sean. We would have made a great team, you know."

"Shut it, Douglas. I'm not like you," I snap.

He raises his eyebrows. "You might not admit it to yourself, but you're more like me than you realize. That head of yours is full of secrets, isn't it? Does your partner really know who you are?"

Catherine takes her eyes off the road for a second to ask, "What's he talking about, Sean?"

"Nothing, Cath. He's talking out of his backside, as always. Keep your eyes on the road."

As she turns away, Douglas leans towards me and whispers, "How is Maria anyway? She's a fine-looking woman. If my situation were different, I would probably have had a crack at that piece of ass myself."

I angrily push him away and point to the entrance to Kings Cross. "Fuck you, Clive. We're here. Where now?"

He laughs and tells me to stop being so sensitive and then points to the car park. "Stop in there and take me to the underground station. The north-bound platform."

As expected, there has been no sign of Inspector Thurgood or his men, but I'm confident that they will be close by. I'm worried, though, that if we go into the underground station it will be much harder for them to follow us without being seen.

My look of concern must be obvious because Douglas smiles and say, "Something wrong, Sean? You look like you've seen a ghost."

"No, everything's fine. Where are we going?"

"I've told you already," he responds. "We've got a train to catch." He then mimics a pair of scissors and says, "Tickety tock, Sergeant McMillan."

Catherine parks and we escort Douglas inside. If Clive has accomplices waiting here to spring him, he has chosen the location well. It's approaching the daily peak time on the rail network and the station is packed with commuters. Even to a trained eye it would be extremely difficult for us to pick out a threat before it was too late.

We force our way through the crowd and take an escalator down into the underground station. With so many anonymous faces coming and going, nobody notices as a hand deftly lifts the back of my jacket and slips something into my pocket. I feel it though and, concerned that the outline might be visible, I subtly straighten my jacket as we cross the bridge to the north-bound platforms. Three trains are lined up next to each other on the tracks and I ask which one we should take.

Douglas checks around to make sure that we are not being followed and then says, "The Glasgow Express. It's the one nearest to the wall."

He is already walking towards the train, but to buy us some more time, I say, "Hang on, Douglas. We are not bloody going to Glasgow."

He stops and turns to face us. "You are if you want to see Kevin Morgan alive again."

He carries on walking and I glance over my shoulder to see if our backup is with us. Catherine whispers to me, "Sean, come on we need to go. Thurgood is with us. I clocked one of his guys watching us as we crossed the bridge."

Reassured, we follow Clive and board the train. He leads us towards an empty carriage, and it suddenly dawns on me that we don't have tickets.

"If a ticket inspector gets on, what then Clive? You didn't think about that, did you?"

Douglas smirks and says, "You really underestimate me, don't you, Sean?"

He reaches under one of the seats and lifts out a padded envelope. It doesn't contain train tickets though. The envelope contains an automatic pistol, which he levels at us.

Pointing to the door facing the station wall, he says, "Don't make yourself comfortable. Both of you, get out."

Catherine opens the door and we drop down into the gap between the train and the wall.

Douglas pushes the pistol into my back. "Get moving, there's a door fifty feet ahead on the right."

We follow his instruction and Douglas pushes us through the unlocked steel door and into a service tunnel. Above us sunlight is streaming through an open manhole.

"Get up the ladder and don't bloody try anything. Any tricks and you both die."

Cath is the first to scale the ladder and as I follow her, I emerge into a deserted backstreet behind Kings Cross Station. Paddy Newman is standing behind Catherine and has one of his huge arms wrapped around her with a knife held across her throat.

"No sudden movements, McMillan. Get in the car."

A white Toyota Landcruiser with the engine running is parked at the side of the road. Paddy gestures again for me to get in and he pushes Catherine in beside me onto the backseat.

Moments later, Douglas joins us and says, "Look out of the window."

We watch as Paddy drops the manhole back into place. Then he walks away and climbs onto a forklift truck. We both already know what he is doing, but it is still a blow to see him place a pallet of concrete blocks over the manhole.

With all hope of backup gone for now, we both turn away from the window and Douglas smirks at us. "Alone at last, but don't look so sad, kiddies. This was always how it was meant to be."

Paddy Newman gets into the front of the car and we pull away into the traffic.

"You've got no intention of going back to prison when this is done, have you, Clive?"

"Do you blame me, Sean? If you were in my position, would you go back to prison, even if a reduced sentence?"

"Where are you taking us?" I interrupt him. "Where is Kevin Morgan?"

"You'll find out soon enough. That's where we are going now."

Cath says, "Earlier on the phone, you said you would take us to the gold first and then to Kevin Morgan."

"Yes, well, I've changed my mind. I've decided to keep the gold for myself. Running away is damn expensive, DC Swain. And besides, Morgan and the gold are in the same place anyway."

I shake my head. "You did plan this from the start, didn't you?"

Douglas nods and then shakes his head. "Yes and no, Sean. I always planned to get my hands on the gold."

"Is that why you helped Rosemary Pinois get a job in central records?" Catherine asks.

"Not exactly. When I helped her get the job it was mainly to help me with my other activities. I was still a Detective Superintendent at that point and having an insider in central records was hugely beneficial to our organization. I did of course know about her history and I knew it was likely that Rosemary and Newman still had the gold stashed somewhere."

"But why would they help you?" I ask. "Why would they be willing to share it with you?"

"Money of course, Sean. They had the gold alright, but they had no way of fencing it. We're not just talking about a handful of sovereigns now, are we? That's where I came in."

"So, you clean the gold and take a big cut in return for Rosemary feeding you information and doctoring files for you. Is that it?" Catherine says.

"Spot on, Catherine. It was a mutually beneficial arrangement that developed into something more after my arrest."

"Something more?" I ask. "What changed?"

Douglas screws up his face and angrily says, "Keep up, Sean. My career was brought to an ignominious bloody end, thanks to you and Catherine. That's what changed."

Before I can stop her, Catherine smirks and says, "You're welcome, Clive."

Douglas raises his hand to slap her and is only stopped by Paddy Newman telling him that we have arrived. He slowly lowers his hand, but he warns Catherine.

"Don't think I won't bloody hit you just because you're a woman. Just give me an excuse, I dare you."

■ ■ ■ ■ ■ ■ ■ ■

Ashdown Forest has barely changed in the more than thirty years since I was last here. Apart from the lines on her face, I get a distinct feeling of déjà vu when I see Rosemary standing next to the recently excavated pit.

Neither of us focus on Rosemary for very long, though. Kevin Morgan is on his knees at the edge of the pit with his head down. His arms are cuffed behind his back and his eyes are covered with a blood-stained yellow bandana. There are also fresh bruises on his face to indicate a recent beating. Douglas urges us forward and, ignoring his instruction to keep quiet, I shout, "Boss, we're here. Don't worry, we're going to get you out of here."

At the sound of my voice Morgan lifts his head, "Sean, is that you? You have to—"

Rosemary hits him across the back of the head with her pistol and roughly yanks him backwards.

"Shut it, Morgan. And you, McMillan. Get them on their knees, Paddy. I want them to see this. I want them to feel my pain."

Newman pushes us both down and keeps us covered with a sawn-off shotgun, while Clive goes to the other side of the pit to join Rosemary.

He stands behind Kevin Morgan and drums his fingers on the top of Morgan's head as he sizes us up. "Okay, now that all the gang is here, we can get on with what we came to do."

"What was she talking about?" Catherine asks. "What does she want us to see? Killing the boss will achieve nothing. Just take the gold and let us go."

Douglas shakes his head and Catherine tries again to appeal to his better nature, if he has one.

"It doesn't have to end like this, Clive," she calls out. "All of you can just walk away now. Be the bigger man and promise me that whatever happens now, you won't kill him. He's got a family, for God's sake."

Douglas mockingly slow claps and then says, "That's very touching, DC Swain. But this is a little more complicated than you realize. I promise not to hurt DCI Morgan, but unfortunately I can't speak for my friends. Nor can I guarantee the safety of either of you."

At this new revelation, we both try to get to our feet, but Paddy roughly pushes us back down and puts his gun against the back of my head. "It's your choice, McMillan. You get the first barrel and the bitch gets the second."

I'm scared myself, but Catherine is visibly trembling. I take her hand and squeeze it, before taking a deep breath to calm myself.

"Okay, we know that we're not leaving here alive," I say, "so how about you let us know at least what all of this has been about."

"That's a long boring story, Sean. I'm sure you don't want to hear about it."

"We're in no hurry," I say. "How about you humor us?" I'm gambling on the fact that clever villains like Douglas have an Achille's heel: vanity.

Douglas smiles and nods. "Good, I was hoping you were going to say that. I do want you to know what this was all about."

Rosemary is clearly impatient. In no mood to waste time, she pushes her pistol against the back of Morgan's head.

"Enough of this dramatic shit, Clive. I've waited long enough for this moment."

But before she can pull the trigger, Clive pulls her away.

"You'll get your moment. You have my word on it, but not just yet."

She reluctantly lowers her weapon and Clive smiles. "Okay, let's start at the beginning, shall we? You didn't have any luck finding Terry Pinois, did you?"

"That's because it wasn't Terry; it was Thierry," Catherine says.

"No, no. You must be mixed up," Douglas chuckles. "I definitely said Terry Pinois the first time I met you in prison, didn't I?"

"Yes, you did," I say. "But that was wrong."

"Not wrong, Sean. I think I just got mixed up. Or maybe I got the letters mixed up. It's easy to get confused at my age."

Cath and I look at each other trying to work out what he means. I'm about to ask him to explain himself when Kevin Morgan lifts his head to say, "An anagram. I think he means an anagram."

In response, Douglas slaps him on the back of the head.

"That was an unwelcome interruption, but yes it's an anagram."

I shake my head. "What the hell are you talking about?"

Douglas looks at me and scowls. "I was going to be generous with my time, but you're really starting to piss me off with that attitude of yours, Sean. You now have sixty seconds to solve the anagram or daddy here gets a bullet in the skull."

Rosemary pushes her pistol back against Morgan's head, then she checks her watch and says, "Sixty seconds and counting, Sean. Fifty-nine, fifty-eight, fifty-seven ..."

"Wait, no. We need more time," I exclaim.

"Fifty-four, fifty-three, fifty-two ..."

"Fuck, okay. Cath, I need you to focus." I spell out the letters to the name Terry Pinois and then I tell her to close her eyes and imagine the letters on a sheet of white paper.

"Come on, Cath. You can do it. You're the brains of this team."

On the other side of the pit, Rosemary continues the countdown, "Thirty-five, thirty-four, thirty-three ..."

My heart is pounding, and I watch nervously as Cath clenches her eyes tightly shut.

"Nineteen, eighteen, seventeen ..."

"Come on, Cath, picture it. Think like Douglas."

"Twelve, eleven, ten, nine. Times running out, bitch. Five, four, three, tw—"

Cath's eyes suddenly open and she shouts, "Wait, please. I've got it. It's iron pyrites."

I have no idea what she is talking about, but Clive Douglas nods and claps his hands. "Congratulations, DC Swain. I am suitably impressed."

"What are you talking about, Cath? What the hell is 'iron pyrites'?"

Kevin Morgan raises his head again and says, "It's fool's gold, son. Iron pyrite, or iron pyrites, is the geological name for fool's gold."

Douglas claps again. Then he playfully ruffles Morgan's hair and comments on what a brain box he is, before removing his blindfold and throwing it into the pit.

"What can I say, folks? In prison time passes very slowly, so I had a lot of time on my hands."

"So, what? That was meant to be funny?" I ask.

Douglas shrugs. "I personally found it to be very amusing, but I guess I'm looking at it from a different perspective to you. Funny or not, though, you have to agree on one thing."

"And what would that be?" Catherine asks sarcastically.

"You have to agree that the reference to fool's gold is highly appropriate to the situation that you find yourselves in now."

He points to a black transit van sitting low on its suspension at the edge of the track. "There is enough gold in the back of that van to ensure that we live the rest of our lives in luxury. And by we, I'm talking about myself, Rosemary, and Mr. Newman. You three, however ... well, I guess you know already that you're the fools and this is not going to end well for you."

I shake my head. "You've got what you want. Just take the gold and go. What good will killing us do?"

Douglas shakes his head and then theatrically drums his fingers on Morgan's head again. "I'm sorry, Sean. It stopped being about the gold after my arrest. With me tucked away inside, in let's say ... a less than advantageous position, I needed something more to keep Rosie and Paddy interested in helping me."

"In helping you escape you mean?" Catherine asks.

"Of course, Catherine. They needed me on the outside to convert the gold into cash, but Rosemary also took advantage of my situation to help her with something else."

"With what?" I ask.

"With me," Morgan says.

Rosemary viciously yanks Morgan backwards by the cuffs again and screams for him to keep quiet. "You shut the hell up, or I will shoot you dead right now."

Douglas allows a few seconds for things to calm down again, then he says, "Another unwelcome interruption, but DCI Morgan is right. In return for a share of the gold and Rosemary's assistance in getting me out, I was asked to help deliver Kevin Morgan."

"But why?" I ask. "What has he got to do with this?"

Morgan is about to speak again, but he is cut off by a vicious slap from Rosemary across his face. "I told you to keep your bloody mouth shut."

Douglas comes to our side of the pit and hands me an envelope before returning to the other side. "Read it. It will tell you all you need to know."

Inside the envelope I'm surprised to find an unredacted copy of the Thierry Pinois inquest report. I scan through to find the names of the officers involved in the death of Thierry, but all mean nothing to me, until I get to the name of the officer that pulled the trigger. I show the report to Catherine and point to the name, then I look back to Douglas who knowingly asks, "You found something, Sean?"

When I hesitate, he says, "Don't be shy. We are all friends here. Go on, what did you find?"

I make eye contact with Kevin Morgan and he nods. "Go on, son. It makes no difference now."

I look back down at the report and read the name of the shooter, "Constable Anthony Morgan. Is that—?"

Kevin Morgan nods, "Anthony Morgan was my father. He was the—"

"He was the murdering bastard that killed my father in cold blood," Rosemary screams. She lunges for Morgan, but Douglas steps in front of her and holds her back. "Soon, Rosie. I promise, not much longer."

"So, this is it," I say. "We all die so that you can escape with a boatload of cash and so that Rosie can get her revenge for what the boss's father did."

"No, no. Sean. Don't sell yourself short. For me it wasn't just about escaping with a few quid in my pocket. Rosemary is not the only one motivated by revenge. You ruined my life, McMillan. I know that killing you both won't change that, but it will make me feel a whole lot better about things."

Obviously concluding that she has nothing to lose, Cath looks over her shoulder at Paddy. "And what about this fat sack of shit? What was his motivation?"

The barrel of Paddy's shotgun strikes her on the back of the head and Catherine topples forward into the pit. It is no more than three or four feet deep, but as an unconscious deadweight, she hits the bottom with a sickening thud.

"For God's sake, Douglas," Morgan protests. "This has gone far enough. Just do what you will with me, but let Sean and Catherine go. They have nothing to do with what happened to Thierry Pinois."

Rosemary grabs Morgan's hair and pushes his face over the edge of the pit. "Don't you bloody dare say my father's name. I've felt the pain of his death for more than thirty years and before you die, I want you to feel the same kind of pain."

She pulls Morgan back from the edge and then turns to Clive. "You owe me this. I kept my end of the bargain."

Douglas nods his head. "Sure, why not. I'm bored with this anyway. How do you want to do it?"

Rosemary points to me and says to Paddy, "Give him a shovel. I want Morgan to watch his princess get buried alive before I kill him."

Before either of us can react, Douglas drops a noose over Kevin Morgan's head and viciously yanks him backwards as Paddy presses the barrel of his shotgun against the side of my head. Douglas then drags Morgan back to the edge of the pit and forces him to look in.

"If it's any consolation, I think she might be dead already. Now stand up and start shoveling, McMillan."

Paddy drags me up and thrusts a shovel into my hands. "You heard the man, McMillan. Get on with it."

Catherine is face down at the bottom of the pit and doesn't appear to be breathing. I appeal again for them to let us go, but Douglas just smiles.

"Sean needs a little encouragement, Rosie. Shoot Morgan in the leg," he suggests.

"Okay, okay," I plead. "Please don't do it."

Rosemary lowers her pistol and to buy time I slowly start to shovel earth into the pit. I'm not completely certain, but as the third load of soil hits her legs, I'm sure that Catherine moves. I stop to check for movement and Paddy jabs me between the shoulder blades with the shotgun. "Enough of the bloody games, McMillan. Shovel faster and get her head covered as well."

"What's he playing at?" Douglas asks.

Before Paddy can answer, we all hear something, and Douglas tells us to be quiet. Two seconds later a Pitbull terrier comes bounding towards us and in the distance, we hear someone whistling and shouting.

"Tyson, here boy. Tyson, where are you, boy?"

The dog stops a few feet away from us and adopts a defensive stance. Moments later, its owner emerges from the woods. His cellphone is held to his ear and he appears not to notice what is going on until he gets to within ten feet of us.

Clive Douglas raises his pistol. "It's not your lucky day, son. Now put the phone down and put that mutt on a leash."

Picking up on Clive's aggression, the Pitbull starts to snarl, and Paddy turns his weapon on the dog. "I'd shut that bleedin' mongrel up right now if you bloody know what's good for you."

The dog owner looks nervously to each of us, then he carefully raises his hands. "Okay, I don't want any trouble. Whatever is going on here is none of my business. If you just let me finish my call and put my dog on its lead, I'll get out of your hair."

"Just stay right where you are," Douglas says. "And hang up that bloody phone right now."

The stranger holds out his hands again. "Okay, you're the boss. Just take it easy." Then, far louder than is necessary, he says, "It's just my Uncle Mike. I'll tell him I'm going to be late for dinner."

From that point on, everything happens very quickly. Thurgood and his hostage rescue team emerge from the woods and challenge Paddy, Rosemary, and Clive to drop their weapons. At the exact same moment, Catherine lunges for Morgan and tries to pull him into the pit with her but instead ends up in a life or death tug-of-war with Clive Douglas, which only ends when the Pitbull clamps its jaws around Clive's wrist. Clive howls with pain and releases Morgan, who then tumbles into the pit on top of Catherine.

While this is happening, I make a grab for Paddy's shotgun, but the old bastard is freakishly strong. He wrestles me to the ground and forces the weapon up towards my face. He pulls the trigger and I jerk my head away just in time, but the shockwave from the blast leaves me stunned and momentarily deaf. Paddy gets to his feet and I can see his lips moving, but I can't hear what he is saying. Neither do I hear the warning from Inspector Thurgood for Paddy to drop his weapon.

I do, though, see the neat line of holes that appear on Paddy's chest as Thurgood opens fire. For a moment, the big fella remains standing, as he looks down at the holes in disbelief that he has been shot. Then the blood comes. At first there are just a few small spots. Then the small spots become small patches that soon merge to form one large dark patch on his jacket.

The shotgun falls from his hand and almost in slow motion Paddy Newman falls forward like a mighty oak tree felled in a forest. I roll away and his body misses me by inches as it slams into the ground.

Inspector Thurgood stands over me, grins, and offers me a helping hand to get up, "You doing okay, Sean? Are you hurt?"

More concerned for Catherine and Kevin Morgan, I turn and am relieved to see them both sitting by the edge of the pit being looked after by two of Thurgood's men. One of them is holding an ice pack to Catherine's head and another is removing Morgan's handcuffs.

Behind them Clive Douglas is face down in the dirt with his hands cuffed behind his back being watched over by the dogwalker, his Pitbull, and another armed officer. Ever the showman, Darren puts his boot on Douglas's back and smiles, but I don't have time to return the pleasantry. I turn around to find Inspector Thurgood. "What about Rosemary? Where the hell is she? We need to get after her."

Thurgood points towards the woods. "She made a run for it while you were grappling with Newman. Don't worry, she won't get far. My other team have gone after her. Just leave it to my boys. This is what they do."

DCI Morgan shakily gets to his feet. "To hell with that. This is our case and I'll be damned if I'm going to let another team bring Rosemary Pinois in. This is personal. Come on, Sean. She can't have gone far."

I point to Morgan's left hand which is wrapped in a filthy blood-stained bandage. "Sir, you've lost a lot of blood. This is not a good idea."

Thurgood backs me up and suggests that Morgan would be better off waiting for the paramedics. "Sean is right, sir. You really need to be checked over as soon as possible. That hand could be infect—"

If any confirmation was needed of Morgan's health and his ability to think rationally, his curt interruption of Thurgood is it.

"Thank you, Inspector. As the ranking officer here, I think I'll be the judge of what I need and what I don't need. This case is under the jurisdiction of my department and my officers. Now, if you don't mind, I would like to borrow your sidearm please."

Thurgood looks uncertain and Morgan holds out his hand. "I'm assuming you don't want us to go after an armed felon without a weapon?"

Thurgood reluctantly hands his automatic pistol to Morgan, then he orders his team to stay with Catherine and Clive Douglas.

"You lot hold fast here. I'm going after our third felon with DS McMillan and DCI Morgan. The paramedics should be here in a few minutes to check DC Swain over. If Douglas gives you any trouble, you have my permission to shoot him."

Darren, who is still standing guard over him, laughs. "Don't worry, they won't need to shoot him. I'll get Tyson here to rip chunks out of his ass."

Morgan scowls at Darren. "Thank you, Mr. Phillips. I think you've done quite enough already."

Then, looking disapprovingly at me, he says, "We can talk about the involvement of Mr. Phillips in this case when all of this is over."

He hands me Thurgood's pistol, "Until then, it's probably better that you have this, son. I'm too involved to remain impartial."

I'm unsure of his meaning and I ask, "Sir?"

Morgan leans in and whispers, "It was Pinois that took my finger with a pair of garden secateurs. Better it's you that is armed, Sean. Come on, let's go get her."

■ ■ ■ ■ ■ ■ ■ ■

We head off in pursuit of Rosemary but have barely covered fifty yards when Thurgood tells us to stop. Away to the right we see Rosemary emerge from the woods with Thurgood's second team flanking her.

Rosemary continues walking slowly towards us. Her hands are raised above her head, but she is still holding her pistol and is ignoring the warnings to drop the weapon and to stand still.

When she gets within twenty feet, Thurgood steps in front of us and raises his MP5K.

"Stop where you are, or I will fire!"

Rosemary stops and lowers her arms.

"I'm warning you, drop the weapon, put your arms in the air where I can see them, and then slowly get down onto your knees."

Ignoring Thurgood completely, she calmly looks all around her and then says, "I want to speak to Morgan and McMillan."

Thurgood takes a step closer. "That's fine. I'm sure they would like to talk to you as well. But first you need to drop your weapon and get down on your knees."

Rosemary shakes her head. "Something has been bugging me since you first came to my house, Sean."

Thurgood starts to shout another warning. But Morgan stops him. "It's okay. Let's hear what she has to say. Go on then, Rosemary. We're listening. What's been bugging you?"

She looks around again, then she says to me, "When you came to my home the first time, you reminded me of someone from my past. And not just me either. Paddy also thought he recognized you. The name was the same, but it's not possible. Perhaps your fath—?"

Realizing that to say more could incriminate her for a yet unrevealed crime, Rosemary stops mid-sentence.

"You're not making sense," Morgan says. "What has this got to do with anything?"

"You're right," she replies. "It doesn't make sense. It was a lifetime ago and it's nothing more than a coincidence."

Morgan looks bewildered. "I'm really not following you. Is that it?"

Rosemary nods. "That's all for Sergeant McMillan."

"Okay. And what about me? You said you wanted to speak to both of us."

Rosemary looks at Morgan's bloodied hand and sighs, "I wanted to say sorry. For your finger, I mean."

Morgan shakes his head. "There really is no need. Just hand over the weapon and come in peaceful—"

"No, you don't understand. I'm sorry that it wasn't your fucking head."

She raises her weapon, but a split second before she can fire, the force of a non-lethal flexible baton round between the shoulder blades hurls her forward. A second round hits her wrist and the pistol falls from her hand. Thurgood's officers pile onto her within seconds and after a brief struggle she is cuffed and lifted back to her feet. They bring her to us, and I ask the boss if he would like to make the arrest. He shakes his head.

"I wouldn't dream of it, Sean. This one is down to you and Catherine. Go on. You do the honors."

■ ■ ■ ■ ■ ■ ■

Despite facing the prospect of spending the rest of her life behind bars, Rosemary remains defiant as I arrest her.

"Rosemary Pinois, I am arresting you on suspicion of conspiracy to commit armed robbery. For incitement to the murder of Michael Davies on the 4th February 1984. For the aggravated kidnapping of DCI Kevin Morgan. For conspiracy to pervert the course of justice, and for the murders of George John Benson and Peter Edwin Lane on or around the 24th of December 1983 ..."

At the mention of the murders of Benson and Lane, the boss gives me a sideways glance, but he allows me to carry on.

"... You do not have to say anything, but it may harm your defense if you do not mention when questioned something which you later rely on in court. Anything you do say may be given in evidence."

I then shake my head and add, "And that's just for starters."

Even listening to such serious charges, Rosemary remains impassive. I shake my head and nod to the officers holding her. "Go on, lads. Take her away."

Rosemary is escorted back to where Clive Douglas is being held and both are placed in the back of separate unmarked police vehicles. Catherine joins us and we watch as they are driven away under armed escort. Once they are out of sight, Morgan turns to us and shakes his head. "What the hell is the world bloody coming to? If Douglas had cooperated, he probably would have got that reduction in sentence and his move to Cat C. Now what has he got?"

"He's got a roof over his head and three meals a day, which is more than he bloody deserves," Cath says. "I'd bring back hanging just for him, if I could."

I nod my agreement and then say, "Forget about him for now. Boss, you need to get that hand looked at."

Morgan looks down at the bloody bandage around his hand. "I will, son. But first things first."

He straightens up and offers his other hand to Inspector Thurgood. "In all the excitement, I didn't get a chance to thank you. You saved our bacon and as soon as I'm up to it, I'd like to take you and your lads for a few pints."

Thurgood blushes slightly. "It was nothing, sir. It was really all down to DS McMillan and his ... Um, sorry, what was your name again?"

Darren has been quietly standing to the side with his dog, but he now comes forward and offers his hand to Kevin Morgan. "It's Darren. Darren Phillips. We met previously at Sean's commendation ceremony."

Morgan nods, "Yes. I remember you, Mr. Phillips. You took both barrels of a shotgun in the chest. I trust that you're now fully recovered?"

"Fit as a bloody fiddle," Darren replies with a grin.

"Good. I'm pleased to hear it."

Morgan shakes Darren's hand and thanks him for his assistance in our rescue. "We appear to be in your debt once again, Darren. I'll be sure to recommend you for some kind of reward or recognition, but for now would you mind leaving us to finish up here?"

Darren looks to me for guidance and I nod. "Go on, mate. I'll give you a call tomorrow. Thanks for everything."

He shakes his head and holds out his hand. "That's not what I meant, Sean. You've still got my phone."

"Oh right, yeh." I reach into my back pocket and hand Darren his iPhone. "Thanks again, mate. I owe you one."

As he walks away, Catherine nods appreciatively. "I was wondering how they found us. That was a smart move, Sean. It would have been nice to have been in the loop though."

"Yeh, I'm sorry about that, Cath. I wasn't entirely convinced it was going to work, so I thought it better that—"

"Yes, yes, save the apologies for later," Morgan interrupts. "Would somebody please tell me what the hell you're talking about?"

"Yes, sir," Inspector Thurgood explains, "Mr. Phillips was able to slip his cellphone into Sean's back pocket as they passed through the crowded concourse at Kings Cross Station. He then called and gave me his iCloud email address and password. From there it was a simple matter of tracing the phone location through the Find My iPhone application. Simple, but effective, sir. Without it, we may not have got to you in time."

Morgan nods his head. "Yes, well, all's well that ends well, I suppose. And, like I said earlier, we can discuss the involvement of a civilian in one of your cases again at another time, Sean."

Catherine doesn't say anything, but I start to burn up when I see her scowling at me. Thankfully, I'm saved from further embarrassment when Thurgood points towards the black transit van. "Would you like to see what two hundred million pounds of gold looks like?"

We follow him to the back of the van and one of his men opens the rear doors. The crates that I last saw more than thirty years ago are neatly stacked on the floor of the van but being buried for so long in damp soil has darkened the wood. The crates have also visibly started to decay. So, when Thurgood reaches inside the van, he is easily able to pull one of them open using just his hands. He carefully lifts out one of the gold ingots and passes it to DCI Morgan.

"The recovery of this should make a few people very happy. You should be very proud of this, sir. It's a great success for you and your team."

Morgan looks down at the ingot thoughtfully, then he hands it back and shakes his head. "Yes, but was it worth people dying for?"

He closes the doors and turns around to face us. "Tell me about George Benson and Peter Lane, Sean. You've just arrested Rosemary Pinois on suspicion of their murder. Who are they?"

Catherine comes closer and says, "Benson and Lane are two of the three Securicor guards that disappeared after the robbery, sir." Then looking directly at me, "Sean can tell us why he thinks that Rosemary might be responsible for their deaths. And why just those two, Sean? What about the third guy?"

Desperately trying not to look uncomfortable, I backtrack and blame the heat of the moment. "Actually, it was just a shot in the dark to see Rosemary's reaction. I meant to say all three names, but the adrenaline was still pumping, and I forgot to mention the third missing man, Stuart Goldsmith. Sorry about that, sir."

"But you think Rosemary was responsible for their disappearance?" Morgan asks.

"Yes, sir, I do. And if I were a betting man, I'd say that their remains are not too far from here."

I point to the pit and say, "That's only a few feet deep, sir, but if you look closer, you can see that it was much deeper originally. My guess is that Pinois, Davies, or Newman killed the missing guards sometime before the robbery and dumped them here. After the robbery, they must have returned here to bury the gold. I can't see them wasting time or increasing the risk of discovery by digging a second hole."

Morgan and Thurgood both nod and then Morgan says, "That's plausible enough, I guess. Let's leave that to the forensics boys, though. It's been a hell of a day and I need to let my wife know that I'm okay."

He now looks noticeably frail and the medical team that have been waiting patiently move in and escort him to an ambulance. We leave him under the care of the paramedics and Inspector Thurgood arranges for another patrol car to take us home.

"Don't worry about your boss," he says to us. "He's as tough as they come and he's in good hands. Just let the driver know where you want to go. Otherwise, you're both welcome to join me and the lads for a drink if you're up for it. We always go for a drink after a successful operation. It's a bit of a team tradition."

We both decline and Thurgood smiles. "That's fine. It's been quite a day for you pair as well." Then looking at Catherine, he flashes a smile and adds, "Another time maybe."

Catherine returns his smile. "Yes, I'd like that, Mike."

When she sees me smirking, she quickly straightens her face and says we should go. We leave Thurgood at the crime scene to wait for the coroner and forensic teams and we wearily climb into the back of the patrol car.

■ ■ ■ ■ ■ ■ ■ ■

As the driver starts the engine, Catherine immediately turns away from me and I ask her if she is alright. She ignores me and continues to stare out the window. It's no great surprise. I can tell that she is pissed off with me for keeping her in the dark. She's reacted this way in the past.

This time, however, the tension is far more palpable than anything I have ever experienced with her before. In an effort to not make the atmosphere any worse than it already is, I remain quiet in the hope that she will change her mind and speak to me.

When twenty minutes pass without a single word or even so much as a passing glance between us, I touch her hand and try to lighten the mood.

"The boss was right, Cath. It has been a hell of a day. In fact, it's been a hell of a few days. I don't know about you, but I'm ready for a long hot soak in the bath. I feel like I've been run over by a herd of elephants."

Catherine turns to face me, but her response is not what I was expecting. "I'd take a shower if I was you, Sean. The last time you took a bath, it didn't work out so well for you. Or have you forgotten?"

Although taken aback by her sarcasm, I laugh it off and try to carry on as if she were joking. "Yeh, I did forget about that for a moment. Thanks for the reminder, mate."

I then point to her head. "That lump looks nasty. You should get it checked out when you can. Just to be on the safe side."

This time her response leaves me in no doubt whatsoever about how annoyed she is with me. "Thanks for that, Sean. If you were half as good at sharing as you are at dishing out your crappy advice, we would make a bloody good team. But as it is, you're a comple—"

"Whoa, Cath, what' all this about?" I interrupt.

"Just forget it, Sean. I'm not in the mood for your shit right now."

She turns back towards the window and tells me that she doesn't want to talk.

"Maybe not," I say, "but if there is something on your mind, I'd like to hear it please."

Cath turns back and shakes her head. "It's the same bloody thing every time with you, Sean. Despite everything we have been through together and all your promises, you continue to lie to me or to keep me out of the loop when it comes to critical information or pieces of evidence."

"Cath, I already explained about Darren and the phone."

"And what about the murders of Benson and Lane?" Cath snaps. "Or was it of Benson, Lane, and Goldsmith? And don't give me any shit about a hunch or getting a gut feeling when you looked at that bloody hole, Sean. You know exactly what forensics are going to find in that hole, don't you?"

I start to stutter a denial, but Cath raises a hand to cut me off. "Stop, Sean. You're a bloody liar and you're just embarrassing yourself."

"Cath, it's not how it seems. If I could tell you, I would. I want to but—"

We are interrupted by the driver telling us we have reached my apartment block. He pulls up outside the entrance and I tell Catherine that I will explain everything in the morning.

"I know how you feel, Cath, but now is not the time to talk about this. We're both pretty beaten up and it will do us both the world of good to get some rest. Let's talk again tomorrow with a clear head. Okay?"

"Would there be any point?" Catherine asks. "No, don't even answer that. Just go, Sean."

I try to speak but she stops me. "Please. Just go before I say something I'll regret."

I reluctantly get out and am about to walk away when the window opens. "Sean, wait a second."

Hoping that she has had a change of heart, I start to ask her if she would like to come up to talk, but she stops me dead.

"When was the last time you were in Ashdown Forest before today?"

I look puzzled and ask, "Sorry. What do you mean?"

"It's a simple enough question, Sean. Just bloody answer me. Have you been to Ashdown Forest before?"

I shake my head. "No, Cath. Before today, I've never set foot in the place."

Catherine shakes her head in dismay and then reaches into her coat pocket to take out a small black leather wallet. She opens the wallet and uses the back of her sleeve to wipe away some of the years of ingrained grime before passing my warrant card through the window. Although badly faded, my ID picture is still clear enough to see and with a sickening jolt, I finally realize why Catherine is so angry with me.

"So how do you bloody explain this then? I saw it sticking out of the dirt when I was face down in that pit waiting to die. You have been to Ashdown Forest before, Sean, and judging by the state of that wallet and warrant card it wasn't recently either."

"Cath, it's really not what you think. If you give me a chance, I can te—"

"Save it, Sean. I'm really not in the mood for any more of your bullshit today. But if I were you, I'd think very carefully tonight about what you're going to tell me. Because tomorrow I want answers and if I don't like or believe what I hear, I'm going straight to Morgan to tell him what I think is going on. And don't think I won't, Sean. Friend or no friend, if you lie to me tomorrow, I will finish you. Take me home please, driver."

Left alone on the pavement watching Catherine drive away there is only one thing I can think of to say to myself … "Fuck!"

Turn the page for an extract from...

Walk With Me

One Hundred Days of Crazy
By Ernesto H Lee

"Walk With Me, One Hundred Days of Crazy is a novel with a powerful tale of romance and one that explores the deep longings of the human heart." Ruffina Oserio for Readers Favorite.

"Walk With Me, One Hundred Days of Crazy by Ernesto H Lee is a fascinating book packed with craziness, emotions, family, and love (lots of love)." Ankita Shukla for Readers Favorite.

At forty years old, Mark Rennie was the man that appeared to have it all. As a successful commodities trader with one of the leading London trading houses, he was happy, healthy and, engaged to be married to the woman he loved. Then came the devastating news that would change his life forever. Less than two years later, his health is in tatters, his fiancée is gone, and his life is reduced to nothing more than a series of difficult choices and harsh realities. In search of answers and, in search of a drink, he walks an unfamiliar part of London.

He doesn't find the answers he is looking for, but he does find Karen. With Karen, he finds hope. With Karen, he finds love. With Karen, nothing is ever going to be the same again.

Available Now

Walk With Me
One Hundred Days of Crazy

By Ernesto H Lee

Preface

"Good morning, ladies and gentlemen, this is your captain speaking. I hope you all had a pleasant flight and were able to get some rest during the night. For your information, we will shortly begin our descent, and we expect to be on the ground by 11.42 am. If you would like to adjust your watches, the current local time is seven minutes past eleven and the weather is a crisp twenty-eight degrees Fahrenheit. For any passengers that are visiting for the first time, I would encourage you to open your window blinds to take in the breathtaking scenery of the Alps as we pass overhead. It really is a sight to see. Finally, on behalf of myself and the rest of the crew, I would like to thank you for choosing to fly with us and we hope to see you onboard another of our flights soon. Thank you, and please enjoy your stay in our beautiful country."

■ ■ ■ ■ ■ ■ ■ ■

Usually, what I enjoy most about flying Business Class on a long-haul flight is the ability to turn my seat into a fully lie-flat bed. My usual routine is to eat, have a couple of drinks, watch a movie and then sleep until just before landing.

On this occasion, however, I have struggled to concentrate on sleep for more than a few minutes at a time. After trying unsuccessfully for more than an hour, I resign myself to a sleepless night and turn my attention back to the inflight entertainment system.

My next four hours were spent absentmindedly surfing the various movie, TV and music channels trying to find something to keep me occupied. It is a great relief then to finally see daylight creeping through my window.

Captain Müller is absolutely right, the Alps are stunning and probably even more so at this time of the year. The morning sunshine reflecting off of the snowcapped peaks is both magnificent and oddly captivating.

Before his announcement, I was so lost in my own thoughts that I only realized how long I had been staring out of the window when Müller's German accent came to life on the PA.

I look down at my watch and am surprised to see that more than an hour has passed since I last checked it. For the life of me, I have no idea what I might have been thinking about during this time. Given the circumstances of this trip, it is hardly surprising I have been preoccupied, but to remember absolutely nothing of the last hour is extremely unusual. I can't decide, though, if remembering nothing is worrying or liberating. I rack my brains for answers for another few minutes before I finally give up and turn away from the window.

Unlike me, Karen has been sleeping soundly for almost the entire flight. Even Captain Müller's chirpy morning announcement has failed to disturb her. I lean in to kiss her on the forehead. Her breathing is slow and relaxed, and I consider for a moment to allow her to sleep for longer. But I know she will be annoyed if I do. This is the last leg of an incredible journey that we started together more than three months ago, and today of all days, she will want to arrive at our final destination looking her very best. I smile at the thought of everything we have done together in these last three months, and then I gently shake her shoulder.

"Karen, we're going to be landing soon; you need to wake up now and get ready."

She doesn't react and I shake her for a second time. This time she reaches up and squeezes my hand.

"Just a few more minutes, babe. Please, I'm so tired. I promise, just give me a few minutes more."

Her eyes remain closed while she speaks, and even though she has been asleep for almost eight hours, I know how badly she needs the rest. The cabin crew haven't yet started their preparation for landing, so I kiss her hand and gently place it back down on her pillow.

"Okay, just a few minutes more, darling. Go on, go back to sleep now."

My gesture is returned with a sleepy smile, and within seconds she is sleeping peacefully again. I take the opportunity to freshen up in the washroom before returning to my seat.

Then, all too soon, the cabin crew start their rounds and politely ask me to wake Karen up. I lean over to speak to her, but there is no need for me to touch her or to say anything. She opens her eyes and after a short pause to get her bearings, she sits up and takes a deep breath.

"I don't think I ever truly appreciated sleep until we started this thing, Mark. No matter what's going on in life, when you sleep, you can take yourself away from everything. You can build your own alternate reality and, to a certain point, you can create your own destiny. Does that make sense, or am I rambling?"

"It actually does make sense," I reply. "It's a reality that doesn't last, but while it does last, it's a comfort. So, how was last night's reality?"

"Ironically, it was probably the best one in a long time, Mark. Do you think that's because we are near the end?"

This question brings back the seriousness of our situation and the expression on my face shows it. The look on Karen's own face tells me instantly that she regrets asking the question. She takes my hand and apologizes for upsetting me.

"Mark, I'm so sorry, that was a stupid thing to say. The words were out of my mouth before I could stop myself. I really am sorry. Please forgive me?"

I squeeze her hand and force the smile back onto my face.

"There is nothing to forgive, Karen. It's just a shame that you didn't bring me along for that reality. I spent the night twiddling my thumbs and listening to you snoring. I had to check under your blanket a few times to make sure it was still you and not an escaped rhinoceros. No offense, of course. To the rhinoceros, I mean."

In response, she playfully punches my arm and then shakily gets to her feet. She steadies herself on the headrest of the seat in front and I pass her handbag up to her.

"Go on, go and get freshened up. The Captain is going to be putting on the seatbelt signs soon and I doubt you'll be allowed into the country looking like a hobo. It would be such a shame if I had to leave you on your own at immigration."

"Yeh, you wish," she replies. "Even if I was refused entry, you wouldn't leave me on my own. It's not possible because you, Mr. Mark Rennie, are completely infatuated with me."

With that, she winks and then blows me a kiss before stepping into the aisle and walking slowly towards the washroom.

Knowing full well that I am watching her, she stops at the door and playfully wiggles her ass, much to the amusement of myself and all the other guys that have been following her progression down the aisle.

She steps inside and closes the door, leaving me alone once again with my thoughts. Like it or not, Karen knows me almost as well as I know myself. I'm not just infatuated with her, I am head over heels, up to my neck, batshit crazy in love with her. Despite the utter irony of our situation, the last few months have been the happiest of my life, and no matter what happens from here on, nothing will ever change that.

Chapter One

Four Months Earlier

After my initial diagnosis, I had spent nearly two weeks researching my condition and looking into who the top specialists in the UK were. My final shortlist had three names on it. After a consultation with each of them, I had sat down with my father and brother to make the most important decision of my life to date.

With his impeccable credentials and an even more impressive track record of success, I finally chose to put my faith and my life in the hands of the eminent Harley Street Consultant Oncologist, Dr. Alan Bleakley. More than eighteen months on, he now feels like a close friend, and I feel like I know the layout of his surgery better than I know my own apartment.

As with all close friends, there is an unwritten rule that no matter how harsh the message or the opinion, friends should always be honest with each other. They shouldn't be afraid to tell the truth and they should never, under any circumstance, try to sugarcoat the message in an attempt to spare the feelings of the other person.

With Alan, this has never been an issue. By the very nature of his profession, Alan Bleakley is as straight as they come when delivering bad news. Unfortunately, this is of no consolation to me, and despite there having always been a chance of this scenario, it's a bombshell none the less. After delivering the latest bad news, Alan tactfully stays quiet and allows me a couple of minutes to fully digest it, before he speaks again.

"Mark, I know we've discussed this possibility before, but I think now is the time to look at the options we discussed prior to your last transrectal MRI scan. You should really consider the—"

"Sorry, doctor, but am I missing something here?" I angrily interrupt. "You've just told me that my tumor has grown and that the cancer may also now have spread to my lymph nodes and bladder. Is there any real point in continuing this conversation? When I first met you, you confidently told me there was a ninety-one percent survival rate for prostate cancer at my age. That was pretty good odds by any measure. So, what the hell went wrong? Did I back the wrong horse?"

My outburst is completely uncalled for, but, ever the professional, Alan doesn't immediately respond. Instead, he allows another short pause for me to compose myself, during which I immediately regret speaking to him in such a way.

My reaction to the news that my cancer is now at stage four is most likely a scenario that he has witnessed many times before, and whilst I have no doubt that he has heard a lot worse from other patients, this is still no excuse for my behavior, and I offer an apology.

"I'm sorry, Alan. I didn't mean that the way it sounded. I'm truly grateful for your advice and support. I just never thought it would ever get this far. I'm forty-one years old and I have no idea if I'm going to see my next birthday. I really don't know what else to say."

"You don't need to say anything," he replies. "I do need you to listen carefully though, and then I suggest you go home and speak to your family."

I nod my agreement and then I ask him how long I have left.

"Well firstly, Mark, let's clear something up, shall we? Stage four cancer doesn't necessarily mean that we are out of options. It's very serious, of course, but it's still possible to beat or to prolong life expectancy with the right combination of therapies and surg—"

"But, how long do I have?" I Interrupt again.

My question causes him to look down at his notes and then he frowns and pushes his glasses further back on the bridge of his nose.

"Your best-case scenario without further treatment is nine to twelve months, but it could be as little as six months. However, with surgery and a more intensive application of hormone therapy and chemotherapy, there is a real chance of..."

Dr. Bleakley is still talking, but he lost me at six months and my mind wanders to a place where all that awaits me is a protracted and painful death. The way I see it, the only two options I have are to continue my unpleasant course of treatment with a slim chance of beating my cancer, or to walk away now and make the best of what little time I have left. Neither option gives me any sense of comfort or hope, and when he realizes that I am not listening, he stops talking and reaches across his desk for my hand.

"Mark, why don't you go home and get some rest. I'll ask my PA to make you another appointment in a few days' time. We can discuss then how you'd like to proceed. Would you like me to arrange for one of our drivers to take you home?"

I can still barely comprehend what is happening, but I get to my feet.

"No, that's okay, thank you. I think I'd prefer to walk for now and get some fresh air."

Alan gets up and walks me to the reception to make my next appointment. His PA is an attractive blonde in her early thirties, and despite her best efforts she is failing horribly to hide the fact that she knows the details of my latest prognosis.

On my previous visits she was chatty and bubbly, but today her smile is forced and I'm almost feeling embarrassed for her. To save both of our blushes, I turn away and pretend to check something on my cellphone whilst Alan checks for the next available appointment.

"Joanna, please check if we have a one-hour slot available on Monday for Mr. Rennie."

There is a short pause and then she asks me if 2 pm would be okay, adding, "If two is difficult for you, then we could also fit you in at four. Which would you prefer, Mr. Rennie?"

"Both are fine," I reply, "so put me down for the 4 pm slot, please. I can finish work early and I'll head straight home afterwards."

"Okay, that's confirmed for you," Joanna says. "Would you like our driver to take you anywhere?"

Alan replies on my behalf, "Mr. Rennie would like to walk to get some fresh air. Mark, please let me show you out."

I turn towards the door, but before either of us can move, Joanna informs her boss about his next appointment.

"Dr. Bleakley, Dr. McKenzie is here to see you next."

We both turn to face the waiting area and the stunningly beautiful woman sitting on one of the leather sofas. I had been so wrapped up in my own thoughts that I hadn't seen her when I came out of Alan's surgery. Now, though, I can't take my eyes off of her. She is in her mid- to late-thirties, around five-feet eight-inches tall, slim with a fair complexion and long black hair. I'm wondering about her connection to Dr. Bleakley when he puts his hand on my shoulder and my concentration is broken.

"Mark, are you sure you won't take that ride? It's no problem, the car is just outside."

I decline again and Alan walks me to the door. He shakes my hand and tells me again to speak with my family.

"This is not the end of the line, Mark. There are options. I'll see you at 4 pm on Monday, but feel free to call me if you have any questions before then."

■ ■ ■ ■ ■ ■ ■ ■

I step out into the street and Alan closes the door behind me. The time is just after three, but I have no appetite to go back to work. My boss and my colleagues are all aware of my condition, and I am in no mood for the inevitable questions, or the barrage of advice and suggestions that I know will be waiting for me. They all mean well, but for now I just want to walk and be on my own. It will be bad enough talking to my father and brother later today, without also having to explain myself a dozen times to my workmates.

Without really knowing where I am going, I slowly walk down Harley Street and take some time to reflect on the frailties of life. Less than two years ago, I hadn't a care in the world. Approaching my fortieth birthday, my career in the city was on the rise, and I was living a life that most can only dream of.

As a successful commodities trader with one of the leading London trading houses, I had it all. I had more money than I could spend. I had the flashy car, a penthouse apartment, memberships to the best clubs and, above all, I had my health and a beautiful fiancée.

I still have the material things, of course, but the things that mean the most are long gone. My body has been ravaged by cancer, and unable to cope with the challenges of my illness, my beautiful and caring fiancée turned out to be not so caring after all and is now engaged to one of my former friends.

I stop for a moment and take in the sight of the impressive Victorian and Edwardian period buildings that dominate Harley Street. It's famous as the center of private medicine in England, for those fortunate and wealthy enough to be able to afford it.

A fat lot of good that has done for me.

Despite the enormous sums of money I have thrown at my treatment, it has still not been enough.

When the odds are against you, it doesn't matter how much money you have. You still can't win.

At the top of Harley Street, I turn right onto Devonshire Street and then left onto Portland Place until I reach the crescent that encircles Regents Park. It's still early September, and although I've been walking slowly, I am sweating.

I take off my suit jacket and tie, and for a moment I consider going into the park, but then decide against it. Inexplicably, I leave my jacket and tie hanging on the railings and I turn right towards Marylebone Road. I've lived in London for more than fifteen years, but I've never been to this part of town before and this is the first time I've seen the John F. Kennedy Memorial close-up.

The memorial itself is beautiful in its simplicity. There is a bust of JFK on a tall black plinth with the simple inscription 'John F. Kennedy 1917–1963'.

I compare my own situation to his, and then completely irrationally I find myself getting angry that he was forty-six years old before he died.

"For Christ's sake, even he made it to forty-six. What the hell have I done to deserve this?"

My question is to myself, but my outburst has caught the attention of a small group of elderly American tourists who are also looking at the memorial. One elderly gentleman wearing a baseball cap emblazoned with a US Navy emblem and the words USS Arizona approaches me and puts his hand on my shoulder.

"Are you okay, son? You look a little pale. Can I help you with anything?"

His words are sincere, and I find myself blushing as his friends crowd around to offer their help. I assure the veteran that I'm okay and then I ask him about his cap.

"The USS Arizona, wasn't that one of the ships at Pearl Harbor?"

My question makes him smile and his chest swells with pride as he confirms that it was. I can tell he is itching to tell me more, but I interrupt him and ask his age. If I thought his chest couldn't swell anymore, I am instantly proved wrong as he answers me.

"Would you believe me if I told you I was ninety-two years old, son? I was just eighteen when the japs attacked us at Pearl Harbor."

I'm stunned at how well he looks for his age and I ask him a final question.

"Would you say you've lived a good life, sir?"

"I think so," he replies. "Don't get me wrong, I haven't led a perfect life and I have plenty of regrets. But, on balance, yes. I think I have led a good life. Is everything all right, son?"

"It is, thank you. You've been very helpful."

I shake his hand and then leave the veteran and his friends to mull over my last comment.

I continue to walk, but now I know what I want. I want some time alone and I want a cold pint. On Euston Road, I stop outside The Green Man pub to check my phone. It has been on silent for the last few hours and I have half-a-dozen missed calls and text messages from my father and brother asking me to call them. I message them both to tell them that I'll call them later, and then I turn off my phone and go inside the pub.

This is my first visit to The Green Man, but if I had to put a label on it, I would describe it as a contemporary British boozer. The clientele, however, are anything but contemporary. Even without needing to hear the accents, most of the drinkers have tourist written all over them. It's likely they are here simply to tick the trip to the British pub off of their bucket list.

I walk towards the bar and signal to the barman. He is a tall, good-looking young man with tightly cropped blonde hair, so it is no surprise when he greets me with a strong Eastern European accent.

I return his greeting and order myself a pint of Stella Artois. Then I take a seat in a quiet booth opposite the bar.

I watch for a few seconds as the condensation runs down the side of my glass, and then I take a large gulp and savor the taste of the cool liquid. If anyone was watching me, they might think that I'd never had a cold beer before, and they wouldn't be too far wrong. After my diagnosis, and on the advice of Dr. Bleakley, I gave my lifestyle a complete overhaul. Healthy eating, a sensible exercise regimen, no more late nights and, most importantly for my immune system, no alcohol.

In retrospect, that all seems to have been a bit of a waste of time, and whilst I'm not entirely sure if I've lived a completely good life, the words of the navy veteran have made me realize that I at least need to live what little of my life I have left.

I finish my drink and head to the bar to order a refill. While the barman fills my glass, I turn towards the end of the bar to watch the early evening BBC news. It's the usual banal rubbish, but when I hear a soft female voice ordering a drink, I turn back towards the barman to see who it is.

"Hi, Pawel, a gin and tonic please, and make it a double."

The accent is distinctly northern and not at all what I was expecting. As stereotypes go, and based on looks alone, I would have put her down as a London girl, or, at the very least, home counties privately educated. The accent is not the real surprise though, and as she catches my eye, we both awkwardly look away.

I take my drink back to my booth and put our encounter down to nothing more than an embarrassing coincidence. Despite this, I keep looking over towards her and more than once she catches me staring.

After catching me for a third time, she smiles, finishes her drink and picks up her handbag. To my great relief, she walks towards the door, but then she turns and walks back in my direction. I look down, hoping she is going to the bathroom, but she stops and puts her bag down on the bench opposite me. I look up from my drink and she asks if I'd mind her joining me.

I'd been hoping to be left alone and, gorgeous or not, her interruption is unwelcome, and my response is suitably curt.

"That really all depends on what you want. Did Dr. Bleakley send you to spy on me, Dr. McKenzie? Are you going to report back that you caught me having a sly pint?"

"Yep, that's right," she replies with a smile. "I followed you with the GPS tracker that he implanted into you earlier today. I take it that you didn't know that Dr. Bleakley is an undercover agent for MI5?"

Her response makes me blush and without waiting for an invitation she sits down opposite me.

"I'm no different from you. I needed a drink and was intending to have one before going home. I didn't follow you. I live close by. What's your excuse?"

"This is my first time in this pub. I started walking and ended up here. You haven't answered my question, though. What do you want?"

"Just some company with a like-minded soul. I'm guessing you came here to get some peace and quiet and to escape reality for a while. Well, so did I, but when I saw you at the bar, it made me think about fate and what really matters most in life."

"I'm sorry, I'm really not following you, Dr. McK—"

"Call me Karen," she interrupts and holds out her hand. "And you are?"

"It's Mark, Mark Rennie. But didn't you know that already?"

"Why would I? Are you famous?" she adds with a smirk.

Now I'm completely confused.

"Sorry, Karen, but can we start again, please? What's your connection to Dr. Bleakley, and what did you mean by a like-minded soul? Did Bleakley discuss my case with you?"

She laughs slightly and then takes me by surprise as she reaches across the table for my hand.

"That would be a massive breach of patient and doctor confidentiality, Mark. And, besides, it wouldn't mean all that much to me. Pediatrics is my specialty. My business with Alan today was completely personal."

"Okay, so, part two of my question?" I ask.

"Yep, part two, that's the real winner for both of us. I wasn't trying to listen as you were leaving the surgery, but I heard Dr. Bleakley tell you that you still have some options. I, unfortunately, am out of options."

My look betrays my surprise, and without thinking I blurt out something about how she looks so normal.

This causes her to laugh again and she thanks me for the compliment. "Thanks. It's amazing what a shitload of medication, makeup and a wig can do. Believe me, though, ovarian cancer is a bitch, and underneath this extremely expensive wig I've got the whole Britney Spears meltdown thing going on. Do you want to see?"

She jokingly tucks her fingers under the wig to lift it off and laughs again when she sees the panic in my eyes.

"For a man knocking on death's door, you really need to loosen up and live a little. What's the worst that can happen?" She says with a lift of her eyebrows.

"I'm sorry, the news today hasn't quite sunk in yet. You seem to be coping okay though. What's your secret?"

"There's no big secret. I knew deep down that my cancer was terminal. So, when Alan confirmed it today, I think I was already mentally prepared for it. The way I see it, I have two choices: I can sit around waiting for the end, or I can make the most of what time I have left."

I nod my head and tell her that I was thinking much the same thing.

"Great, so we're in agreement," she says, before calling to the barman. "The same again for both of us, please, Pawel. And two shots of the tequila gold."

"Oh no, no tequila for me," I protest. "I've got work in the morning."

Pawel looks at her for guidance, and after squeezing my hand and telling me to relax, she tells him that we'll both have a tequila. He smiles and starts to prepare the drinks, and I tell Karen that she is playing with fire.

"You do realize that with the medication I'm on, there is a distinct possibility that I'm either going to pass out or throw up?"

"Well, the same applies for me, but let's hope we don't pass out. Throwing up might not be such a bad thing though."

"And why would that be?"

"Two reasons. Number one, it will do us good to get some of that medication out of our system."

"Wonderful! And number two?"

"Number two, Mark, is that we'll have room for another tequila."

She looks at me with the wickedest of smiles and I can't help but smile back.

"You really are quite crazy aren't you, Dr. McKenzie?"

"Not yet," she replies. "But I'm hoping to get there quite soon. Now, are you going leave me to drink alone or are we going to have some fun?"

Ernesto H Lee

Also by Ernesto H Lee

Out of Time, The Dream Traveler Book One – published August 2018.

The Network, The Dream Traveler Book Two – published October 2018.

Finding Lucy, The Dream Traveler Book Three – published March 2019.

Walk With Me, One Hundred Days of Crazy – published July 2019.

For questions about any of his books or other enquiries, the author can be contacted at – ernestohlee@gmail.com

Printed in Great Britain
by Amazon